Paul R. Robbins

Unfinished Symphony, Unsolved Murders

A Harry Ellison Mystery

iUniverse, Inc.
Bloomington

iUniverse books may be ordered through booksellers or by contacting:

iUniverse
1663 Liberty Drive
Bloomington, IN 47403
www.iuniverse.com
1-800-Authors (1-800-288-4677)

ISBN: 978-1-4502-5424-3 (sc)
ISBN: 978-1-4502-5425-0 (ebook)

Printed in the United States of America

iUniverse rev. date: 11/18/2010

To my brother, Larry,

with love and respect

I would like to thank Leroy Resnick and James Robbins for their helpful comments about the novel and Sharon Hauge for her many contributions in editing the manuscript.

Prologue

On a blustery morning in December, the body of Edward Todd Griffith, a distinguished professor of music at Yale University was discovered lying in the snow not far from the entrance to his New Haven home. After a brief investigation, Griffith's death was ruled a suicide. His colleagues at Yale were surprised and dismayed. They didn't believe it.

In June of the following year, Aaron Wolfson, a highly respected professor of music at Princeton University was murdered in a vacation apartment at Rehoboth Beach, Delaware. The motive was apparently robbery. No suspects were found. No leads were uncovered.

The unnatural deaths of two of its luminaries threw the New York music world into shock. In September, the noted conductor, Sir Charles Southwick, held a memorial concert at Lincoln Center for the two men, performing the Brahms Requiem to a hushed audience. Afterwards, in Lincoln Center's Cafe Vienna, there was much talk about the unhappy coincidence of the passing of these two eminent scholars. Then, an elderly woman, who once worked for the magazine, *Musical America*, voiced an unspoken thought. "What if the deaths were not coincidences? And, if so, would there be more?"

Part I

Chapter 1

A glass of iced champagne with a sumptuous dinner, an evening spent in a lively restaurant with Debbie, the woman splashing in the shower--these images of soon-to-come events brought delight as they flooded the mind of journalist Harry Ellison. The thoughts gave rise to a feeling of complete contentment as Harry sank his body a little deeper into the soft cushions of the expensive oversized couch that Debbie had talked him into buying. When she moved in with him, she said, "Why not be comfortable?" So, they went on a buying spree: a lovely landscape of Provence to hang on the wall, a bevy of green plants, African violets and angel wing begonias to put around the windows, and a deep-seated easy chair for Harry to use when Debbie sprawled on the couch after a hard day's work. Thus it was that Debbie ended up making his apartment and his life more comfortable at the same time. Comfortable was not the right word, Harry thought. He was a wordsmith; he could do better than that. Not comfortable, nicer. Life was simply much nicer with Debbie. That was the right word.

The apartment, a spacious two-bedroom, was located on the seventh floor of a condominium not far from Washington Circle, close to the nerve centers of the Nation's Capital. From the pool on the roof of the building, one could see the Circle with its green benches that looked upon a weather-beaten statue of the Father of Our Country. The statue itself gazed upon an unending flow of traffic--busses, cars, taxis--that wound its way eastward down Pennsylvania Avenue toward the White House. Up the Avenue, in the opposite direction, lay Georgetown with its carefully restored townhouses, upscale shops and jazz clubs.

The day had been hot and humid, more typical of Washington in mid-August than the mid-June day it was. It was probably still sticky outside, Harry thought, as he relaxed in the cool stirrings of the air conditioning. In his lap he held a legal-size yellow note pad. In large, barely legible handwriting, he had scribbled three pages, a draft of his biweekly syndicated column. As was often the case, his topic was foreign policy for it was in foreign affairs that Harry had won his reputation as a correspondent reporting nightly from Middle East trouble spots for the network television news. His current job, writing a syndicated column, was a far cry from his humble beginnings as a newspaper man reporting on the city's robberies, rapes, swindles and homicides. It had been many years since he exchanged the garb of a determined, almost bulldog investigative reporter for the relaxed robes of a columnist and frequent television pundit on the Sunday morning talk shows and PBS specials.

His links to the local crime scene were not entirely severed, though, for the lively young woman who shared his life and whom he would soon be escorting to dinner, was a member of the Metropolitan Police Force. He thought of Sergeant Debbie Simmons and concluded that he was a lucky guy. Harry's reverie was interrupted by Debbie's voice calling from the bathroom, "I need a towel Harry. Could you get me a towel?"

Harry's smile broadened as an image flooded his mind of Debbie, petite, pretty and delightfully wet as she waited behind the half-open glass door that shielded the shower. Dropping the yellow tablet on the coffee table that fronted the couch, he stretched his arms and arose slowly. He ventured a few steps toward the linen closet when the sharp ring of the telephone stopped him in his tracks. What was it to be, the telephone or the towel? "Decisions, decisions," he muttered to himself.

"Answer the phone, Harry," Debbie called, simplifying his life.

"What about the towel?"

"I'll get it myself. Answer the phone. It might be important."

"I doubt it," Harry muttered in barely audible tones. "Probably someone trying to sell me a vacation lot in Florida."

"We could use a vacation home," Debbie replied as she stepped out of the bathroom, water dripping from her legs onto the Oriental rug that Harry had brought back with him from Lebanon.

Debbie looked at the spreading pools of water. "Oh, my God! I'm sorry about the rug, Harry."

Harry ignored the rug. "Boy, you look good," Harry observed, making an exaggerated lunge in her direction.

Debbie laughed. "Get the phone."

"The phone. The phone. Oh, yeah, the phone." Harry made a beeline for the phone, now ringing for the eighth time. He grabbed it, said hello, and seconds later, a smile filled his face. "I'll be damned--Stephanie! It's been a long time."

Harry covered the phone's receiver for an instant with the palm of his hand. He turned towards Debbie. "It's my niece, Stephanie. My brother Dick's girl. She's in town for a few weeks staying in Georgetown with a friend of hers from college days."

Debbie nodded, picked up a large red fluffy towel from the linen closet and walked to the bedroom to dress. Harry resumed his conversation on the phone. Debbie entered the living room 20 minutes later, now clad in a trim, black evening dress. Dangling golden earrings highlighted her soft brown hair, recently cut and styled to suggest the look of an impish street urchin, a gamine. Harry was still talking on the phone. Debbie edged her way in front of him. Her large, brown eyes that usually radiated a pleasant concoction of warmth and mischief offered a pleading look. "I'm starved," she whispered. Harry nodded, waited briefly, said goodbye, and then hung up the receiver.

Debbie asked, "Well, what's that all about?"

"Interesting," Harry replied. "I'll put on a coat and tie and I'll tell you all about it at dinner."

In a few minutes, Harry locked the door to the apartment, took Debbie by the arm and walked down the hall to the elevator. The elevator whisked them down to the parking garage, where they climbed into Harry's blue Volvo and drove off into the summer twilight. Harry drove east, down Pennsylvania Avenue.

Debbie asked, "Where are we going for dinner?"

Harry grinned. "It's a surprise."

Debbie smiled, but did not reply. After a moment, Harry explained, "You said you wanted to try something different?"

Debbie nodded.

"I asked the dining columnist at the *Post* for a recommendation. She suggested--well, you'll see."

Debbie pondered. In a few minutes she ventured, "It must be Chinese. We're heading towards Chinatown."

"We are, aren't we."

Debbie looked smug.

"But you're wrong!"

"Wrong?"

"It's Brazilian."

"In Chinatown?"

"Yeah. Well, near there."

Right on the fringes of Washington's Chinatown, they came to Harry's surprise, a Brazilian churrasqueria. It was wildly Latin, with brilliantly colored canopies hanging over the bar.

Harry turned toward Debbie. "Like it?"

She smiled and replied, "Wow!"

They started with champagne, and then feasted on roasted shrimp topped with garlic, followed by skewers of pork roast and ribs. Debbie's hunger pangs rapidly became history. Now it was her turn for a smile of contentment to fill her face. "Tell me about your niece," she said, as she nursed a strong drink the waiter called a Caipirinha.

"Stephanie? Nice kid," Harry mused. "I guess she's no longer a kid though I always think of her that way. She grew up in Amherst, in Western Massachusetts. Her father is a professor there. He's a physicist."

"That's impressive."

"Dick is impressive. So is her mother, Rita. She is a musician, or was one. Stephanie takes after her. She's a very fine violinist. Oh, she's not in a class with someone like Itzak Perlman or Anne-Sophie Muter. But she's awfully good. She's played in chamber recitals in Chicago, Denver, San Francisco and, I believe, in St. Louis."

"Is she the one you said studied at Julliard?"

"Yeah. I thought for awhile she was going to go into conducting. She studied with Sir Charles Southwick, the renowned conductor. He liked her work."

"She sounds impressive."

Harry grunted. "She's an Ellison."

Debbie looked demure. "When do I get to be an Ellison?"

Harry laughed. "I didn't think you wanted to become one."

Debbie smiled. "You're right. Not yet, anyway." She sipped her drink. "Maybe, one of these days."

Harry took her hand. "You've already stirred up the embers of passion. Now you've raised my hopes."

Debbie laughed. "I hope your column this week is better than that."

"I thought what I said was rather good."

"The sentiment is nice. But the double entendre--well..." She stopped and smiled. "What's Stephanie doing in town?"

Harry grinned. "Stephanie's been working on a Ph.D. in music at Columbia University. I think she's given up the idea of being a full-time performer. I believe she's planning on teaching college like her dad. Anyway, she's doing her dissertation now and spending some time looking through records at the Library of Congress. We didn't talk about her research. I have no idea what it's about."

"So, it was just a friendly call to you...to touch base?"

"Not exactly."

Debbie raised her eyebrows. "There's more?"

"Yeah. Something strange has happened to her. She wanted my advice."

"Is it confidential? Can you tell me?"

"Sure. Maybe you can help."

Harry cut the last sliver of roasted pork on his plate. He twirled the meat with his fork and then raised his eyes toward Debbie. "Somebody's been following her. Maybe, even stalking her. I don't know."

"That sounds like police business, Harry. Should I talk to my boss, Lieutenant Jackson?"

Harry shook his head. "No, not yet. From what she says, it doesn't sound malicious. If anything, the guy--if it is a guy--sounds like he's trying to be helpful."

"I don't understand."

"I don't either. I'm not sure she does. The weird part of this is that she's only been in town overnight. Nobody knows she's here, other than her old college friend Cynthia. Actually, she flew in from Vienna yesterday. She's been doing research there for the last six weeks. She got in last night, went to the Library of Congress this afternoon, took a seat in the reading room and ordered some books. While she was waiting for the books, she went to the snack bar for a hotdog. When she returned to her seat, the books were there. And right in the middle of the books was this nicely typed note stating that he--or maybe she--had some information that would be invaluable for Stephanie's work."

"Does she have any idea who the note is from?"

"No. Not the foggiest. I doubt if it was someone from the library staff. They're much too busy to do something like that for a stranger."

Debbie nodded. Then, she recapitulated, "She was in Vienna, right?"

"Right."

"She flies in last night. Almost no one knows she's coming. And the next day, someone leaves a note for her--unsigned--right?"

"Correct."

"In the Library of Congress where no one knows where she's going to sit--offering to help her."

"Yeah. Strange business."

"I'll say," Debbie reflected. "Must be some logical explanation-- something she's overlooked." Debbie smiled. "Why don't you invite her over? Maybe we can figure it out."

"I'm one step ahead of you, BLP. She'll be here at six tomorrow. Do you think Lieutenant Jackson can let you go by then?"

"Yeah, I can be there. But what's BLP?"

"That's an acronym."

"What's it stand for?"

"Beautiful Loving Partner, of course."

"Oh, Harry, how sweet. But Harry, don't mix it up with BLT."

"What's BLT stand for?"

"Bacon, Lettuce and Tomato. I used to work in a restaurant."

Chapter 2

Stephanie Ellison did not look at all like Harry. While Harry had a big, wide frame of a body (Debbie said he reminded her of a bear), Stephanie was tall and willowy. Her eyes were blue, her hair reddish brown, and except for her large eyeglasses, she would have passed more for a model than a scholar. Harry greeted her with a hug, and then introduced her to Debbie. "Debbie, meet Stephanie, almost Allison Ellison."

Stephanie laughed. She turned toward Harry. "You've got a memory, Uncle Harry."

Harry explained, "It's an old family joke, Debbie. Stephanie's mother Rita wanted to name the baby Allison. Dick balked at the idea, but finally agreed--but only if Rita accepted his challenge. She would have to say Allison Ellison twenty-five times as fast as she could without stumbling. Rita almost pulled it off. On the twenty-fourth time she blew it. And so, Stephanie was named after Rita's favorite aunt, Stephanie Edwards."

"It would have been a little tough to go through life as Allison Ellison," Stephanie admitted.

Harry conveyed his agreement in a smile, and then said, "Let's talk about this business with the note."

"Notes, Uncle Harry," she said as she shifted her weight. "There are now two of them. When I went for a snack at the Library of Congress today, I found another note on my desk. And look at this!" she exclaimed, "It came with the note." She thrust a sheet filled with musical notations into his hand. Harry put on his reading glasses and studied the paper. It was a photocopy of a pen and ink manuscript. The pen marks did not look like the work of a modern ballpoint pen, or even an old-fashioned fountain pen. The script reminded Harry of the signatures he had viewed on the Declaration of Independence. The pen marks looked as if they had been made by a quill.

"This looks old to me," Harry observed. "Very old."

"It does, doesn't it?" Stephanie replied. She cast her eyes about the room and saw a small spinet standing unobtrusively in the corner. "Hey, you got a piano!" she said excitedly.

"It was your great grandmother's," Harry explained. "She left it to me in the hope I'd learn how to play it. Never got beyond picking out a few tunes."

Stephanie smiled. "I'd like to use it, if it's okay. The music on this sheet is scored for a symphony orchestra, but let me see if I can play some of it on the piano. At least the melodic line."

"Go ahead," Harry said.

Stephanie walked over to the piano. Moving aside a book titled, *Easy Melodies for the Piano*, she set the page of music in front of her. She began to play, haltingly at first, and then with more fluency as she became comfortable with the penned notations. When she finished, she said, "I'll try it again, throwing in more of the orchestration." Her second version sounded like a piano transcription of a symphony.

Harry and Debbie applauded. Stephanie smiled. "What's it sound like to you, Uncle Harry?"

Harry scratched his head. "There's not a lot to go on, but it sounds like it might have been written around Beethoven's time."

Stephanie beamed. "Excellent."

"But it ain't Beethoven," Harry remarked. "It's too cheerful...too light hearted. Not ponderous enough. Maybe Mendelssohn or Schubert. I'd say it's Schubert."

"Bravo," Stephanie replied. "You're incredible, Uncle Harry."

Debbie beamed. Harry demurred, "A lucky guess. I never heard it before."

"I'm not sure anyone else has either. Except the person who left it on my desk. If this music is anything, it's Franz Schubert. I'm very familiar with Schubert's works. If it is Schubert, it's never been published. It's something he wrote that's been missing, possibly from one of his uncompleted symphonies."

Harry looked flabbergasted. "You don't mean the Symphony in B Minor? The famous Unfinished Symphony?"

"No," Stephanie replied. "It's a fragment from one of his other uncompleted works." She rubbed her eye, "if it's real."

"I'm lost," Debbie remarked.

"So am I," Harry agreed. "I don't understand any of this. Who is this stranger? Why did he give this fragment to you? It must be priceless." Harry paused. "It's time to fill us in," he said. "How did you get involved in all of this?"

"It's a bit of a story," Stephanie said.

"Sit down. I'll get you a drink," Harry said.

"No thanks. A cup of coffee would be good, though."

"I'll heat up some," Debbie volunteered. "Harry just made some coffee".

"Thanks."

While Debbie walked into the kitchenette, Stephanie sat down on the couch and began her narrative. "How much did Mom or Dad tell you about my dissertation project?"

"Zip. Not a thing."

"Well, it's about Schubert."

"I see a glimmer of light."

"And it's about his unfinished works."

"I see two glimmers of light."

"I think that's all you're going to see. Everything's foggy after that."

"Try me."

"Okay."

Debbie returned with the coffee and some croissants. "Wonderful," Stephanie said gratefully. "Well," she began, after taking a bite of a croissant, "Schubert didn't finish everything he wrote. Besides the famous Unfinished Symphony in B Minor which only has the first two movements and a sketch of the third, there are other symphonies, for example, the seventh, piano sonatas, chamber music, and a mass. None of them were finished. The question I posed for my research was, 'Why?' My method was three fold." She smiled. "Stop me if I get too pedantic."

"No," Harry said. "Go on."

"First, I'm examining the unfinished works and comparing them in musical terms with his other completed works which were written at about the same time. Second, I have a friend on the faculty; she's also my thesis advisor, Johanna Hoffman. Johanna teaches music history. Her specialty is Nineteenth Century German and Austrian composers."

"Which includes Schubert, of course," Harry interjected.

"Yes. The thing about Johanna is that she's not only a brilliant musician, she's also a fine mathematician and a whiz with computers. What we're planning on doing is to use computer programs she's developed to compare samples of Schubert's unfinished works with contemporaneous samples of finished works. Using the computer, I want to see if I can spot any differences."

"Interesting," Debbie reacted, as she too had a strong interest in computers.

"The third approach is historical," Stephanie continued. "Schubert wrote many letters to his friends and his friends wrote many to him. These letters--and there are other documents as well--shed light on his compositions. Much of this material has been translated into English, but I thought I had better look at the originals."

"So, you went to Vienna," Harry finished her thought.

"Exactly. I spent most of my time in the Vienna Stadtbibliothek, which has a marvelous collection of Schubertiana. I also talked to an eminent Schubert scholar there."

"Maybe our mysterious note dropper picked up your trail there."

"I think it's likely, Uncle Harry. I made no secret of my being in Vienna. In fact, I placed advertisements in several newspapers asking for information about hitherto unpublished letters or documents relating to Schubert. These things keep turning up, you know." Stephanie smiled, "And to top it off, look at the notes." She handed the notes to Harry. They were typed on an old, manual typewriter, not a computer.

Harry smiled. "Ah ha! The notes are written in German. It's clear our mystery begins in Vienna." Inspired by the idea, Harry sauntered over to the piano and began picking out the notes to *The Third Man Theme* from J. Carol Reed's movie masterpiece that was set in post World War II Vienna.

"Is he always this way?" Stephanie inquired.

"Usually," Debbie replied. "But you get used to it."

Harry took the hint and turned around on the piano bench so that he faced Stephanie. "Read the notes, Stephanie. You'd better translate. My German is as rusty as the underside of an old car, and Debbie speaks beautiful French but doesn't know a word of German."

Stephanie nodded. She gazed at the first note. "This one is very short: 'Dear Miss Ellison.'"

"He knew your name," Debbie interrupted.

"Oh, yeah."

"'Dear Miss Ellison,'" Stephanie repeated, "'I am familiar with your interest in studying our dear Schubert. I am in possession of information which may have a profound influence on your work. Wait'"

She paused, and then added, "The letter is signed Schubert Friend."

"I can see why you were startled by receiving the note," Harry observed. "But there's not much there. Read the second note."

Stephanie nodded and once again read aloud.

Dear Miss Ellison,

I trust my note did not disturb you unduly. I am not at liberty to divulge my identity to you at this time; therefore, you must be patient with me. If you are patient, I think I can demonstrate to you that much of our dear Schubert's unfinished work is not at all unfinished, simply misplaced and lost. Kindly examine the enclosed fragment of a musical score. It is almost certainly Schubert. If you would like to see a much larger section of this score, be so kind as to leave a note affirming your interest on your desk at the library when you leave to take your lunch.

Stephanie smiled. "Once again, it is signed Schubert Friend."

Debbie observed, "That chap is sure keeping an eye on you."

"Chap or Chapess," Harry said.

"It's a chap, Harry," Debbie replied with conviction. "A man wrote that. No woman would write that way. It's a man and an elderly one at that. Sounds like a real gentleman."

Harry raised his eyebrows. "Describe him."

Debbie considered. "Well," she said, "I'd say he's about 60 or 65. He has graying hair, maybe a bit white. I bet he has a white mustache."

Harry laughed. "Sounds like one of those pictures of Albert Einstein."

"Not in the least," Debbie replied. "I would say he's very neat and dapper. His hair would never stick out all over the place like a porcupine."

Harry observed dryly, "Stephanie, now that we know what he looks like, he should be easy to spot. Just keep your eyes open for a dapper elderly gentleman when you're at the library tomorrow."

Debbie frowned, but began to laugh when Harry added, "And particularly one who carries an attaché case, an umbrella, and also speaks with a thick German accent."

Stephanie smiled. "All kidding aside, you clowns, I'd like to know who this guy is."

"So would I," Harry agreed with sudden seriousness. "Look, when I finish writing my column tomorrow morning, I'll go over to the Library of Congress--say about 11:30 or 12:00. When you see me, don't give any sign of recognition. Just wait ten minutes, then take off. If our phantom shows up, I'll get a look at him."

"It won't work, Harry," Debbie objected. "Your face is too well known. Somebody's bound to recognize you. They always do. They'll want to shake your hand or talk to you."

"I haven't been on the tube that much lately. It's not like when I was a correspondent in the Middle East and I was reporting every day."

"Debbie's right, Uncle Harry. I just saw you last week on public television in that discussion show on the history of the Arab-Israeli conflicts."

Harry reacted dryly, "Who watches public television?"

"People who use the Library of Congress do," Debbie reacted quickly.

"Touché, my dear." He kissed her on the cheek. He shrugged his shoulders. "If not me, then who?"

Debbie let out a little squeak. "Me!"

Chapter 3

Sergeant Debbie Simmons of the Metropolitan Police Force was in plain clothes today on stake-out assignment in the Adams-Morgan section of the Nation's Capital. The string of restaurants on 18th Street where Debbie had been hanging about spoke of the area's ethnic diversity. The names of the restaurants--Meskerem Ethiopian Resturant, Saki Asian Grille, La Fourchette, Jyoti, Indian Cusine--made one feel that one was at the United Nations. In this cosmopolitan mix of peoples of different colors and languages, Debbie was hoping to catch a glimpse of Howard Jones, an elusive con artist who had been fleecing residents in the neighborhood. She had been working the streets since early in the morning, but had nothing to show for it except two propositions from eager middle-aged males. Debbie had half a mind to run them in, but didn't want to blow her cover. She simply frowned and shook her head.

Debbie glanced at her watch. Her relief, Officer Bernice Johnson, was due in a few minutes. When Bernice arrived, Debbie planned to hail a taxi and spend her lunch hour doing some unofficial detective work at the Library of Congress.

Bernice, who came originally from Trinidad, was glad to shed her police uniform for the day and wear a loose fitting white dress splashed with dabs of rose color that she had worn in the islands. She carried what looked like a coiled wicker basket. "Lovely basket," Debbie remarked upon greeting her.

"No basket," Bernice replied. "It's a purse. My cousin who lives in Granada gave it to me. It can hold a lot of things, including one item that will cause Mr. Jones to stand at attention if I chance to see him."

Bernice opened the purse and Debbie laughed as she spied a revolver.

Bernice inquired, "Any sign of Jones?"

Debbie shook her head. "I think he may be on to us. He's pretty slippery."

"Like an eel."

Debbie smiled. "I hope you have better luck than I did. And watch the heat. It's getting bad."

Bernice returned the smile. "I'm used to it."

Debbie walked east toward 16th Street. She spotted an empty Yellow Cab, waved to the driver and was soon on her way to the Library of Congress. Mid-day Washington traffic was heavy. The going was slow, and the cab driver trying to save on gasoline expenses kept the air conditioner off. Debbie was sweating profusely when she finally arrived. She checked her watch again. It was ten minutes to twelve when she stepped out of the cab.

She walked up the wide concrete steps that led to the Library of Congress. The entranceway was crowded with tourists, men and women carrying cameras and guidebooks, flanked by young children, often restless, dashing ahead of their more slowly moving parents.

The inside of the building seemed comfortably cool compared to the oppressive heat and humidity she had experienced on the streets and in the taxi. Debbie walked briskly to the elevator which took her near the main reading room. A uniformed officer stood in the entrance way of the reading room monitoring the comings and goings of people. Standing a few feet from the officer was a pretty young girl in a white summer frock with a ribbon in her hair who looked as if she could have been the subject in a Renoir painting. Debbie smiled at the girl who smiled back. When Debbie entered the reading room, she experienced a sense of deja vu. It didn't seem that long ago when she had come here to write her term papers when she was a student at George Washington University. Now she was a veteran police officer and she had Harry. She smiled. "Not so bad."

Debbie walked around the cavernous reading room, looking one-by-one at the people occupying the seats and desks, searching for Stephanie. Ah, there she was sitting in the corner between a young man in a naval uniform and an elderly woman. Slowly, Debbie walked towards Stephanie, hoping to make eye contact. But Stephanie's eyes remained buried in an oversized book. "Come on, Stephanie," she muttered to herself. "Look up!" Then, as if by magic, Stephanie raised her eyes; she nodded almost imperceptibly. She began fussing with the books on her desk, arranging them into a manageable pile. She placed a handwritten note on the top of the pile of books, arose from her chair and left for lunch. Debbie kept walking until she reached an alcove where medical journals were stored. Here she stopped and pretended to look through the *Journal of Psychosomatic Medicine*. "Dreary stuff," she thought, as she browsed through an article on anger and ulcerative colitis, all the while keeping an eye on Stephanie's now vacant desk. For several moments, she waited expectantly, but no one in the room stirred. Then, she noticed that the girl in white who had been standing in the waiting area at the entrance to the reading room began talking to the guard. The guard nodded. The girl entered the room. As if guided by radar, she walked directly to Stephanie's desk, picked up a slip of paper, examined it, and then deposited a manila folder.

Debbie shook her head in disbelief. What happened to her dapper 65-year-old white-haired Viennese? As the young girl walked out of the reading room, Debbie followed her at a discrete distance. Rather than take the elevator, the girl walked slowly down the steps, and then quickened her pace, heading for Pennsylvania Avenue. Debbie quickened her own pace to keep the child in view. Fortunately, the girl stopped at the corner and waited. The traffic light turned red, then green, then red again; the crowds moved into the street, but the girl waited, almost impassively, never looking one way or the other. Then, a black limousine came into view. Right behind the limousine was an oversized tour bus. The limousine stopped in front of the girl. From behind black curtains, a hand opened the door to the limousine. The girl quickly entered the car, the door shut, and the limousine sped off. Debbie tried to identify the license number of the vehicle, but the tour bus blocked her view. When the limousine drove away, it was too late.

Chapter 4

When Stephanie examined the contents of the folder on her reading desk, she could hardly contain her excitement. It was an entire movement of a symphony. The movement was labeled Scherzo and appeared to be the third movement of Schubert's Seventh Symphony which was thought, like the B-Minor Symphony, to exist only in sketch form. But here it was, fully orchestrated and ready to play.

Stephanie picked up the manuscript and nearly stumbled as she dashed down the corridor to find a quiet spot to telephone Harry. When she found a quiet alcove, she stopped, fumbled through her purse which was crowded with ticket stubs, travel notes, and Austrian coins, to retrieve her cell phone. She dialed Harry's number. At the sound of his voice, she blurted out the news of the discovery. Then, she asked whether she could come right over and try out the score on the piano. Harry replied that while he had to be at his office during the afternoon, he would leave a key for her at the front desk. Stephanie said that would be fine and that she was on her way.

Harry did not return home until eight in the evening. When he entered the apartment, he carried a white paper bag with an imprinted red dragon containing cartons of Chinese food: imperial shrimp and fried rice, General Tso's chicken, and egg rolls. The food was a welcome sight to Debbie, who had just returned from police headquarters, and to Stephanie, who sat half slumped on the piano bench, still teasing out a hard-to-read passage from the score. Unceremoniously, Harry passed the cartons around. Then, he added some chopsticks from the bag and some paper plates that had been stacked in the kitchen cabinet.

Harry settled into his oversized chair and poured himself a shot of bourbon to sip with his food. After tasting the hot sting of the bourbon, he glanced at Debbie, who was reclining on the couch, eating Roman style.

He grinned, and then turned to his niece. "Well, what do you think of the score?"

She shook her head. "The whole thing is just amazing. It's like I'm in a wild dream, waiting to wake up." She reached for two pieces of paper on the edge of the piano bench. "Let me read you the note that came with the manuscript. It's in German, again, and it's much longer." She began to read slowly:

Dear Miss Ellison,

I hope this finds you in good health. I am pleased that you find yourself able to cooperate in this endeavor. To hear our dear Schubert's lost works performed by a modern symphony orchestra will be a magnificent experience. Perhaps I am getting ahead of myself. It is my belief, no stronger than that--a conviction--that what I present to you today is no less than the orchestrated score of the Scherzo from Schubert's Symphony No. 7.

I would like to address myself to two issues. One, what had happened to this manuscript--that is to say, what was its fate since Schubert composed it, and two, what you must do to substantiate my claim that the work is truly Schubert.

To begin with, as you well know, Schubert experienced a severe illness not long after he wrote The Symphony in B Minor--the so-called Unfinished Symphony. As you know, he was hospitalized. That would be in May of 1823. For much of the year Schubert was ill and dispirited. As always, he depended on his large circle of friends to see him through. Most of them behaved admirably. As you know, Schubert had wonderful friends: Johann Mayerhofer; Franz von Schober; Moritz von Schwind; and, of course, Josef von Spaun. But, there was one man who, like Judas, betrayed him and posterity. Some of Schubert's manuscripts including the Scherzo from the Seventh Symphony and the jewel of all jewels in music were left in the hands of a certain Herr _____. As a caution, I will delete his name for the present. If I revealed the name of the scoundrel who kept these manuscripts from the public--through malice and jealousy--I would open up this matter to a monumental legal challenge. No one has a clear claim to these manuscripts. But if word were to get out prematurely of what I have discovered through what I must say frankly was a prodigious research effort--the line of claimants would be long and dreary. As such, I must remain in the shadows and not reveal myself until the project is a fait accompli."

"Project," Harry muttered. "This guy--or whoever it is--is beginning to sound a little like a nut."

Stephanie nodded. "He certainly seems obsessed," she reflected. "I can understand why a person could develop a passion for such an undertaking. Think about Heinrich Schliemann and the discovery of Troy. People thought he was a nut."

Harry replied, unconvinced, "Maybe so."

Debbie wondered out loud, "Is it true what he says about the long line of claimants to the manuscripts?"

"I can think of a bunch of claimants without even trying," Stephanie replied. "While Schubert left no will, his principal heir was his younger brother Ferdinand. He ended up with a lot of Schubert's music and sold it. Ferdinand had many kids and Lord knows how many descendants there are in the hills and valleys of Austria."

Harry nodded. "I see what you mean." He paused. "I bet Austria would put in its claim, too. Treasure hunters in this country have to divvy up to Uncle Sam when they find things like sunken Spanish galleons."

"And then there is the scoundrel," Debbie added with emphasis. "His descendants would have a claim, I suppose, whoever he was, whoever they are."

Harry nodded, "Speaking of the so-called scoundrel, how do you suppose our mystery man," he smiled at Debbie, "or little girl," Debbie grimaced, "spirited the manuscripts away from the heirs of the scoundrel?"

Debbie replied defensively, "I still bet there's an elderly Viennese gentleman at the bottom of this."

Harry smiled. He inquired, "Who's the girl?"

Debbie smiled, "It's his granddaughter. I bet her name is Maria like in *The Sound of Music*."

"Well, let me rephrase the question. How did Maria's grandpappy rustle this stuff away from whomever or whatever had it?"

"Skullduggery," Debbie answered with a broad smile. "I think Grandpappy is a crook."

"You suspect a con game?"

Debbie shrugged, and then laughed. "Who knows? I sure don't trust the guy."

"You think he's a crook; I still think he's a nut."

Stephanie laughed. "I think you all had better listen to the rest of the note."

Stephanie read further:

Now as to your role, Miss Ellison. I have watched your research in Vienna with great interest. You strike me as a woman of both intellect and integrity, a person who would be the ideal conduit to bring these treasures to the ears of the public and to posterity. I realize that you do not have the musical authority to announce these discoveries to the world, but I ask you to kindly do the following. Select two people of standing: The first should be a conductor--someone who would revel in the opportunity to present not only the Scherzo of Schubert's Seventh Symphony, but even more importantly, to present the world premier of the completed score of the Unfinished Symphony. Yes, Miss Ellison, I and I alone can make that possible.

Harry shook his head. "Megalomania. He's nutty as a fruitcake."

"Who knows," Stephanie remarked, shrugging her shoulders. "I'll finish the note."

Your second person should be a Schubert scholar. You choose, not I. I am confident that when you bring to these people the score of the Seventh Symphony, they will be only too eager to see the complete Symphony in B Minor.

Now, what do I want for myself? Two things. First and foremost, I want to know that our beloved Schubert's work will be performed after all these years. Second, I have incurred considerable expense.

Debbie interrupted. She slapped her hands together. "I was waiting for that. He is a crook!"

Stephanie smiled and continued to read.

Considerable expense in pursuing my inquiries. It seems only fair that I be recompensed for my efforts. If these manuscripts are deemed to be authentic, please ask the conductor you choose to make inquiries from foundations and other sources to see if something suitable might be arranged.

"I bet he'll want it in unmarked twenty dollar bills," Debbie observed.

"More likely, he'll want his own picture on the bills," Harry added.

Harry turned toward his niece, who had bent over with laughter. Harry smiled and waited for her to recover herself. He spoke slowly. "Let's talk about the score, Stephanie. Long before your time there was a song called, 'Is She Is Or Is She Ain't My Baby?' Here is a question for you, soon-to-be Dr. Ellison: Is she or is she ain't Franz Schubert?"

Stephanie smiled. She did not answer immediately. Instead, she averted his eyes and looked out of the window into the darkening hazy sky. She arose from the bench and then walked over to the window, stopping to peer at the profusion of newly-lit rooms in the large apartment building across the road. Then, she paced about the room, passing between Harry and Debbie in her meanderings. She had a troubled look; she was clearly distressed. Finally, she said haltingly, "To be honest, Uncle Harry, I don't know. Stylistically, it's as Schubert as Schubert can be. It has every nuance of Schubert written into it from the joyful use of woodwinds to his driving intensity." Stephanie looked directly at Harry. Her voice became more intense. "But, I feel there's something missing. Schubert had a creative spark, a genius for song-like melodies. The world has produced only one Schubert, just like there was only one Beethoven and one Mozart. I'm not sure I hear that spark here, Uncle Harry." Suddenly, she buried her head in her hands. "It worries me, Uncle Harry. I don't know one way or the other. I just don't know!"

Harry sighed. "You're overtired Stephanie; but, I can sense your dilemma. You may be on top of the biggest sensation in classical music of the century--and then again, you may not be." He paused. "What do you plan to do?"

Stephanie's voice was resolute. "I've thought about it--a lot--and I've made a decision. I am going to follow the instructions he or she gave me in the letter. I'm going to send out copies of the manuscript to two musical authorities and await their judgment."

Harry nodded. "I think that's wise. Who are your choices?"

Stephanie smiled. She flashed a look of reassurance. "The conductor's easy. It's a cinch. Sir Charles Southwick. I studied with him. He knows me. If I picked anyone else--someone who didn't know me--I'd never get to first base if I came in claiming to have Schubert's unfinished symphonic scores. They'd think I was a nut. Sir Charles won't react that way. He'll find this very interesting."

"And your musical scholar?"

"That's harder. When I was in Vienna I met Leopold Rieder. He's probably the foremost authority on Schubert in the world, but I don't think our mystery man--" she added, "or woman--would want me to go near Vienna."

Harry nodded. "You're probably right. But if he's as good as you say, I wouldn't rule him out so quickly. Tell me more about Rieder."

"Leopold Rieder is an extremely knowledgeable man and his opinion could be decisive. But there's another reason I think he is out. I couldn't afford him! I think he'd want to charge me for the opinion, and plenty." She paused and shook her head. "You see, he's stone broke, Harry. He got involved in some kind of a botched up real estate deal. He invested heavily--everything he had in an Alpine ski resort that went bankrupt. The government declared the site unsafe. There was an unacceptable risk for avalanches. They didn't want another tragedy on the evening news. When I visited Rieder, he and Irmgard--that's Mrs. Rieder--were selling off their furniture and paintings to pay off their creditors. We had our talk on two hard chairs in the kitchen." She sighed. "Everything else in the house was gone." She waved her hand expressively. "Everything. Their house is up for auction. It's really very sad. He didn't know what he was getting into."

Harry considered, "I've heard stories like that. In fact, I have a friend who is a novelist. He invested in a diamond mine in Southern Africa. The problem was there weren't any diamonds. He went broke, too. Should have stuck to writing." Harry picked up his reading glasses and began to clean them with a tissue. He inquired, "What about American musicologists? Do we have any top scholars on Schubert?"

Stephanie nodded. "We had three really distinguished Schubert scholars in this country. Edward Todd Griffith of Yale, Aaron Wolfson of Princeton, and Thaddeus Cochrane who was at Julliard and is now retired. Unfortunately, Griffith and Wolfson died recently."

"Edward Todd Griffith," muttered Harry. There was a flash of recognition. He smiled. "Sure! Didn't he used to write musical reviews? I remember reading him. He could be pretty acid, sometimes, but he was a great critic. They used to compare him with Deems Taylor."

Stephanie replied, "That's the man. He was very much admired. It was a sad ending. Some children found him in the snow in front of his house. An overdose--or something like that. They said it was suicide." She hesitated. "I heard that his colleagues at Yale never believed it was suicide."

Harry thought for a moment. "Interesting," he said. He asked, "What about Wolfson?"

"I can tell you about that one." Debbie volunteered. "I followed the story closely. No question of suicide there. He was murdered. In Rehoboth Beach. He was vacationing there. I saw a copy of the report. It happened suddenly. No clues, no suspects, no nothing."

Harry shook his head. "That's a strange coincidence--two eminent Schubert scholars dying suddenly. Get out of the music business, Stephanie. It seems to be a hazardous occupation."

Stephanie laughed. "Speak for yourself, Uncle Harry."

Harry had an all-too-vivid memory of how his leg had been almost shattered by a bomb blast in Lebanon years back. He nodded. "Touché!"

"Now that you mention it, Uncle Harry, it was unnerving that both men, distinguished scholars with nearly identical interests, died unexpectedly, so close in time. You know--Southwick opened the fall musical season in New York with a memorial concert for the two men. I was there. They played the Brahms Requiem. It was a beautiful performance. Afterwards, I heard a lot of talk about the deaths."

Curious, Harry asked, "What kind of talk?"

Stephanie shrugged. "Just talk. People wondering what happened. It bothered people. It was a hard thing to accept."

Harry picked up his glasses and put them on. He studied his niece. She looked tired and troubled. Maybe he should stop. No, there was more to talk about. He asked, "Tell me about the third chap you mentioned, Stephanie--Cochrane. The name doesn't ring any bells."

"Thaddeus Cochrane has written a book and some brilliant essays on Schubert's work. But Johanna--Dr. Hoffman--says Cochrane's a difficult man to approach. Johanna used to know him pretty well. He has been living in Salem, Massachusetts for a number of years. Johanna says he's a recluse, prefers the company of seagulls to humans. When I started doing my research, I wrote him a letter asking for some guidance. He never even answered my letter."

"Pleasant fellow," Debbie commented.

Stephanie nodded. "Johanna wasn't surprised by his behavior. After Cochrane, there's no one who is really outstanding. I think Johanna's certainly as good as anyone else around, maybe better." Stephanie smiled. "Maybe, I'm prejudiced, but I think I'll send it to her." Stephanie nodded. She smiled brightly. "Uncle Harry, I think it's a good decision. I'll call them both in the morning."

Around 11 p.m., Harry saw his niece safely to a taxi. When he returned to the apartment, Debbie was in bed. Harry spent a few minutes cleaning things up. He tossed the paper plates into the trash. He was about to do the same with the bag with the red dragon when he felt the bottom of the bag. There was still something there. He shook the bag and two fortune cookies fell out.

Harry walked into the bedroom and spied his lady dressed in shorty pajamas curled on her side. He asked softly, "Are you awake?"

"Um hmm," she muttered.

"Want to know your fortune? I found two fortune cookies in the bag."

"Sure."

He handed her the two cookies. "Pick one."

Debbie crunched her cookie into two pieces and silently perused her fortune: "You will soon meet an attractive stranger." Debbie smiled. This she would keep to herself.

"Nice fortune?"

Debbie replied matter-of-factly, "Okay."

"What's it say?"

Debbie thought quickly. She replied, "Patience is a virtue."

"Kind of nondescript," Harry said. Cracking his own cookie in half, he read the message out loud. "This is not a propitious time to take risks. Exercise caution." Harry laughed. "What conservative fortune cookie writers they have these days. A bunch of foggies. I don't see any risks out there, but if one comes along, I'll bear it in mind."

Harry took off his clothes and snuggled up to Debbie. "You feel good," he said. "This is a joy."

Debbie smiled. "Thank you, Lover." They kissed and he massaged her shoulder for awhile. His touch was gentle and pleasing.

"You know how to relax a girl," she said. She uttered a deep sign of contentment. Then, she said, "Before I drift off to sleep, I wanted to ask you something."

"Ask."

"What do you think about it all?"

"All what?"

She began to play with the hair on his chest. "The business with Stephanie. Do you think the music is genuine?"

Harry thought for a moment. "Sometimes I act like an ass. But I'd be a bigger ass than I am to voice an opinion on that question."

Debbie laughed. "If you're an ass, what does that make me? I moved in with you."

Harry stroked her gently behind the ear. "I think I better plead the Fifth Amendment on that one."

Debbie laughed again. "I don't know if the music is phony or not," she said. "But as they used to say in those old gangster movies, 'I smell a rat.'" Debbie nudged her head so she could look at Harry's eyes. She asked, "Was it James Cagney who used that line first? 'I smell a rat'?"

"No, it wasn't Cagney. It was Samuel Butler around 1600 and something."

Debbie pulled at the hair on his chest. He said "ouch" loudly.

"Harry, you're incredible."

"I also know some useless batting averages. Do you know what Joe DiMaggio batted in 1938?"

"Go to sleep, Harry.

"Goodnight, BLP."

Chapter 5

Harry spent the morning at home writing his bi-weekly column. It was entitled "Choices in Afghanistan." He gave it a final perusal, nodded his head and put it aside. It wasn't bad. He glanced at his watch; it was nearly twelve. He walked into the small kitchen and began preparing Shrimp Fra Diablo for himself and Debbie, who was coming home for lunch today. Harry learned the recipe from his Uncle Bob's wife, Gina, a woman whom he had met, courted, and married while serving in the U. S. Embassy in Rome. Gina was far from the dark-haired beauty of her youth, but she still was a fantastic cook. And she always had been one of Harry's favorite people..

The enticing aromas of the Italian sauces filled the air when Debbie returned. Upon entering the apartment, she held her head in the air, sniffed, and said "Um-m-m!" before flinging herself into Harry's arms.

When she extricated herself, he smiled and asked, "How did it go? Did you spot the elusive Mr. Howard Jones?"

Debbie shook her head, sniffed the air again, and ventured only, "Let's eat."

The Shrimp Fra Diablo tasted as good as it smelled. While they were both savoring the remnants of the meal and sipping cappuccino, the telephone rang. Harry lumbered to his feet and answered the phone.

It was Stephanie. She had a lot of news to report and Harry listened attentively, voicing only an occasional comment. Finally, he said, "Hold for a minute and I'll ask her."

Holding the palm of his hand against the receiver, Harry spoke to Debbie. "Stephanie's teacher Dr. Hoffman is out of town, vacationing in Canada, but Stephanie did speak to Sir Charles Southwick. He's extremely interested in the manuscript and asked Stephanie to see him in New York tomorrow afternoon. Stephanie wants us to go to New York with her if we can. Debbie, I've been wanting to interview some people at the United Nations for a future column--if I can arrange the interviews, I'll go with her. Now, what about you? Can you go? We could take in a Broadway show."

"Oh, Harry, I'd love to," Debbie replied enthusiastically, "but I can't."

"Mr. Jones?"

"Mr. Jones."

"Damn Mr. Jones."

Debbie shook her head. "I've got to catch the bastard, Harry, before he fleeces someone else out of a life savings."

Harry nodded. "I know. I'll miss you. It won't be the same."

"Thanks for saying that, Harry." Debbie poured herself another cup of cappuccino, took a few sips, headed for the door, stopped momentarily, blew him a kiss, and then dashed off.

After washing the dishes, Harry resolved to do a little research on Schubert himself, before he undertook the trip to New York City. He took a taxi to the Library of Congress and checked through the list of available books on Schubert. There were a number of books listed. Three caught his eye: The classic work by Deutsch, which he had heard of, and books by Leopold Rieder and Thaddeus Cochrane...the two scholars that Stephanie had mentioned. Harry ordered the three books, and then sat at his desk patiently.

An aide dropped a slip of paper on his desk, notifying him that Deutsch's book on Schubert was "not on shelf." However, the books by Rieder and Cochrane were available and Harry began to read through them. As he read, he pondered. Was it possible that the final movements of Schubert's Unfinished Symphony had actually been completed and the score misplaced? Or even worse, deliberately withheld from the public? Could Stephanie's mysterious correspondent be telling the truth? Or was it as Debbie suspected, an elaborate con game?

The facts about the symphony proved to be somewhat sketchy and for some particulars, ambiguous. As far as it was known, Schubert began the symphony as a piano sketch in October, 1822. He quickly orchestrated the first two movements, and sketched the beginning of a third. Then, for some reason, he put the work aside. During the following spring, Schubert was elected to honorary membership in the music society in the town of Graz. A Certificate of Membership was given to one of Schubert's friends, a Mr. Anselm Hüttenbrenner, to give to Schubert. Anselm forwarded it to his brother Josef who lived in Vienna. Josef personally presented the certificate to Schubert. Schubert was quite taken with the honor and wrote the society a note of thanks in which he included the statement, "I shall take the liberty before long of presenting your honorable society with one of my symphonies in full score."

Harry checked the dates carefully. The note was written in September of 1823, almost a full year after Schubert began working on the Unfinished Symphony. Schubert was a quick worker, so there would have been plenty of time for him to complete the symphony if he had intended to. Harry read further. According to Josef Hüttenbrenner, Schubert gave him the symphony, which was still incomplete, to give to his brother Anselm, presumably to transmit to the music society in Graz. Then, inexplicably Anselm kept the symphony for over 30 years, until a clever conductor named Johann Herbeck tricked him into giving it up, on the promise of playing some of Anselm's own compositions.

Harry puzzled over the story. If Josef were telling the truth, Schubert only gave him the first two movements of the symphony and the sketch of the third. Could Schubert have finished the symphony after that point? From his letter to the Society, it looked as if he intended to. But, if he did, what had happened to it? Harry read on. Schubert became very ill after working on the symphony. He was hospitalized and depressed. It was a chaotic period for him. The theory that some of the music he wrote during that time could have been mislaid in the homes of friends and gathered dust seemed plausible. Harry recalled what Anselm did with the first two movements of the symphony. Then, Harry remembered the story of how the composer, Sir Arthur Sullivan, and musicologist, Sir George Grove, found one of Schubert's loveliest compositions, the incidental music to the play *Rosamunde* in a cupboard covered with 50 years of undisturbed dust in the chambers of a Viennese barrister named Dr. Schneider.

Harry shrugged. There might be something to the theory proposed in the note Stephanie received. There certainly was no way of discounting it entirely. Some of Schubert's manuscripts had been mislaid or lost. The idea that someone had deliberately held onto the final movements of the B-Minor Symphony was not out of the question. Perhaps, the writer of the note had uncovered new evidence concerning the fate of the symphony. It was a possibility, but still a long shot. The fate of the Unfinished Symphony had become a puzzle within a puzzle.

Rieder and Cochrane's books had piqued his curiosity. He wondered what the redoubtable Sir Charles Southwick would have to say when he examined the alleged Schubert score that Stephanie had in her possession. Well, they would know soon enough.

At 8 a.m., Harry waited in the driveway entrance fronting the apartment building. In his right hand, he carried a briefcase and in his left hand a small overnight bag. His eyes searched up and down the street for Stephanie's cab, but so far all that he saw was the morning flow of traffic--cars carrying workers to their government and corporate jobs. There was a brisk pace of pedestrian traffic, too--men carrying briefcases, young women in business suits, everyone looking cleaned and scrubbed, but, few looking fresh in the early morning hour. The busy life pulse of the Nation's Capital was only beginning to show itself.

At a quarter past eight, Stephanie's cab pulled into the driveway after its journey from Georgetown. Harry climbed into the back seat beside Stephanie and the cab driver began to fight his way through the morning traffic towards Union Station. The cab arrived at ten minutes to nine. Harry and Stephanie dashed through the spacious confines of Union Station like two soccer players to catch the nine o'clock train. They had barely enough time to board the train and seat themselves when the speedy train began its trip to New York.

Harry spent most of the journey reading through a folder of briefing papers and newspaper clippings about refugee problems in Africa and the Near East. He would be meeting with the United Nations High Commissioner on Refugees tomorrow morning and wanted to be ready. Stephanie seemed pensive during the trip, looking through the wide windows of the train at the countryside as the train rolled through Maryland, Pennsylvania, Delaware, and New Jersey.

As they approached the tunnels leading to New York City, Harry put aside his work and turned to Stephanie. "Going home, eh?"

"In a way. I spent so many years in New York, first at Julliard, then at Columbia."

Harry nodded. He asked slowly, "Do you want me to see Sir Charles with you?"

She smiled. "Would you? That would be nice."

"He won't mind?"

"Oh, no. You're a celebrity. He likes celebrities." She smiled. "Just as long as they're not as big a celebrity as he is."

Harry laughed. "Sounds like he has a big ego."

"A lot of people think so. It may be an occupational disease."

"What do you mean?"

Stephanie thought for a moment. "Uncle Harry, imagine you were standing in front of ninety highly trained musicians, each an accomplished performer on his or her own instrument, flute, violin, French horn, or whatever. There you are standing up there, telling these fine musicians to play faster or slower, louder or softer--how to phrase a particular part of the score. You're telling all of these men and women what to do. It's your conception of the music that matters. It's a pretty heady experience."

"Yeah, I can see that."

"Some conductors can really get worked up during rehearsals. Toscanni used to call his musicians--some of the best in the world--Bambinos."

Harry laughed. "How about Sir Charles?"

"Well, he doesn't have an explosive temper. At least, not usually. I like that. Stephanie paused. "I better phrase this delicately. Let's say he's very confident of his own judgment."

Harry laughed. "Doesn't listen to anyone else, eh?"

Stephanie smiled. "No." She added, "Some people think he's arrogant and a bit pompous. That may be true. But, he is a first rate conductor. He's done some splendid Beethoven recordings. They're among the best I've ever heard."

"I have his recording of the Fifth Symphony," Harry observed. "It has some real fire in it."

Darkness suddenly enveloped the train as it plunged into the tube under the Hudson River and rolled toward Manhattan and their destination, Pennsylvania Station. "It won't be long," Harry muttered, "and I shall meet your Sir Charles."

Harry and Stephanie made one stop on the way to Lincoln Center. For Harry it was a pilgrimage; it was at a restaurant that served thick, hot corn beef sandwiches on pumpernickel, along with potato salad and dill pickles. Harry stared at the heaping plate in front of him. "Boy, I miss food like this," he exclaimed, savoring the corn beef. "It will kill your cholesterol count, but what a way to go."

The meeting with Sir Charles was scheduled at 2:00 in a small office not far from Avery Fisher Hall. When they arrived at the office, they could hear the orchestra practicing for an upcoming outdoor concert they would be presenting at Lincoln Center Plaza. The strains of Tchaikovsky's Nutcracker Suite filled the air.

At twenty minutes to three, Sir Charles arrived. He was a tall, solidly built man with large shoulders and powerful arms. He had a large face. His hair was gray, turning white and neatly combed. He had an imposing, almost commanding presence.

"Sorry to be late," he said in crisp tones. "Had some problems in the woodwind section. Couldn't get it right."

Stephanie introduced Harry. The conductor extended his hand. "Ellison, of course. I've read your work. Good column. Glad to have you here. I wasn't aware that Stephanie had a famous uncle."

Harry laughed. "It won't be long before I will be referring to Stephanie as my famous niece."

Sir Charles smiled faintly. "Indeed," he replied. He turned to Stephanie. "Now let's see this score."

Stephanie opened up her attaché case and handed the score to the conductor. He took one look at the score, and then walked over to a desk. Rummaging through the top drawer of the desk, he pulled out a magnifying glass. "Now, let's take a good look at this." With the aid of the magnifying glass, he looked through the score. "It's not Schubert's handwriting, obviously," he said. "Wouldn't that be nice if it were?" He paused. "It's a copy, but that shouldn't be too surprising. Some of Schubert's works that we most prize today were copies."

He turned toward Stephanie. "There's a piano in a room down the hall. Why don't we go there and play it through?"

Stephanie and Harry followed Sir Charles through the corridors of Lincoln Center until they came to a room that contained a grand piano. Sitting down on the piano bench, the conductor began to play through the score. He had a strong, forceful touch that glossed over errors and lacked delicacy and nuance. Sometimes as he played, he muttered to himself, "I see..." "...interesting..." and "...well, now." It wasn't the superlatives that Harry fondly recalled from his childhood days listening to New York sportscasters describing the big moments of baseball and football games, the "Wow, what a play, unbelievable!" Still, it was clear that Sir Charles was deeply interested. How deeply came as a revelation when he arose from the piano bench, walked over to Stephanie and exclaimed, "This is astonishing. It's pure Schubert! My Dear, you have done me a colossal favor by bringing it to me."

Stephanie was both relieved and concerned. She felt compelled to express her doubts. "Technically, it's vintage Schubert, I agree. Still, I feel there's something lacking in it--that wonderful creativity--that makes me wonder whether it really is...Schubert."

"Oh," the conductor explained, "it's certainly not Schubert at the top of his form. No, far from it. I'll grant you that. But, Schubert it is. And if there is more, if this mysterious gentleman really has the rest of the Unfinished Symphony--well then I must have it. I simply must." He slapped his hands together.

"It will cost," Harry interjected. "He wants money."

"I have resources," the conductor replied, exuding confidence.

Stephanie inquired, "What do you want me to do?"

"Return to Washington. Make contact with the gentleman. Find out what he wants." The conductor sighed. "This is just amazing. Imagine! The world premiere of Schubert's complete Symphony in B Minor right here in Lincoln Center. The musical world will have waited since 1865 for this day." The conductor wiped the sweat off of his face. He sighed once again. "What an event!"

Chapter 6

Harry's interview at the United Nations with the High Commissioner for refugees and members of her staff went well. He had a good discussion about the problems resulting from years of conflict in the Sudan. He would have plenty to write about. Before taking the train for Washington, he checked with Stephanie. She would be staying in her New York apartment for several days, as she had additional meetings scheduled with Southwick. Southwick's instructions were unequivocal: "Get the manuscript!"

When Stephanie returned to Washington, she resumed her daily visits to the Library of Congress. Each day, she waited for word. It came on her fourth trip.

As usual, the note was typed and in German. It was brief.

Dear Miss Ellison,

I trust you remain in good health. Please let me know whether a decision has been reached concerning the B Minor Symphony. If the people you represent would like to have the manuscript, what financial arrangements can they make? Finally, make no effort to identify me. Your earlier effort to do so was both clumsy and childish. I will make myself known when I see fit.

Your humble and obedient servant
Schubert Friend

When Stephanie showed Debbie the note, she sizzled, sticking out her tongue in contempt. She muttered, "Clumsy and childish, my Aunt Minnie! I'll fix that guy."

Harry laughed. Debbie turned toward him. "Don't laugh so loud, Lover. It was your idea to follow him."

Harry grinned. "Come to think of it, you're absolutely right."

On the following day, Stephanie left a note on her desk in the reading room offering $100,000. The offer was summarily rejected. A counter offer was proposed of $300,000. And the payment was to be in cash, in $100 bills.

It could prove to be an expensive fiasco, but Sir Charles was ready to take the risk. Using his good offices and considerable prestige, he was able to raise the money quickly. Then, he telephoned Stephanie, asking her and her uncle, who he described cheerfully as a "man of the world," to make the transaction.

When Stephanie relayed the message to Harry, he reacted with irritation. "He's gotta be kidding," Harry said. "I don't mind the cloak and dagger stuff, but I'm not buying anything where there's no clear title. Hell, that's like buying stolen goods."

Stephanie asked sheepishly, "What do we do, Uncle Harry?"

Harry thought for a moment. Then, he said, "Get a piece of paper from Southwick, something written by his lawyers stating that all of us are acting solely in the interest of the musical public and that when we secure the score it will be turned over to the proper authorities to determine its ownership. That might be the state of Austria or, who knows, maybe the International Court of Justice. That's up to the lawyers."

"And if he doesn't give us such a paper?"

"Forget it! We're not going to stick our necks out."

"Okay, Uncle Harry. I'll talk with him."

Sir Charles was miffed at the delay. He wanted to move quickly, but realized that he had no real alternative but to do things Harry's way. Reluctantly, he agreed and set his legal staff to work. Working feverishly, in three days' time, the lawyers produced a twelve-page document disclaiming any proprietary interest in the manuscript. Rights to performances would be in the public domain while the matter of ownership was adjudicated in the courts.

The document satisfied Harry. It also satisfied Sir Charles, who knew that possessing the score would give him first crack at performing it. That world premiere at Lincoln Center was becoming a dream larger than life. He sent the money carefully wrapped up in a box to Stephanie, by special courier.

Stephanie crafted a note to the unknown correspondent asking whether it would be acceptable if Harry could join her in carrying out the swap. She pointed out that lugging around a suitcase with $300,000 worth of bills might be more than she could manage. Much to Harry's surprise, the response to her inquiry was that "Mr. Ellison's presence would present no obstacle."

Harry and Stephanie waited patiently for further instructions. On Saturday morning the phone rang in Harry's apartment. Debbie was catching up on some sleep, so Harry answered the phone. The voice he heard was badly garbled. It was a recording; an electronically altered voice that repeated the same message three times and then ceased.

The voice instructed Harry and Stephanie to go to a German restaurant that Harry often dined in. They were to be there at eight o'clock tonight, bringing the money. They would give their names to the head waiter, who would escort them to a private dining room. They would make themselves comfortable and wait.

Harry immediately called Stephanie. She was half asleep. "Show's on tonight," Harry said. "Pick you up at 7:15. You got the money?"

"Yeah," she replied, yawning. "It's sitting in the bedroom closet in a suitcase. I'm sitting here right now guarding it. I have a broom handle in case of trouble."

"Broom handle?" Harry burst out laughing. "I guess that's better than nothing. I'll be there early."

At 7 o'clock, Harry arrived at the Georgetown townhouse on N Street where Stephanie was staying. It was an attractive red brick house with oversized dark green shutters. "Nice," Harry murmured as he looked for a place to park. There was nothing to be had. Everything resembling a parking space was occupied. He began to cruise the streets. It took him fifteen minutes to find a place about a block from the house. When he finally rang the doorbell, Stephanie was waiting with her broom handle and $300,000 in a suitcase just inside the front door. Harry picked up the suitcase, opened the front door cautiously, and peered down the street. There was no one there, so off they went.

Chapter 7

Holding the suitcase tightly in his right hand, Harry shepherded Stephanie into the restaurant. As he walked through the door, he could hear singing and the clinking of beer glasses downstairs in a rathskeller that catered mainly to college students. Harry's eyes glanced about the dining room: it was all very familiar to him--from the bar decorated with steins, to the old piano which would be serving up familiar melodies to the dining room customers as the evening lengthened. The waiters were familiar too. Harry did not have to signal the head waiter. As soon as Harry entered the restaurant, the head waiter approached. "Ah, Mr. Ellison," he said, "We are expecting you." The head waiter nodded graciously to Stephanie and ushered them into a small private dining room.

"Well," Harry said as he pushed the suitcase under a table elegantly set with polished silver and long-stemmed goblets, "it looks like we eat."

"Your dinner has been ordered, Mr. Ellison," the head waiter replied. "Sauerbraten and roast goose."

Harry thought to himself. "How appropriate. I wonder whose goose is going to be cooked tonight?"

There were three settings on the table. Harry wondered, would they at long last meet their elusive correspondent who thus far had been dangling them from a distance, like so many puppets?

They waited and wondered. In a few minutes, the waiter entered bringing a bottle of vintage Rhine wine. Harry sniffed the wine, and then tasted it. It was superb. He thought that the evening might not turn out badly after all.

At about 8:30, the waiter escorted a woman into the room. She was about sixty, her hair was gray, piled high and set with a silver comb. She wore glasses and she was slightly plump. She carried an oversized purse and a brown folder tied with a string. There was nothing whatever menacing about her. She looked like somebody's doting grandmother.

Harry arose when she came in. She nodded and took a seat at the table. She handed the folder to Stephanie, and then spoke with the unmistakable traces of a German accent, "This is the manuscript I was instructed to give you. I do not know much about music--I only know a little--so you will have to examine it for yourself. Take as much time as you need." She looked at Harry and smiled. "I shall comfort myself with the wine." The waiter entered carrying a large platter. "And the goose," she added.

Harry replied, "It looks good, doesn't it?" He added, "Do we get to meet the person who sent you?"

She shook her head. "No. Not now."

Harry smiled. "When?"

She shrugged. "I was instructed to say 'at the appropriate time.' I am sorry I can answer no further questions."

As Stephanie pored through the manuscript, the woman and Harry began to eat the goose and sauerbraten along with red cabbage and fried potatoes. Outside the private room, in the main dining room, a violinist and pianist began to play Fritz Kriesler's *Libesfreud*. Touching Harry's legs was a suitcase with $300,000 in cash.

The goose went fast, with the exception of a slice Harry carved out and put on Stephanie's plate, and Stephanie had to be content with that and the remains of the Sauerbraten when she completed her inspection. "Well," asked Harry as she began to devour her share of the dinner. "What do you think?"

Stephanie nibbled at the remains of the delicious roast before looking up at Harry. "Whoever wrote the earlier manuscript--the one we gave Sir Charles--wrote this. If that was Schubert, then this is Schubert."

"Is it of the same quality as the first two movements of the Unfinished Symphony?

Stephanie shook her head. "No. I don't think so. Far from it. But it's still very workmanlike. I'm almost certain Sir Charles will be happy with it."

Harry winked at the woman seated across from him. "There's some money for you...under the table."

She laughed. "I understand your little pun. It's very good."

"Do you have some way to transport it?"

She nodded. Slowly she arose from the table. She opened the door to the main dining room. She nodded her head. Seconds later, a tall dark haired man dressed in a chauffeur's uniform walked into the room. Harry took a very good look at him, and then pointed to the bag below. The man in the uniform nodded, picked up the bag, and disappeared from the room.

The woman returned to the table to eat her dessert, apple strudel. Harry asked, "You came in style--a limousine?"

She smiled, but did not answer.

"The strudel reminds me of Vienna," Harry observed. "It's marvelous, there."

The woman nodded and replied. "Well, I must be going. It was pleasant." She sipped some coffee, rose to her feet and left.

"Should we follow her, Uncle Harry?"

"Naw. No point. The limousine's long gone." He smiled. "Enjoy your strudel."

Chapter 8

The first thing Stephanie did upon obtaining the $300,00 manuscript was to walk over to the neighborhood photocopy store and make a copy for herself. The second thing was to fax the score to Sir Charles in New York. Sir Charles's reply was a cryptic two words. "Well done." He then dispatched a courier to the house in Georgetown where she was staying to pick up the original manuscript, which would remain under lock and key at Lincoln Center.

Sir Charles was determined to include the composition in the first concert of the fall season. The score was quickly fashioned into "parts" for the various sections of the orchestra. Rehearsals began immediately. The musicians were told that they would be giving the world premier of this "realization" of Schubert's B-Minor Symphony (Sir Charles no longer referred to it as The Unfinished) and that they would damned well be ready. He was tightlipped about where the manuscript had come from and offered no explanation. He admonished his musicians to "say nothing whatsoever" about the score to anyone--that he wanted it to be a surprise to the musical world.

Despite Sir Charles' admonition for secrecy, leaks began immediately. Husbands talked to wives, wives to friends. Rumors began to circulate. The gentlemen and ladies of the press soon got wind of the fact that something very unusual was going on in the rehearsals of the symphony orchestra and began to badger Sir Charles for information. Sir Charles' only comment was "no comment."

Sir Charles' lack of disclosure only increased the curiosity of the media which redoubled efforts to find out what was happening. Stories began to appear daily in the newspapers about a monumental discovery. A national tabloid featured an article revealing that Franz Schubert had communicated the score to a new symphony from beyond the grave to a psychic who would soon be receiving scores from Beethoven and Bach as well. As rumors mounted, music critics became featured guests on television talk shows, voicing learned if not necessarily informed opinions about what Sir Charles had discovered. To prevent the whole thing from turning into a circus, Sir Charles scheduled a press conference for Thursday afternoon, three weeks before the beginning of the fall concert season.

On Tuesday of that week, two days before Sir Charles' press conference, Stephanie received a letter from her thesis advisor at Columbia University, Dr. Johanna Hoffman.

Dear Stephanie,

I returned from my long vacation in Canada on Monday. My daughter lived in a cabin on a remote lake and it was a wonderful experience--something I needed. When I went to my office, Ms. Havens, the department secretary, gave me the manuscript you left for me.

Stephanie--I was astonished to say the least. Part of Schubert's Sixth Symphony? Could it really be so? After playing the score on the piano, I was left with a feeling of uncertainty. It is, certainly, a very interesting piece of music. Stylistically, it was clearly Schubert, but was it the "real McCoy"? Like you, I had serious doubts.

I decided to run the computer program on the score --- you are, of course, familiar with my computer program that enables one to compare musical scores on a wide range of stylistic features. As you know, I have worked out a "model" for Schubert. The model is based on a number of his compositions, written at about the time the Sixth Symphony was sketched. The model provides a composite view of Schubert's musical tendencies. When I compared the score you sent me with my computerized model, the results were astonishing. I have never seen anything like the results I obtained. It was amazing. I was so bewildered by my findings that I needed to talk with someone, so I telephoned a colleague who had seen a copy of my program some years ago. He agreed that the results were wildly improbable and suggested that I should discuss the whole matter with you as soon as possible. Accordingly, I am coming to Washington, D.C. on Thursday. I have reservations at the Mayflower and will be in my hotel at about 9:00 p.m. I will call you just as soon as I settle in.

Cordially,
Johanna Hoffman

P.S. To paraphrase Shakespeare, "Something is rotten in Vienna."

Stephanie shared the letter with Harry and Debbie. Harry turned to Debbie and said, "Hey, Beautiful, do you know what the functional equivalent of 'Something's rotten in Vienna' is?"

Debbie replied, "No."

Harry bent over and whispered in her ear, "I smell a rat."

Debbie smiled. "I was right. He is a crook."

Harry nodded. "Could be." He turned toward Stephanie. "Shouldn't we warn Sir Charles? I heard he's having a press conference Thursday afternoon. He could make a bloody fool of himself if this thing proves to be phony."

Stephanie reflected. "I don't know, Uncle Harry. Johanna's method is very controversial. Some musicians question its validity. They have been very skeptical. A few have been scathing in their comments. I'm not sure how Sir Charles feels about Johanna's work, but they were colleagues at Julliard and I'm sure he'll take it much more seriously if Johanna talks to him directly. I'll ask her to do that when I see her Thursday night."

Harry nodded. Then, he asked, "What about the press conference? He's going to hold that before you see Johanna."

Stephanie laughed. "Don't worry about that. Sir Charles will be fine. He's a smoothie."

At 3 o'clock on Thursday afternoon, Dr. Johanna Hoffman watched a television press conference from her home in Scarsdale. Sir Charles Southwick faced a bevy of reporters from local television stations and the city's major newspapers. There were also reporters from the networks, cable news, public radio and television, and a few correspondents from abroad.

Sir Charles began the conference by reading a brief statement announcing that his opening night program would include a recently discovered realization of Schubert's Symphony in B Minor. After he read the statement, he deftly negotiated his way through a minefield of tough and persistent questions. Johanna admired his dexterity. While never quite claiming that the work he would soon be giving its world premiere was in fact Schubert's complete score of the Unfinished Symphony, he left that distinct impression time and time again. "The musical public would have to judge for itself," he said, adding, "I'm confident the public will welcome this work enthusiastically." Asked what he thought of the work by a correspondent from London, he replied, "It is extraordinary; Schubert through and through." And when asked in a follow-up question, was he sure that the music was Schubert's, he replied, "Obviously, one can't be fully certain, but there are compelling reasons to believe it may be authentic." Sir Charles looked confident, sounded confident, and in truth was confident.

Within two hours of the press conference, Avery Fisher Hall was sold out. Dr. Hoffman repeatedly tried to order a ticket but was unable to break through the jammed phone lines. Disappointed, she straightened up her desk and left a memo to herself to call Sir Charles first thing upon returning. She placed the printout of the computer results in her attaché case, picked up a packed overnight case and headed for Pennsylvania Station.

Stephanie waited impatiently for Johanna's arrival. At 9:30 she called the hotel and was told that Dr. Hoffman had not yet arrived. When she called at 10:30, she received the same answer. She tried again at 11:30; the same response. Johanna was running very late. Perhaps, she stopped somewhere for dinner. But, that seemed unlikely; she would probably check into her hotel first. Perhaps she had to cancel her trip. Better check on that. She called Johanna's home.

Johanna's daughter Maria answered the phone. Maria had been sleeping. "No," she answered in a half daze, her mother had definitely gone to Washington.

Stephanie's concern mounted. At midnight she called the hotel once again. Dr. Hoffman still had not yet registered.

Shortly after midnight, Stephanie woke Harry out of an early dream. When he shook off his slumber, he listened attentively. "I don't like it," he said. "It doesn't sound like your professor. Describe her to me and Debbie will check with the police."

Moments later Debbie made the call. Did they have any reports on a forty five year old white woman, about 5'4", stocky build, brown hair, ruddy complexion, wearing glasses--who was planning on staying at the Mayflower Hotel?

The reply was immediate. An unidentified woman, meeting that description, was found dead, shot twice at close range in the chest. Her purse, bags, or anything else she may have been carrying, were gone. The apparent motive was robbery. The case had been assigned to Captain Tony O'Meara at Homicide.

Part II

Chapter 9

When Debbie first joined the metropolitan police force, she worked for Tony O'Meara, then a lieutenant in the Sixth Precinct. Harry knew Tony from way-back-when, in the days when Tony was a rookie police officer and Harry was reporting on local crime. It was a meeting of old friends, though the circumstances were grim, particularly for Stephanie who only hours earlier had performed the miserable task of identifying the body of her teacher and friend. One awful look and she knew that it was Johanna Hoffman.

The three of them sat with Tony in his office at Homicide. Tony was tall and athletic. He wore a heavy pair of glasses that gave him a thoughtful look. Tony had been a scholar-athlete at Yale, one of the first African-Americans to have that distinction. Pictures of his wife and children adorned the desk. His oldest son was in a football uniform. He was a senior at St. John's High School, Tony explained. He had received scholarship offers from Howard, Wake Forest, and Illinois. Tony beamed when he talked about his son.

Harry noticed that Tony looked leaner than he used to. He asked, "Lost some weight?"

Tony nodded. "It's the job. We're on the go all the time. You wouldn't believe the number of shootings we have in this town. Some of them are drug related. Some are robberies. Some domestic violence. Some for no reason at all. It's these teenage kids that are driving me crazy. 'He disrespected me.' If I hear that line again, I may shoot somebody myself. It's just unbelievable what's going on these days."

Harry nodded.

Tony continued. "My guess is that Dr. Hoffman was a victim of random street violence. We have so much of it. Probably a robbery. Her purse and bag were taken. It was dark. There was only one witness, an elderly man.

He was pretty far away. He said the assailant was white, male, tall. Grabbed her stuff and fled."

Harry shook his head. "I doubt if it was random street violence, Tony. Got time to listen to a long story?"

Tony grinned. "Are you involved in it?"

Harry grinned back at his old friend. "Only at the margins, Tony." Harry settled back in his chair. He talked slowly. "First, there is a chance--I don't know how much of a chance--but it's possible that this murder may be connected to two earlier deaths. I don't know that this is the case but it's something to think about. You remember the Wolfson murder in Rehoboth?"

Tony nodded. Harry continued, "Like Dr. Hoffman, Dr. Wolfson was an eminent musicologist with the same specialization, early 19th Century music--Beethoven, Schubert, and Mendelssohn. And a few months before, a Yale professor of music by the name of Edward Todd Griffith died an unnatural death which was ruled a suicide--but nonetheless was very suspicious."

Tony interrupted, "Same specialty?"

Harry nodded. Tony mused, "This is getting interesting." He shook his head. "Still, it could be a coincidence. Both the Wolfson case and Dr. Hoffman appear to be robberies." He paused, "There's more, I take it."

Harry smiled. "Oh, yeah, a lot more. Enter Stephanie Ellison. Exceptional graduate student in music. Goes to Vienna to gather data for her doctoral thesis on Schubert. The day she returns she finds someone has been shadowing her--perhaps stalking her." Harry turned towards Stephanie. "Stephanie, why don't you tell Captain O'Meara about what happened at the Library of Congress?"

In a halting voice at first, and then with more steadiness, Stephanie described her trip to Vienna. Then, she related how when she returned to the States, she decided to continue her research at the Library of Congress. She told about the succession of notes she had received and the fragments of musical scores that appeared to be the work of Franz Schubert. She described the trip she had taken with Uncle Harry to see Sir Charles Southwick in New York City and how Sir Charles was determined to obtain the completed version of the Symphony in B Minor. Then, she related how she and Uncle Harry had gone to the restaurant where they had exchanged

$300,000 for the manuscript. Finally, she showed Tony Dr. Hoffman's letter revealing her skepticism about the authenticity of the score.

Tony scratched his chin. Turning towards Stephanie he asked, "Who knew that Dr. Hoffman was coming to Washington?"

"Her daughter--Johanna lived with her daughter Maria in Scarsdale. Johanna's divorced. Her ex-husband lives in Seattle. Apart from Maria, maybe the music department secretary--I'm not sure of that--me, of course--Harry and Debbie--and, oh yes, she mentioned a colleague whom she had talked with who advised her to see me."

Tony asked, "Do you know his or her name?"

Stephanie shook her head. "I have no idea."

"Not much to go on," Tony observed. He turned towards Harry. "Any ideas, Old Buddy?"

"Yeah. Three to be exact."

Tony chuckled. "I knew it. Wouldn't be Harry Ellison if he weren't two steps ahead of everybody."

"Or behind," Harry muttered.

Tony laughed. "Well, spill it out."

"Harry took a deep breath. "Number one," he began. "Dr. Hoffman was carrying some analyses she made of the Schubert score with her when she was murdered. Everything she had with her--purse, bags, I would imagine a brief case--was taken by the killer. If we are right and this is not a random street crime, then the killer not only wanted her out of the way, but wanted her papers as well."

Harry paused. "It's clear from her letter that she relied heavily on the computer in her work. The analysis must still be on disk in her office. We ought to get it."

Tony nodded.

Harry continued, "And while we're at it, it wouldn't be a bad idea to search her office. Maybe, we can find out the name of her colleague that urged her to see Stephanie."

Harry's eyes searched around the room, and then he looked again at Tony. "Point two. Somebody has been stalking Stephanie. This shadowing may have started in Vienna. It certainly looks that way. The stalker kept such a close eye on her--he or she knew exactly when Stephanie arrived in Washington, where she went after she arrived--that it's very likely the stalker came from Vienna on the same airplane. Can we get the passenger list for that flight? Maybe, we can draw up a list of suspects."

"Can do," Tony replied.

Harry scratched his chin. "Let me throw in an addendum to the Vienna investigation. Stephanie had one major contact in Vienna, a musicologist by the name of Leopold Rieder. From what Stephanie tells me, Rieder knows more about Schubert than anyone else on the planet. If anyone could orchestrate a swindle, he could. Besides, he was familiar with Stephanie's itinerary." Harry looked at Stephanie who nodded her head. Swiveling in his chair, Harry smiled at Tony. "And he had a motive for a swindle. He's desperate for money. He put his money into a real estate venture that went belly up. His house was up for auction. Maybe, the police in Vienna can do some checking for you about Dr. Rieder."

Tony replied, "Interesting. I'll look into it."

Harry continued in a bulldog manner, "Point three. There were two prior deaths, Griffith and Wolfson. It's time we took a closer look at these cases ourselves...to see if there's anything that ties in with Dr. Hoffman's killing." Harry moved his body towards Tony. "Now, I know you're undermanned as it is, but suppose I do some digging. I've always wanted to take a look at Yale University--being a plebeian who went to Columbia. I'll go up there and see what I can find. Nothing like being a journalist to give you cover for snooping."

"Fair enough," Tony replied. "Who goes to New York to look through Dr. Hoffman's office?"

"Stephanie, for one. She knows what the stuff means. And Debbie, if you can pull her off the Jones' case from the bunko squad. She's very good with computers."

"Jones' case. You don't mean Howard Jones? Is he at it again?" Debbie nodded.

Tony laughed. "That man is as elusive as The Scarlet Pimpernel."

Harry asked, "Can you spring Debbie for a few days?"

"Yeah. I can do it. I still think the odds are that this case is street crime, pure and simple, but I can't ignore what you've told me. I'll call the New York Police Department right now and ask them to set things up for Debbie and Stephanie to look through Hoffman's office."

When Tony called Lieutenant Alverez in New York and began to explain about the murder of Dr. Hoffman and the need to search her office, he did not get very far. "Somebody beat you to it," the lieutenant interrupted. "Somebody broke in about 6 o'clock this morning. Must have been surprised by the security guard. Shot him three times. Died this morning. Never regained consciousness. Looks like we'll be working together on this one. Send your people up tomorrow. Our criminalists should be through with the office by then."

When Tony O'Meara hung up the telephone receiver, he grimaced and shook his head. "Ain't no street crime, Harry. This is turning into a big mess. Dr. Hoffman's office was ransacked--the security guard was killed. May have some kind of a nut on our hands."

Harry nodded. "That's what I've been saying all along."

Tony reflected. "Look, I don't want to alarm you folks, but you're both involved in this thing and you could be targets." He turned towards Harry. "Stephanie knows more about this business--whatever it is--then anyone else now. I think she should have more security."

Harry nodded. "I agree."

Tony said, "You have a couch she could sleep on?"

"Better. We have an extra bedroom."

"Sure. I remember. That would be fine." Tony looked directly at Harry. "You can help, Harry. You're good in a pinch. But it's Debbie I'm thinking about. She's got a gun and she's a crack shot."

Harry smiled, "Yeah. She's good all right."

"I'll have her assigned to Homicide on a temporary detail. She'll go with Stephanie to New York as planned. And she'll stay with her wherever she goes."

Tony turned toward Stephanie. "Okay with you?"

"More than okay. I'm very grateful."

Tony smiled faintly. "Well, we have our work cut out for us--New York, New Haven and a passenger list of a flight from Vienna...which may or may not include a demented serial killer."

Chapter 10

Lieutenant Frank Thomas of the New Haven Police Department looked tanned and relaxed after two weeks of vacation, mostly spent fishing with his son and grandson. He was nearing retirement, but didn't look his age as he had a full head of curly black hair, clear unwrinkled skin, and a well-muscled body. He greeted Harry in his office with a warm handshake. "Captain O'Meara called this morning," he said. "He told me that you were an old crime reporter and was working unofficially on a homicide case. He asked me to give you any assistance I could."

Harry smiled. "Thanks," he said, "I appreciate it." Then, he added, "Do you know Tony?"

Thomas nodded. "Yeah. We met two years ago." He thought for a moment, "More like three. Time flies, doesn't it? It was at an International Chiefs' of Police Convention. Both our bosses were participating in a symposium on youth violence. Tony and I were helping out as staff. We had dinner together. Nice guy--Tony--and smart."

"Went to school here," Harry said.

"Yeah. Played some football. He was a wide-out. In those days they used to call them ends, like bookends."

Harry laughed. "I remember."

Thomas continued. "My dad and my grandfather were big Yale fans. None of us went to the school but we were big fans anyway. We used to go to the games. I saw Tony get banged up. When I met him at the convention, he told me it was a knee."

"The doctor told him not to play anymore. He would risk a permanent injury. So he concentrated on academics. Just as well. He's a very fine detective."

"He has an excellent reputation." Thomas shifted his weight in the chair. "Now, Mr. Ellison, I understand you want to discuss the Griffith case."

Harry nodded. "It was your case, right?"

"Um-hum."

"Well, there's a chance that Griffith's death might be linked to some more recent killings. It's only speculation at this time, but worth looking into. So, I would appreciate it if you would tell me whatever you can about Griffith's death."

"All right," he said. "We'll drive to his house. It's not far. I'll show you where it happened."

Harry nodded. "I have a rental car outside if you want to use it."

Thomas shook his head. "Thanks, but we'll use mine." He smiled. "It's a nice day. I'll give you the scenic tour."

They left the police station and walked to Lieutenant Thomas' police cruiser. They fastened their seat belts and Thomas drove slowly through the streets near the campus. He pointed out art galleries on Chapel Street and Audubon Street, and then passed by the Peabody Museum of Natural History. "Not exactly the Smithsonian," he quipped, "but it's nice."

Harry nodded. Thomas continued to cruise along at a leisurely pace. In a few minutes, he turned into a side street. It was a pleasant lane with detached houses and well-kept lawns on both sides of the street. The detective parked the car across from a white wooden house with a single large evergreen tree on the lawn. He pointed at the house. "That's it," he said. "Try picturing the lawn with a foot of snow on it. That's the way it was the morning the body was discovered. Right there on the lawn, near the tree. The body was half covered with snow. I remember that morning well. It was cold and blustery. We had a heavy snowfall the preceding night, followed by northwest winds."

Harry inquired, "Who discovered the body?"

"One of the boys who lives next door. His name is Rod. Must be about six or seven years old. Anyway, Rod and his older brother were having a snowball fight on their front lawn." The detective pointed to the lawn. Except for two small bushes, it was open space. "Well, the older boy, his name--let me think--yeah, it was Tom--was pummeling his younger brother--and Rod, like any good general, retreated. The nearest cover was the big spruce tree on his neighbor's lawn. He made a dash for it and nearly stumbled over the body of Professor Griffith. The kid was shocked. He screamed, called for his brother, who came running, took one look at the body, grabbed him by the arm and ran home to tell their mother. She called the police."

Harry nodded. Thomas took a long look at the lawn across the street, as if he were re-experiencing the scene of last winter; looking at the body of Professor Griffith in the snow. Then, he shook his head and said, "We've seen all we can see here. Now, I'll tell you what happened next." Thomas looked at his watch. "We have some time," he said. "Rather than go back to the office, I'll take you up near Science Hill. There's a nice spot to park near there and we'll have more privacy than in the office." He shrugged. "There are some delicate aspects to this case."

Harry smiled faintly, but did not comment. Instead, he inquired, "What is Science Hill?"

"It's part of the University where some of the science buildings are located. It's a pleasant area with lots of trees. There's a large newer building that's the biology center and more traditional, college buildings that house other science labs. The medical center's out that way, too. I like the area."

Science Hill proved to be an impressive sight. From the vantage point of the parked police cruiser, Harry spied a large tower perforated with rectangular open facings. The tower dominated the surrounding buildings that seemed cast from an earlier age. Some had small towers resembling the bell towers that would have been at home in an Italian Renaissance landscape.

Thomas observed, "That's where the men and women in the white lab coats work. Somewhere in there, someone will discover something that will win a Nobel prize."

"Smart people," Harry replied.

"You bet," Thomas said. He shifted his body and looked toward Harry. "Now, back to Dr. Griffith. We went into the house. The door was open. That's probably not too significant but it does seem to rule out an accidental death--Griffith locking himself out and dying in the storm from exposure. The inside of the house was very orderly. Everything was put away--the dishes, glasses and cups. There was no sign of anything unusual. Certainly no sign of a struggle. If there had been an intruder, Griffith had not put up a fight. But then again, he was aging and somewhat frail. He couldn't have fought very much, if he wanted to. But, as I said, there is no evidence that anything happened.

The medical examiner's report was interesting. It would have been easy to assume that Griffith died from hypothermia--the appearances were all that way. But the medical examiner found that Griffith died from an overdose of barbiturates. A very large overdose, I might add." Thomas scratched his head. "Based on his doctor's testimony, the death was ruled as suicide."

"Why did Griffith go outside after trying to kill himself with all those pills?" Harry inquired.

"Good question to which there is no good answer. The thinking was that Griffith might not have been sure that the pills would kill him, but he knew the freezing temperatures would."

Harry scratched his head. "The same reasoning would apply if someone forced him to take barbiturates at the point of gun and then when he was unconscious dumped him outside."

"Exactly."

Harry looked at the detective. "Were you convinced it was suicide?"

Thomas smiled. "Should I be frank?"

"Please."

"No. Not at all. I argued rather vigorously that the cause of death was indeterminate--equivocal if you prefer--and that we should carry out an extended psychological autopsy before a definitive ruling was made."

"Psychological autopsy? I've heard the term. I can't pull it back."

Thomas smiled. "It's just a fancy name for an extended investigation trying to reconstruct the state of mind of the decedent. They had a unit out in Los Angeles for many years--detectives, psychiatrists and others that would conduct interviews with people who knew the decedent. They would ask whether the decedent had been depressed, was he under stress--things like that. The suicide team was often able to resolve equivocal deaths-- determining whether the death was an accident, suicide or homicide."

"Interesting," Harry observed. "And you wanted to do something like that for Griffith?"

"Oh, yeah. I started to. I talked to Griffith's neighbor Mrs. Hart--the boys' mother. The professor had come over for a cup of coffee the day before he died. She said he seemed quite cheerful. I also talked to Dr. Rubinstein, the music department chairperson at Yale. He couldn't believe the suicide verdict. But that's as far as I got. Griffith's physician, Dr. Ian MacGregor, said that in his professional judgment, the death was a suicide. Dr. MacGregor has a lot of clout around here--he's on the hospital board and is an officer in the State Medical Association. When he pronounced the death a suicide, it was ruled a suicide. That was it."

"You're still not convinced?"

"Not at all."

"What's Dr. MacGregor like?"

Thomas paused. "I'd almost rather not comment. You're not going to publish this, are you?"

"Nothing you say about MacGregor. Not a word."

"Okay." He reflected for a moment. "You may not have been around long enough to remember the Ben Casey Show on television. Anyway, Casey was an idealistic young doctor always dealing with medical crises. And there was this older, more experienced guy named Dr. Zorba who was his mentor. This scene sticks in my mind. Casey has been facing a monumental problem. Maybe, one of his favorite patients is dying. Then, Zorba says something like, 'Ben, you're a doctor, not God!' Well, it was a pretty good line in the show. It also makes a lot of sense. The problem with Dr. MacGregor is that he doesn't recognize the distinction."

Harry laughed. "I've known one or two people like that including an editor. You know, I think I'll pay a call on Dr. MacGregor."

"Don't tell him what you want to talk to him about or he won't let you in the door."

"Thanks for the tip. Who else would be worth seeing?"

"I would go see Dr. Rubinstein at Yale. He knew Griffith well. Better than anyone."

Harry nodded and wrote Rubinstein's name down on his note pad. Then, he asked, "Anyone else?"

"No. I'd start with those two and see what you think."

Harry smiled. "Thanks a lot. You've been very helpful."

"I'm glad. Say 'Hello' to Tony when you get back."

When Harry returned to the police station, he telephoned Ian MacGregor's office. A recorded message greeted him stating that the office was closed for the day and that Dr. MacGregor would be available in the morning. Harry wondered whether the doctor was at home. He checked the telephone book again. The home address was listed. Harry thought about calling him, but remembered Thomas' caution. "What the hell," Harry muttered to himself. "I'll just drop in on him."

Harry's name and reputation gained him admittance to the doctor's large, comfortable, expensively furnished home. The couch looked like it cost a mint and the coffee table tops were made of polished marble, fashioned in Italy. The walls were covered with original paintings, including drawings by Picasso. But whatever good will Harry's reputation engendered evaporated immediately when Harry broached the subject of Edward Todd Griffith. The expression on the doctor's face became a scowl. His reaction was abrupt and gruff, almost menacing. And MacGregor had the body to be intimidating. He was a large man, tall and bulky with powerful-looking arms.

"I don't talk about my patients," he said. Then, he punctuated his sentence with the word, "period," almost spitting at Harry in the process.

Harry was solidly built himself. He was not used to being intimidated and did not plan on starting now. He continued his conversation about Griffith as if he had not heard MacGregor's Sherman-like statement. Grinning at Dr. MacGregor, he asked "Are you certain that Griffith killed himself?"

MacGregor replied in spite of his protestation that he would have nothing to say. "Of course, I was certain. He committed suicide. I said so, didn't I?"

When Harry replied that the professor's friends didn't think it was likely he killed himself, he replied angrily, "Those fools! What do they know?"

The interview went from bad to worse when Harry asked, "Did Griffith tell you he was thinking about suicide?"

"Tell me? Of course he didn't tell me. Do you think I wouldn't have done something to try to prevent it? What do you take me for?"

"You didn't know--then--that he was planning to take his own life?"

"Of course not."

"Then what made you so sure that he did?"

The doctor's face reddened. His fists clenched. "Damn it! I told you it was suicide. He was depressed about the loss of his wife. That's all that I'm going to say. Now kindly get out of here Mr. Ellison before I throw you out."

Harry grinned once more, but took the hint. As he left the house, Harry wondered whether Dr. MacGregor would examine a man with an ax blade in his back and call it a suicide.

Dr. Eli Rubinstein, Chairman of the Yale University Music Department was much more forthcoming. Rubinstein was a man of short stature. He had a very high forehead. His eyes were deep brown and had a piercing quality. He seemed a picture of concentration. His office was very small and crowded with books. On the wall were autographed photographs of American composers--Leonard Bernstein, Aaron Copeland and Samuel Barber. Harry began the conversation by stating that he was looking into the deaths of three eminent musical scholars, the latest being Dr. Johanna Hoffman. Rubinstein replied quickly, almost interrupting Harry in his eagerness to talk. He said that he had found the news of Dr. Hoffman's murder deeply distressing and he had been wondering whether there were any connections between her death and the deaths of Professor Griffith and Professor Wolfson. Now that Harry had broached the subject he was anxious to talk about it.

Dr. Rubinstein asked Harry how he had become involved in the matter. Harry replied, "My niece--who has been staying with me, Stephanie Ellison--was a friend and pupil of Dr. Hoffman. Dr. Hoffman was on her way to see Stephanie when she was killed."

Dr. Rubinstein smiled. "Stephanie--Stephanie Ellison--sure. I didn't realize the connection. I've met her. Brilliant young woman. I'd like to have her on the staff here someday. She has the makings of a first rate musical scholar."

Harry smiled, feeling a surge of family pride. Stephanie would be pleased by Rubinstein's comments. "That's very kind of you," he replied. He leaned back in his chair. "Professor Rubinstein, how likely is it that Edward Griffith took his own life?"

Professor Rubinstein answered without hesitating. "Not at all. Sure, he was still grieving for Jean, his wife. She died two years ago. She was a wonderful woman. My wife and I knew her well. We were very good friends. But, Ed not only loved her, and deeply, he loved his work, too. He loved teaching. I saw him the day he died. He was talking enthusiastically about the new book he was writing. He didn't sound at all like a man about to commit suicide. I didn't believe it then. I don't believe it now."

Harry nodded. "What about Dr. MacGregor's opinion?"

"You met the man?"

Harry nodded.

"I think he's an ass, but draw your own conclusions."

Harry smiled and thought to himself, "I already have."

Harry fiddled with his glasses, and then asked, "Did Dr. Griffith have any enemies?"

"That's not an easy question to answer. If you're talking about Yale, I doubt it. Ed was well liked. He was an engaging conversationalist. He was one of the wittiest men I ever met. But as you probably know, Mr. Ellison, Ed had a long career before coming here. He worked as a music critic in New York about 10 years before joining our faculty. He may have made enemies there."

"What was he like as a music critic?"

"Ed had terrific musical sensibilities. He had a great sense of what was well performed and what wasn't. When something was well played, he would say so. He could be very complimentary."

"And when it wasn't?"

"He'd say that too. He wasn't afraid to criticize something that he thought was badly done. And when something was really awful, with his wit, he could be scathing."

"I imagine he bruised a few people's feelings along the way."

Dr. Rubinstein smiled. "I wouldn't be at all surprised if he did, Mr. Ellison. We have some terrific egos in the music profession. You'd be surprised at the grudges some people harbor." He sighed. "Even in my own department. We have a guy who was turned down for a national endowment grant and blamed me for it. Said my recommendation wasn't glowing enough. Since then, he's done everything he can in small ways to make my job as Department Chairman miserable."

Harry shook his head. "I know what you mean." Harry thought of Percy Williams, an editor who had done the same thing to him. Harry rubbed his glasses. "Do you know Leopold Rieder?"

"Sure. But not very well. Why do you ask?"

"The deceased were all Schubert scholars."

Rubinstein nodded. "True," he said slowly. "Yeah, they were. I met Rieder a few times at conferences." He smiled. "The way he speaks English--it's worse than the way I speak German." His smile broadened. "His phrasing sounds so stilted at times. And his conversation is so analytical. He puts his points into numerical order: von, two three. Reminds me of--"

"Kissinger?"

"Exactly. Henry Kissinger." Rubinstein laughed.

Thinking of the notes Stephanie translated, Harry wondered whether they might possibly have come from Rieder. There was something pedantic about the style. Harry asked, "Did you ever correspond with him?"

Rubinstein shook his head. "No." He paused, "But Ed did. He and Rieder were trying to put on an international symposium on Schubert's music. They tried to set it up for two or three years, but the project finally fell through."

"How come?"

"Funding," he said slowly. "It's difficult to get money for something like that. The humanities are not a high priority in today's world. Ed was very upset when it fell through. I imagine Rieder was too. I understand he put a lot of work into it. The whole thing must have been frustrating."

"Was there any hint of animosity between the men?"

"Ed never mentioned anything. But he wouldn't have told me if there were. He would have kept it to himself."

Harry glanced at his watch. He would have to be leaving soon. A final thought took hold of him. "Just one more thing," he said. "What happened to Griffith's personal papers?"

"I don't think you'll find much. His nephew--can't remember his name--was executor of his estate. Ran a nursing home in Seattle. He said he wasn't into classical music and couldn't see any point in keeping the papers. He said he was going to shred them."

Harry shrugged. "So much for that idea."

He arose, smiled, and extended his hand to Rubinstein. "Thanks a lot," he said. "You've been very helpful."

The professor shook his hand. "Nice to have met you. Come again some time."

When Harry left Rubinstein's office, he strolled through the campus, venturing into several lovely courtyards. He paused for a moment and looked at an old building with turrets on the roof that were punctuated with spikes. The turrets reminded him of the helmets worn by German soldiers during World War I. Smiling at his fanciful association, he walked on over to College Street and continued along until he found a restaurant.

He ordered a cup of coffee, and then took out his cell phone. He dialed his apartment. There was no answer. He hung up and dialed Tony's office. Tony was in the office. After an exchange of pleasantries, Harry asked, "Is Debbie around? I telephoned the apartment. She wasn't there."

Tony answered, "She and Stephanie left here a few minutes ago. They had overnight bags with them. They're on the way to New York."

Harry thought briefly. Then, he said, "Tony, there's still a lot of daylight time left. I'm in the mood for a drive. I think I'll drive to Rehoboth on the way home. I'd like to look into the Wolfson case. Could you call the police in Rehoboth and pave the way for my visit?"

Tony said he would be happy to oblige. They exchanged a few more pleasantries. Harry said goodbye and hit the road.

Chapter 11

In the morning, Harry awoke, walked to the window of his efficiency apartment, opened the drapes, and gazed outward at the Atlantic Ocean. The waves were surging over the shore line, lapping up onto the beach. The sight exhilarated him. Quickly he shaved, showered and dressed. He wanted to walk down to the beach and fill his lungs with the ocean air before beginning his tasks for the day.

In a matter of moments he was outside, treading his leather city shoes on the nearly-deserted beach. Sandals and a swimsuit would be more appropriate dress, he thought, but the early morning's allure of the ocean was irresistible and thoughts about dress codes soon vanished from his mind. He walked on the sand, stopping a few feet from the amorphous line separating the dry sand of the beach from the sand wet from the morning splash of incoming tide. Then, he turned and walked along the beach, enjoying the sound of the waves and the sight of seagulls that soared overhead or alighted on the beach. For a few moments, he stopped and admired a group of seagull chicks parading along the shore line. It had been a grinding drive from New Haven the night before; he had encountered heavy traffic around New York and on the Jersey Turnpike, but the morning walk soon erased any feeling of weariness. He walked almost two miles before halting at a tall lifeguard observation post. Turning around, he retraced the steps along the beach. There were now the glimmerings of activity. He passed a teenage couple with their arms locked around each other's waist and an elderly man who doffed his captain's cap as he walked by. Harry returned to his apartment and started up his rental car. Next on his agenda was a good breakfast, perhaps hot coffee and waffles, and then on to the police station.

If Lieutenant Frank Thomas were nearing the end of his career as a police officer, Officer Yvonne Drake must have been close to the beginning of hers. She looked about twenty-three or twenty-four if that. Her hair was a lovely auburn color and it set off her pale green eyes. She had rosy cheeks and a nice smile. She was a little on the plump side, but the weight seemed to go well with her. The proverbial girl next door, Harry thought, "Why not?"

Harry introduced himself, and Officer Drake said she had been expecting him. "The person who you'd really like to see is Detective Shoemaker, but he left the department about six months ago to take a job with the FBI. He's out West in one of the field offices. I think it's Kansas City. Shoemaker was in charge of the case, but I worked with him on it, so I can tell you about it."

Harry was about to make a comment about Willie Shoemaker, the legendary jockey, but held his tongue. Officer Drake was probably too young to have heard of Shoemaker unless she was a horse-racing fan.

"Sounds good," Harry said. "Tell me what happened."

"Well," she began, "we don't have many homicides in Rehoboth, so when something like that happens, you really remember it. It really sticks in your mind. It happened on the morning of July second, just about a year ago. It was just after ten in the morning. Dan, that is Detective Shoemaker, answered an emergency telephone call from Mrs. Acosta. She was very upset. By the way, Mrs. Acosta and her husband own a house on a side street about a block from the beach. They live in the downstairs part of the house and rent the upstairs part during the summer season. There is a separate entrance to the upper floor. You get there by a wooden staircase."

Officer Drake paused and looked at Harry as if to see that he was following her. Harry nodded and she continued. "Mrs. Acosta had rented the apartment upstairs to Professor Wolfson for two weeks, July first through July fourteenth. Wolfson arrived on July first. His wife and teenage son were expected to drive down from Princeton and join him on July fourth."

Officer Drake took a deep breath and continued. "On the morning of July second, Mrs. Acosta knocked on the door of Wolfson's apartment. She wanted to make up the bed and change the towels. No one answered, so she used her own key to unlock the door. When she walked inside, she found Wolfson's body on the rug. There was blood all over the rug. She called her husband who was downstairs and then called us.

Shoemaker and I rushed right over there. Wolfson had been dead for some time. The medical examiner estimated the time of death at 8:00 p.m.

the preceding night. He extricated two bullets from the victim's chest. The gun was fired at close range. The murderer couldn't miss."

Harry asked, "Did anyone hear the shots?"

"Mrs. Acosta said that she had heard shots between eight and eight-thirty." Officer Drake shrugged her shoulder. "She said that she thought the shots came from the T.V. Her husband watches T.V. all the time. He loves shows with chases and shootouts, and one was on at the time. Mr. Acosta is deaf in one ear and won't wear a hearing aid, so he turns the volume up."

"Mrs. Acosta has a tough life," Harry observed dryly.

Officer Drake smiled. "I guess she does."

"What did you find in your investigation?"

"We got some assistance from the state police to go over the crime scene. The only fingerprints uncovered were the victim's, the landlady's-- Mrs. Acosta's--and those of a previous tenant. We checked her out. She was in Buffalo at the time."

"The gun ever turn up?"

"No. No sign of it. We talked with Mrs. Wolfson after she arrived in the afternoon. She told us that her husband had taken an expensive camera and a laptop computer with him. They were missing. There was no money in his wallet and his credit cards were missing."

"Sounds like robbery," Harry mused.

"That's what we thought."

"Did Wolfson have any enemies?"

"His wife said that she didn't know of any. Dan talked to some people at Princeton. Wolfson was highly regarded. They said he was a brilliant man and well liked."

Harry thought for awhile and then asked, "Any other witnesses at all?"

"Just one. A teenage girl named Doris Chapin. She's a high school student who lives with her aunt. She had a summer job at the Napoli Pizzeria as a waitress. Doris reported that she saw a large black automobile leave the street at about the time the murder was committed. She couldn't give us any details. She didn't hear any shots fired."

"I'd like to talk with her and Mrs. Acosta. Would you mind?"

"No, not at all. I'll give you the Acosta's address. It's an old house. Doris is working at Napoli's again." She smiled. "If you find anything, let us know."

Harry nodded. "You can count on it."

The Acosta house was a gray wooden house that was badly in need of fresh paint. It looked seedy. Harry studied the wooden steps that afforded a separate entrance to the apartment that Wolfson had stayed in so briefly. The entrance was secluded. Anyone walking up the steps would not have drawn notice from passersby. The upstairs apartment was a good candidate for a burglary. If there were no deadbolt lock, it would be easy pickings. But a burglar, he reasoned, would probably have to know that Wolfson was there and would have waited for another time. Unless, Wolfson was asleep.

Harry knocked on the door to the house. When the door opened a tiny crack, Harry was nearly knocked off his feet by the blare of the television set. The sound grated in his ears. He grimaced. Wolfson wasn't sleeping. Not with that volume.

Mrs. Acosta was unwilling to let any strangers into her house, even after Harry presented the good offices of Officer Drake. Harry smiled and said that he understood perfectly well why she should be cautious and wondered whether they could sit outside on the nice comfortable lawn chairs near the entrance to the house. He added it would only take a few minutes of her time. Mrs. Acosta reluctantly agreed.

Mrs. Acosta was a white-haired woman who looked like she might be about seventy years old. She was plainly dressed in a faded blue summer frock. She wore no makeup or jewelry, only a pair of thin speckled eyeglasses which she touched now and then in a nervous gesture. In speech that was rapid, one sentence quickly following another without seeming pause, she related how she and her husband had been unable to rent the apartment since the murder, what a nice man Mr. Wolfson was, how awful he looked lying on the floor, how she had nightmares ever since she discovered the body, how the police had found nothing, and how she dreaded the possibility that the killer might come back again. Now, she said they had installed a burglar alarm system but still that might not be enough.

Harry felt a wave of sympathy for Mrs. Acosta. Her life had been torn upside down by this improbable event. She had been deeply traumatized by discovering Wolfson's bloodstained body. It was as if she had been in a war zone or had been the unlucky resident of a house demolished by a tornado or earthquake. But she told him nothing that shed new light on the murder. So he listened sympathetically until she had played herself out, and then left.

Harry drove to the Napoli Pizzeria, parking his car in front of the restaurant. As he walked inside, he sized up the place. It wasn't very large. There were several tables, covered by checkered red and white table cloths in the middle of the room; two booths in the back of the room and a carry-out stand flanked by several chairs near the cash register. Large posters of Venice, Rome and Naples decorated the rear wall. It was too early for the lunch time trade so the restaurant was nearly deserted. One customer was seated at a booth, sipping coffee. Two waitresses stood in the corner, talking in low tones.

Harry sat down in the other booth. One of the waitresses, a short girl with cropped blonde hair, walked over to the booth. The name "Doris" was printed in block letters on her shirt. "I'm in luck," Harry thought.

Harry ordered a hamburger and an orange crush. Then, he introduced himself, telling her that he had obtained her name from Officer Drake and asked if he could speak to her for a few minutes about the car she had seen the night of the Wolfson murder. She nodded, put in Harry's order, asked the other waitress to cover for her and joined Harry in the booth.

"I'm not sure there's much I can tell you," she said. "I was working half-time here last summer. This summer I'm full-time, trying to save money." She smiled. "I'm going to the University of Delaware in the fall. Last summer I was just having fun hanging out at the beach and working in the early evening until 8:00. After work, I walked home to my aunt's house. It's on the street past the street where Dr. Wolfson was killed. That night I saw this big black car pull out in a hurry."

"Was it larger than your average car?"

"Oh, yeah. It was twilight and the light was fading, of course. But I would say it was a limousine. Yeah. I'm sure it was a limousine. That's what I told Detective Shoemaker."

"Did you get a look at the driver?"

"No. I couldn't see inside the car. It was like my view was being blocked by something."

"Blocked?"

"Yeah."

"Curtains?" Harry suggested.

"Yeah!" she exclaimed. "It might have been curtains. I only got a glimpse, of course. But I couldn't see inside the car. And I tried to. You see, I was curious. You don't see limousines around here. It must have been curtains or a screen of some kind."

"A screen would be kind of awkward in a car," Harry mused.

She laughed. "It would, wouldn't it? But there was something definitely blocking my view. It must have been curtains."

Two customers entered the restaurant. Doris eyed them. "I have to work," she said. "Do you need me anymore?"

"No," Harry replied. "You've been very helpful. Thanks."

Harry ate his hamburger and returned to the car. His work at Rehoboth was over. But he was in no rush to drive home to an empty apartment. Debbie and Stephanie would be in New York. It was a sunny, breezy day. The beach looked inviting. "What the hell," he thought. "Why not enjoy it?" He strolled down the boardwalk until he found a shop that sold tee shirts, straw hats and sandals. In a few minutes, he looked half the part of a vacationer.

Harry found an empty bench on the boardwalk that overlooked the beach and the ocean. With his straw hat shading his eyes from the sun, he looked at the beach, now spotted with large umbrellas and at the water's edge, where children splashed into the incoming waves. He looked out further into the ocean where he spied two sailboats shimmering in the sun. One sail was a gleaming white spec, the other a brilliant red. "Red Sails in the Sunset," he said affectionately. It was a song his grandmother had sung to him when he was a child. A wave of nostalgia swept over him as he thought in turn of his grandmother, his father long dead, his mother living in San Francisco, and his brother, Dick. The professor, he thought, smiling. Then, his thoughts turned to Dick's only child, Stephanie, and to the ugly mess she had stumbled into. Somehow, he would have to shepherd her through it. He knew deep down that there was only one way to be sure that she would be safe and that was to find out who was responsible for these killings and bring them to justice.

Chapter 12

Debbie and Stephanie scurried through the campus of Columbia University seeking shelter from a sudden summer shower. Debbie had wanted to take a quick tour of the campus because Harry had gone to school here and had often reminisced about his college days. But their brief excursion through the grounds of the University had been cut short by a cloudburst, and they dashed past buildings whose names were all too familiar to Stephanie, having spent the last two years here completing the requirements for her doctoral degree. They dashed past Schermerhorn and Avery and the Law Library, finally stopping at Dodge, which housed Dr. Hoffman's office. They stood for awhile inside the entrance way of the building, shaking off the water droplets from their clothes. Then, they ascended a flight of stairs, walked down a corridor and halted when they encountered a policeman guarding the entrance to Dr. Hoffman's office.

Debbie identified herself and they were admitted into the office which was now a crime scene. Dr. Hoffman's office had been torn apart; not so much in a blind rage, as in a systematic dismemberment, like an anatomy instructor might strip the flesh from a cadaver while lecturing to students about the arrangement of muscles. Whatever the killer had been looking for, there was little doubt that he or she had found it and carried it off. Debbie tried the computer. The memory banks had been wiped out. She opened a box labeled, *Disks for Analyses of Musical Compositions*. There were three subdivisions in the box: Bach through Grieg; Haydn through Rossini and Schubert through Wagner. The last batch of disks was gone.

They spent two hours looking through the office. Their efforts were in vain; they found nothing helpful.

The rain had stopped when they left Dodge, although the sky was still overcast and threatening. They walked away from the campus, down Broadway until they stopped in a small cheerless restaurant where they sat on stools at the counter and ordered coffee. Stephanie looked at Debbie. "Uncle Harry's idea didn't pan out. What do we do now?"

Debbie pondered. "I've been thinking about that. Harry had the right idea--but maybe the wrong place."

Stephanie was curious. She asked, "What do you mean?"

"Look--I use computers at the office. I also have one at home in our study. Many people have more than one computer. Maybe Dr. Hoffman has a computer at home. Maybe she has duplicates of her computer files there."

Stephanie brightened. "She does have a computer in her home. Her daughter, Maria mentioned it to me when I was visiting them. She was joking about how her mother was turning into a workaholic."

"How well do you know Maria?"

"Well enough."

"Do you think she'll let us take a look around?"

"Sure."

"I'll clear it with Lieutenant Alvarez. Then we'll give Maria a call." She smiled. "Scarsdale sounds fancy. I've always wanted to go to a fancy place."

Johanna Hoffman's residence did not turn out to be all that fancy but there was a large sunlit room filled with healthy looking potted plants and dominated by a Steinway grand piano--all one could wish for as a practice studio. There was also a comfortable office that contained rows of bookshelves stretching from floor to ceiling crammed with books and journals about music and music history. Bulky gray metal file cases containing correspondence and research notes filled up one corner of the room while a computer work station was in the other.

Johanna's younger sister Louisa had moved in to stay with her niece during the funeral period, and both she and Maria had granted permission to Debbie and Stephanie to look through Johanna's office. The two women went immediately to the computer. While Debbie switched on the machine, Stephanie searched for a box containing disks that was similar to the one that had been rifled at the University.

Stephanie's search did not take long. She yelled, "Bingo!" There it was, meticulously arranged, a box of disks for analyzing musical scores arranged by composers. Only this time, the files from Schubert to Wagner were intact.

Stephanie thumbed through the disks until she came to one labeled *Composite Schubert Model: Modal Tendencies for Schubert's Orchestral Compositions for Representative Samples, Years 1817-1827.* She withdrew the disk from the box and handed it to Debbie.

Debbie placed the disk in the drive slot and called up the directory of files. There was a series of files, each dealing with specific stylistic features that were the components of Dr. Hoffman's model. Stephanie read aloud from the list of file names as she scanned them: "Use of Sonata Form, Use of Lengthy Introductions, Length of Melodic Lines, Characteristic Phrase Structure, Use of Dissonance, Use of Chromatic Scales, Frequency of Key Changes." She shook her head and skipped further down the list. "Prominence of Brass, Incorporation of Folk Melodies." Her eyes darted further down the list. Suddenly she smiled as her eyes encountered the listing she wanted, "Overall Graphic Profile." She exclaimed, "This is it! Johanna's computerized model of Schubert's musical tendencies--his musical profile."

Stephanie handed the disk to Debbie who put it into the computer. A long graph appeared on the screen: on the abscissa of the graph were listed the specific stylistic features of the model, on the ordinate, a scale of values from 0 to 100. The value for each component of the model was represented by a thin line rising from the abscissa.

Debbie looked at the screen, shaking her head. "I hope this means something to you. It's Greek to me."

Stephanie thought for a moment. Then, she spoke slowly in a professorial tone. "Let me try to put Johanna's program into perspective. Debbie, think about a person who is very familiar with classical music. Now, imagine that she hears a recording of a classical piece that she is unfamiliar with--something she has never heard before. Chances are that she might make a pretty good guess as to who composed the music. For example, if she heard a piano piece that had a haunting melody with lots of delicate grace notes and embellishments, she might say, 'It sounds like Chopin' and chances are that she would be right. Chopin had a very distinctive musical style. And the same is true for many other composers. It would be difficult to mistake Handel or Mozart or Tchaikovsky. And who else constructs musical monuments like Beethoven? What Johanna did was to dissect the common ingredients of musical style, and put them into this program. The program helps one analyze musical compositions and comparing composers."

Stephanie took a deep breath and continued. "Now, some aspects of the program are quite objective and easy to use, hardly more than counting key changes. Other aspects of the program are more subjective and only a trained musician could use them, and that's only after considerable study of Johanna's codes and procedures. Even then, two scholars might differ somewhat in their analyses."

Stephanie reflected, "Obviously, Johanna's approach is limited. Despite her best efforts, the program could miss holistic features of the music, the uniqueness in the way these musical building blocks are used-- some would argue that the program might miss the very essence of the genius that went into the composition. Still, I find her program very useful in differentiating composers and a valuable analytical tool. Johanna was anxious to improve the program to make it even more useful, but, sadly, this task will have to fall to someone else now."

Debbie nodded. Stephanie continued. "The vertical lines you see on the screen represent a kind of average tendency for the way the composer--in this case, Schubert--writes his music. If you put any one of his compositions into the computer--it would differ from the model in some respects--just like you or I would differ from the profile of an average woman."

Debbie smiled, "Like I'm shorter."

"Right--and I'm taller."

Debbie's smile broadened. "And we're both thinner."

Stephanie giggled. "Right again!" She reached into the box and pulled out a disk labeled *Schubert's Symphony No. 9, The Great C Major*. "Here, I'll show you what I mean. Print out the model that's on the screen, and then we'll run this one--Schubert's Ninth Symphony."

Debbie printed the graph of the model, and then ran the profile for the Ninth Symphony and printed it. Stephanie placed the two sheets together so that the two graphs were flush against each other. Then, she held the papers in front of a bright desk light. "You can see how much difference there is in the length of the lines," she observed. "The symphony deviates in many respects from the composite model."

Debbie leaned closer to Stephanie to get a better view. She nodded. "I see what you mean."

"Now," Stephanie pondered, "where is the movement of the Sixth Symphony I sent her?"

Stephanie searched through the Schubert listings, but the disk was not there. She shook her head in disappointment, but then suddenly she noticed at the very end of the box a small white envelope. She opened the envelope and there it was. *Scherzo Movement, Schubert's Symphony No. 6* with a large question mark following the title.

Excitedly Stephanie picked up the disk and handed it to Debbie. Quickly, the computer generated the graphic portrait. When Debbie gave the printout to Stephanie she held the thin sheet of paper flush against the graph of the general Schubert model. Her eyes opened wide. She exclaimed, "I don't believe this! Debbie, look! Do you see what I see?"

Debbie looked at the printouts illuminated by the light. She gasped. "They're almost identical. It's almost as if they had been traced."

Stephanie nodded. "The print-out for the scherzo movement of the Sixth Symphony fits the general model for Schubert like a glove!" She shook her head, and then stood silent for a moment; as if she were trying to comprehend the meaning of what she had seen. Then, almost unconsciously she moved toward the window of the office and peered through beige colored curtains at the world outside. The heavy clouds were breaking up, although the sun was still hidden. The street was empty except for a solitary boy throwing a tennis ball into the air and trying to catch it. Suddenly, Stephanie felt a flash of anger. She realized that she was being used as a pawn in some kind of crazy scheme. And Johanna had been murdered because of it. The feeling sickened her. She felt her body begin to shake. She stared blankly ahead, not really focusing on anything as she tried to regain control of her emotions, to let the anger and grief subside. Finally, she turned toward Debbie. In a voice that cracked with emotion, she said, "This is either an amazing coincidence or this symphony is as phony as a three dollar bill. Debbie, I think I've been used and I'm mad as hell."

Debbie nodded. Her eyes radiated concern. "I understand what you're saying," she said. "You have every right to feel angry. Very angry."

Stephanie shook her head in dismay, but she seemed soothed by Debbie's words. When she replied, her voice was steadier. "Debbie--you thought this whole thing was phony--from the beginning."

Debbie smiled. "Yes, I did. But I couldn't prove it." She touched Stephanie's arm. "Try not to get down on yourself, Stephanie. You were always skeptical about the score. You came right out and said as much--that evening in the apartment. I remember."

"Yeah," she replied reluctantly. "I did." Then, she added slowly, "Still."

"I know," Debbie sighed and was silent for a moment. Then, she said, "You know, Stephanie, we still can't prove anything. And we don't know who did it or why. I think we should get back to work. We need to go through Dr. Hoffman's files. Harry suggested that we ought to find out who Dr. Hoffman had talked to about her analysis of the score you sent her. I think we'll have to go well beyond that now. Let's check all of her correspondence and see if we can discover the names of anyone who has been using this model. It could be our Schubert friend."

Stephanie nodded. They walked over to the file cabinets. The cabinets were unlocked. Dr. Hoffman's correspondence files proved voluminous. Debbie took half of the files over to the computer work station and began to read through them while Stephanie sat in a large brown easy chair by the window and looked through the remainder. As Stephanie began to read, she noticed a statistical journal on the floor beside the chair. Curious, she picked up the journal and looked through the table of contents. One of the article titles was circled in red. Its title was "A More Precise Method of Calculating the Probability of Rare Events," by a mathematician named Bakshi. Stephanie turned to the article and found a small piece of paper inserted in the journal. The paper was replete with calculations and there was a note scribbled at the bottom of the page: "The probability of the alleged Sixth Symphony fitting the model so closely are approximately 1:999999 or about one in a million."

When Stephanie showed the note to Debbie, Debbie grinned. "It's a terrific find, Stephanie!" Harry and Tony will go bananas over this one. Somehow I'm not surprised. I think we have one hell of a con game going on."

They returned to the files, reading through them for about thirty minutes. Then, Debbie called out. "I think I've found what we're looking for. There's a list of people who have requested reprints of her articles on her computer model and also some correspondence with people who wanted copies of her computer programs and her coding procedures. I think the correspondence is the important stuff. I doubt that anyone could use the model without the computer program and the coding procedures."

Stephanie agreed. "The article just summarizes her procedures and presents some of her findings. You would need the program and the coding scheme to do anything."

Debbie pulled out the correspondence file. There was a bundle of letters. "Let's see who wrote her," she mused to herself as she began to look through the pile. "The first letter is from a guy at MIT. He wanted to see if he could simplify the program to make it run more efficiently."

Debbie perused a second letter. "This one is from a professor in Milan, Italy. He wanted her program on Vivaldi."

Stephanie laughed. "You can throw him out. She doesn't have a program on Vivaldi. She used to joke about Vivaldi. Said he wrote the same concerto 400 times. They all sound pretty much alike."

The next letter was from an assistant curator of the Art Institute in Chicago. She wanted to study the possibility of adapting the technique for comparative analysis of painters. "Nothing there," Debbie remarked, tossing the letter into the discard pile.

There were several letters asking for the program on Beethoven, two correspondents wanted the program on Brahms, and one on Wagner. Debbie continued sorting through the letters looking for interest in the Schubert program.

"Hey! I got something!" she called. "There's a guy in Sykesville, Maryland named Oliver Queen who wrote Dr. Hoffman about the Schubert program. Let's see. He apparently had the program and this is a thank you note. Get this, Stephanie." Debbie's voice rose in excitement. "He said he used the program to create Schubert-like melodies. And--hey--he had been a computer programmer and worked on projects in artificial intelligence."

"Wow!" Stephanie replied. "That's right on target. Creating Schubert-like melodies. He's got to be a suspect."

"Yeah. Maybe, Number One."

Debbie put Queen's letter aside and continued to peruse the remaining letters. Suddenly, she let out a squeal. "This will interest you, Stephanie. It's from Salem, Massachusetts, from Thaddeus Cochrane. Isn't he the guy you mentioned who wouldn't answer your letter?"

Stephanie nodded.

"Well, let's see what Mr. Nice Guy says." She read aloud:

Dear Johanna,

A thousand thanks for sending me your article. It is extremely interesting. I am sure the powers that be in the musical world will under appreciate your contributions as they always do for truly creative work. As we are both painfully aware, innovators and artists always pay the price. That interview Sebastian had on television in which he ridiculed your work was outrageous. I felt like shaking him by the ears or his long hair. I am sorry you had to endure that. I appreciated the computer programs you enclosed for Haydn and Schubert. I had hoped to use them to see if I could detect some of the more subtle influences of the former upon the latter. However, I must tell you that computers absolutely baffle me. I discussed the possibility of buying one with the salesperson at our local store and he started talking in a strange language about gigabytes and ram. I'm afraid I panicked and bolted out of the store. I'm afraid if the adage, 'You can't teach an old dog new tricks' applies anywhere, it applies here. So, I am returning your program with thanks.

Cordially,
Thaddeus

"That's interesting," Debbie mused. "Doesn't sound nasty at all-- does he? Sounds like a real gentleman--and compassionate." She looked at Stephanie. "Who's this Sebastian he mentions? It's not *the* Sebastian, by any chance?"

"None other."

Debbie smiled. She sighed. "Oh, wow."

Stephanie returned the smile. "He is dreamy, isn't he?"

Debbie thought of Sebastian's almost shoulder-length blonde hair, his deep blue eyes and that aristocratic yet soulful face. She sighed again, replying with a slow "Yeah."

Stephanie voiced a thought. "I bet Uncle Harry can't stand him."

Debbie laughed. "You're right about that. Every time I turn on the television for one of his concerts, when Sebastian walks over to the piano in that gorgeous white cape, Harry mutters an obscenity and acts like he's going to throw his can of beer at the tube. He says Sebastian reminds him of Liberace. My mother used to tell me about Liberace. He used to put a candelabra on the piano." She laughed again. "Harry says that Liberace was a hack. He says at least Sebastian can play decently. Sometimes he admits grudgingly that he plays very well. But, then, Harry complains that it's all show biz. And does Harry go ballistic when Sebastian starts throwing all that B.S. about how he's on a crusade to deintellectualize music and put passion and feeling back into it. You know what I mean. Breaking down the barriers between the performer and the listener. It's too much for Harry."

"It's show biz, all right. He makes a pile of money."

Debbie asked, "Did you ever see his face when he's playing Chopin? He looks like he's tormented, in agony." She smiled, "Or maybe ecstasy? You're a performer, Stephanie. Is that for real?"

"About as real as the Scherzo Movement we just analyzed in the computer. I think he practices his expressions before a mirror."

Debbie broke up, falling into a helpless fit of laughter. "You're disillusioning me," she said, catching her breath. Regaining her composure, she asked, "What happened between Sebastian and Dr. Hoffman?"

"Sebastian's on this go-back-to basic emotions kick. He's been arguing that contemporary—particularly mid and late twentieth century classical music had become much too intellectualized and simply bores people. While this polemic is all part of his act, he's got a point. Some compositions lack any interesting melodic line and some are so dissonant, they're downright ugly. When Johanna announced her computer programs for analyzing music, Sebastian jumped all over her. She--her work--was the perfect foil. Sebastian is, of course, big time--a celebrity who gets on all of the late-night TV shows. On one show--he might have been stoned, the way he went over the limit. He was downright rude and abusive."

"How did Dr. Hoffman react?"

"Johanna was mad as a hornet. She was furious. I've never heard her swear before. She told me she wrote a letter to Sebastian that would scorch the little bastard's ass."

Debbie smiled. "A little bad blood between the two of them, would you say?"

"More than a little."

"I don't know if he's involved in this business," Debbie mused. "But he might be. Somebody's got to interview him." She smiled impishly. "I think I'll volunteer."

"Harry will love that."

Debbie laughed. "I know." She cast her eyes at the remaining letters and began to look through them. For awhile, there was nothing interesting, no mention of the Schubert program. Then, she came to the last two letters in the folder. The writers both wanted the Schubert program. After scanning the content of the first letter, she spoke to Stephanie. "This letter is from someone named L. C. Houston. She's a psychoanalyst in New York City. Ever heard of her?"

Stephanie shook her head.

"I'll read it to you."

Dear Dr. Hoffman,

I would very much appreciate a copy of your computer program on Franz Schubert's music. I am interested in doing some scholarly work, analyzing both Schubert, the man, and his music through the lens of psychoanalysis. I have the required background in music, having degrees in music from Princeton, and I am a practicing analyst. There are excellent computer programmers in my husband's corporation to assist me in using the program.

Thanking you in the advance.

L. C. Houston

"Sounds like a very interesting project," Stephanie observed

"Yeah. Doesn't sound like a murderer."

"No. Not at all."

"Still. We're going to have to check her out. You never know."

Debbie picked up the last letter. "Hey," she said. "This one's from Vienna. It's in German. You better read it."

Stephanie picked up the letter. "Why, it's from Professor Rieder... Leopold Rieder. Remember I mentioned that I met him when I was in Vienna?" She scanned the letter. "He wanted the Schubert program, too. He said he wanted to compare the scores Schubert wrote as a student with his mature works. He offers four hypotheses underlying his investigation. They're rather technical."

"I can imagine," Debbie replied. "But this is getting interesting. Think about it, Stephanie. Rieder lives in Vienna. He knew you personally. He certainly was in a position to keep track of your whereabouts. He had Johanna's Schubert program, and he had a motive."

"Motive?"

"Yeah. He was broke; you told us that."

"He was broke all right. He needed money in a bad way."

"Three hundred thousand dollars would look real good to someone who was broke." Debbie put the letters back in the folder. "That's three, four—maybe five--leads. Not a bad day's work," she said. She slapped her hands together. "Let's go back to New York City, report to Lieutenant Alvarez, and then call Harry and Tony."

"And get some lunch," Stephanie added. "I'm starved."

"And get some lunch," Debbie agreed. She looked at her watch. "Maybe dinner."

When Debbie finished her conference with Lieutenant Alvarez, the lieutenant made a telephone call to the Scarsdale Police Force requesting that Dr. Hoffman's files be secured and that the house be kept under surveillance in the event the killer might try to break in. Then, Debbie telephoned Tony reporting what they had found. When she finished her story and told him that she was gong to phone Harry, he replied, "I doubt you'll find him in. He's in Rehoboth, or maybe on the road back. You two struck gold in New York. When you talk with Harry, he'll be green with envy."

"Thanks, Tony. But the only time I've ever seen Harry turn green was after eating my lasagna."

Chapter 13

At three o'clock on the following afternoon, Harry, Debbie and Stephanie joined Tony in his office. It was time to share information and ideas. Hot coffee in styrofoam cups was passed around, as well as powdered sugar donuts. The women accepted the coffee but passed on the donuts. Harry took both donuts and coffee but let them sit. He was anxious--almost impatient--to talk. His eyes darted back and forth from one of his companions to the other, as he waited for them to settle down. Finally, he seized the moment and began to speak. His tone and manner were didatic, as if he were giving a lecture. "We've had four deaths," he began. "The security guard is the anomaly in the group. He was just trying to do his job, but was in the wrong place at the wrong time. The other three were all distinguished musicologists, all Schubert scholars. The first death, Griffith's, was ruled a suicide, the second, Wolfson's, and the third, Hoffman's, were apparently killed during robberies. My trips to New Haven and Rehoboth were undertaken to look into the first two deaths.

Let's consider Griffith. Was it a suicide? The detective who led the investigation--and he is a veteran police officer--is not at all convinced that it was. The people who knew Griffith best don't believe it was suicide. Not for a moment. The case for suicide rests entirely on his physician's statement. He said Griffith was depressed because his wife died two years ago and he committed suicide because he was depressed. The problem with his theory is that most depressed people don't commit suicide and that Dr. Rubenstein, Griffith's colleague at Yale, saw him on the day he died and said Griffith didn't act at all depressed. On the contrary, he was completely engaged in his work.

I went to see Griffith's physician, Dr. Ian McGregor. He's a big, boorish man." Harry grinned. "When I asked him about Griffith, he nearly threw me out of his house"

Tony laughed. "That would be pretty hard to do, Harry."

Harry smiled. "I think if I had spent another thirty seconds there, he would have tried."

Tony asked, "So what do you think, Harry?"

Harry sipped his coffee and tore off a piece of the donut. "I think like the detective. McGregor carries a lot of clout up there. They went on his opinion, and he's an opinionated man. The case was closed much too quickly. At best the verdict of suicide is questionable. It could just as easily have been murder."

Tony nodded, and then asked, "What did you find in Rehoboth?"

"There's no question that Wolfson was murdered, gunned down at close range in his vacation apartment. The question that remains unanswered is whether the murder happened during a burglary or whether it was premeditated." Harry nibbled at the donut. The sugar coated his chin with a faint streak of white. He wiped off the powder with his fingertip. "I saw the apartment house," he reflected. "It would have been a perfect setup for either robbery or premeditated murder. The apartment has a secluded, separate entrance. Anyone could have entered unobserved by passersby. To make things even easier for an intruder, the television set in the apartment below is almost always on and turned up to an extreme volume. The landlady's husband has a severe hearing loss.

The evidence for a burglary is that cash, credit cards, a camera, and a laptop computer were taken. Of course, if it were premeditated murder, taking those things would make it look like burglary, and that would be a smart thing to do. And we all suspect our killer is very smart."

Harry looked at Tony. "The Hoffman death looked a lot like a street crime."

Tony nodded. "Touché."

Harry continued. "An experienced burglar would not have bungled the job so badly. He would have watched the house and robbed it when he knew Wolfson was out. That would have been very easy to do. If it were a burglary, the person doing it was a novice.

The police investigation yielded only one clue, but it provides a tantalizing though admittedly tenuous link to the Schubert forgery and by extension to the Hoffman killing." Harry turned toward Debbie. "Debbie, describe the automobile you saw that picked up the girl you followed at the Library of Congress."

"It was a big, black limousine," she replied.

"What were the passengers like?"

"I couldn't see. There were curtains in the limousine."

Harry nodded. "About the time of the murder in Rehoboth, a teenage girl was walking home from her part-time job as a waitress. Near the house where Wolfson was murdered, she saw a big black car start quickly and move rapidly up the street. She described the car as a limousine."

Debbie exclaimed, "Oh, boy!"

"There's more," Harry went on. "The girl--her name is Doris--told me that she was curious and tried to see who was inside the car. She said that she couldn't see inside, that something was blocking her view. Now the light was poor, but there was definitely something obstructing her view. A screen, perhaps, or..."

"Curtains," Debbie said.

"Yes. In retrospect she believes it probably was curtains."

This time it was Tony who said, "Oh, boy!"

"So, to summarize: three Schubert scholars die unnatural deaths, there is an ongoing scam relating to a Schubert manuscript and a big, black limousine keeps cropping up. Oh, I almost forgot," he added. He turned towards Stephanie. "Stephanie, you remember when we were in the restaurant with the lady from Vienna?"

"Sure. How could I forget?"

"Remember that man who came in to carry the money?"

"Yes."

"How was he dressed?"

Stephanie's eyes popped. "In a chauffeur's uniform."

Harry mused, "I wonder if there was a black limousine parked outside the restaurant? I could kick myself for not stealing a look. Stephanie suggested I should."

Tony spoke slowly, "So there are links between the cases. Tenuous, but still there are links." He looked at Harry. "Debbie briefed me yesterday about what she and Stephanie found in Dr. Hoffman's home in Scarsdale. Did she tell you?"

Harry sipped more of his now cooling coffee. "Indeed, she did. She and Stephanie took turns. They did a great job, didn't they?"

Debbie beamed. Praise from the professor, she thought. Tony agreed with Harry's sentiment. "They struck gold." He turned toward Debbie. "Why don't you go over it again so we're sure we're all on the same page.

Debbie nodded and with Stephanie's help repeated the story of their trips to Columbia University and to Scarsdale. And, then they all studied the correspondence from Johanna's file about the Schubert Program to refresh their memories. When they had finished, Harry looked at Tony. "Last time we talked about checking the telephone calls Dr. Hoffman made before leaving for Washington. I wonder if she made any long distance calls, or even out-of-the-country calls?"

"Austria, eh?" Tony grinned. "I had the same idea. I called Alverez yesterday about it. He said he'd look into it."

"Good," Harry replied. "Now that we've filled each other in, I suggest that we go over the list of suspects."

"I agree," Tony said. He reached for a manila folder on his desk. Opening the folder, he withdrew a lined yellow sheet of paper filled with notes.

"Okay," he said, "Let's start with the easiest, Oliver Queen. I checked him out this morning. Queen has been living in Sykesville, Maryland for a good part of the last eighteen months." He turned toward Debbie. "I hate to tell you this, Debbie, he's been a resident of the mental hospital in Sykesville for much of that time. Diagnosis: bipolar illness--he is manic-depressive. When he wrote Dr. Hoffman from the hospital, he was probably recovering." Tony shrugged, "Or who knows, maybe he was in a manic state...in a frenzy of creativity. I've read that many highly creative people are bipolar. At any rate, the guy in Admissions is checking his admission and discharge dates carefully to see whether he was in or out of the hospital during the murder dates."

"Darn," Debbie said. "He really looked like a possibility."

"Yeah, and he still could be. We just have to wait and see." Tony replaced his scribbled notes into the folder, withdrew another yellow sheet of paper filled with notes, and then deftly shoved the folder to the side of his crowded desk. After glancing at the notes, he turned towards Harry. "The second person on our list is Sebastian, a.k.a. Bjorn Sabatini. Mother born in Stockholm, father in Milan. Pianist, showman, big supporter of Green Parties, heartthrob to thousands if not millions of young women."

He turned toward Debbie, and then Stephanie, "Present company, of course, excepted."

Debbie blushed. Harry smiled. "I'm not so sure of that, Tony."

"Well," Tony went on, smothering a chuckle. "Sebastian had a public dispute with Dr. Hoffman, but beyond that, what do we know? Is he tied up in any way with the Schubert scam? Did he know Griffith or Wolfson?"

Debbie added, "Or Rieder?"

Tony scratched his head. "My information is scanty. Somebody's going to have to talk with Sebastian." He looked at Debbie. "He's in Los Angeles. Feel like flying out there to interview him?"

"Sure," she said, trying not to sound too eager. She added casually, "When?"

"I'll see if I can set up an appointment for tomorrow morning. Police business should get his attention."

Harry asked, "While Debbie's in L.A., who's going to keep an eye on Stephanie?"

Tony grimaced. "Damn. I forgot about that." He paused and turned toward Debbie. Maybe we...'"

Stephanie looked at Debbie, and then interrupted Tony with a burst of enthusiasm, "I could spend the day at Harry's office. Nobody ever shoots anyone in a newspaper columnist's office."

Tony responded dryly, "Maybe someone should."

Harry quipped, "Anyone special in mind?"

"Yeah, but not you old chum. Not until we finish that chess game, anyway."

Harry thought of the chessboard on the coffee table in his living room, half filled with delicately carved ivory chess pieces. Tony and he had been playing a game off and on for nearly a month and it still wasn't clear who would win. Harry spoke. "Stephanie can spend the day with me at the office. We'll be fine." Then, he added, "Tony, if Debbie flies to L.A. later, why don't you and Claire come over tonight and we'll finish the chess game. Bring your revolver, too. You can ride shotgun in Debbie's absence."

Tony nodded. "Sounds good. I'll check with Claire." He looked at Harry, his expression having changed to all business. "Debbie brought up Rieder. Let's talk about him." He reached across his desk for the manila folder. As he was about to open the folder, the telephone rang. Tony picked up the receiver. "This is Captain O'Meara," he said. He listened, and then said, "Wait a minute." Reaching for a pencil, he jotted down some dates. "You're sure?" He listened again and replied, "Um hum." Once more he listened. Then, he inquired, "Do you happen to know where Mr. Queen is now?" Tony listened and nodded. "That's very helpful," he said. "Thanks."

When Tony hung up the phone, he looked at Debbie. "Be of good cheer! Mr. Queen is back on our list of suspects. He wasn't in the hospital at the time of any of the murders. Moreover, he's living right here in Washington, D.C. It should be easy to find him. He's playing at one of the jazz clubs." Tony smiled. "You know how much I love jazz, Debbie. I'll look up Queen myself, after hours. Now, let's get back to Professor Rieder."

Opening Rieder's folder, he scanned it before reading aloud. "Leopold Rieder, lifelong resident of Vienna, professor of music, distinguished scholar--late classical and early romantic periods. Married to Irmgard Hochbaum. One child, Franz, who lives in Switzerland. He manages a brewery. Two years ago, Rieder invested heavily in the development of an Alpine ski resort, which was found to be not only unsuitable but dangerously situated because of possible avalanches. The project collapsed. Rieder is now bankrupt. His partner in the enterprise has a shady reputation. Charges of both fraud and embezzlement are pending against his partner. Rieder himself is still under suspicion, although it is possible that he was simply duped and was a front man."

"Not exactly Mr. Clean," Harry commented.

"No," Tony replied.

Debbie asked, "Has Rieder been in the United States during the span of these murders?"

"Once." Tony smiled faintly. "It was the week of Griffith's death."

Harry raised his eyebrows. "Interesting," he mused.

Tony scratched his head. "Oh yeah! I wonder if Rieder had any contact with Griffith during his trip here?"

"They did write each other," Harry observed. "Dr. Rubenstein, the music department chairman at Yale, told me they were trying to organize a symposium. They both worked hard on it, but it fell through for lack of funds. I thought about looking through Griffith's correspondence to see what I might learn about their relationship, but Griffith's papers have most likely been destroyed. From what I heard, Griffith's executor, his nephew, didn't see any point in keeping them." Harry looked at his now empty coffee cup, and then ate the last morsel of his donut. "Tony," he inquired, "What was Rieder's destination in this country?"

"Right here. Washington, D.C."

"I wonder if he went to New Haven that week?"

Tony smiled. "So do I. Harry, he could have. We'll ask him of course. But if he lies, it might be a job proving it."

Debbie said, "We do know that Rieder had a motive and he had the Schubert program. Did he have enough skill in musical composition to use the program to fake a Schubert score?"

Harry turned to Stephanie. "What do you think, Stephanie?"

Stephanie thought for a moment. She shook her head. "I really don't know, Uncle Harry. He's never published anything that I know of. Certainly nothing major that's been performed." She paused. "Of course, he is well trained in composition, and he probably knows people who could help him do it. For example, he may know gifted students in musical composition or people who write film scores. The person would have to be well trained and talented. Yeah, Uncle Harry, It is certainly possible he could have managed it."

Tony thought out loud. "We certainly can't write Rieder off. As Debbie said, he had a motive and with Griffith, at least, the opportunity. Probably not so with Wolfson or Hoffman. Unless, of course, he arranged something. He has an unsavory associate, so who knows?"

Tony continued to muse, half to himself. "We'll have to follow up on this. I'm not sure how. I suppose I could fly to Austria, but I haven't spoken a word of German since college days." He smiled at Harry. "How's your German, old chum? You speak German halfway decently."

Harry returned the smile. His mind took flight and the image of Sergeant Schultz, a character in the early television series *Hogan's Heroes* came to mind. He clicked his heels and bowed slightly. "Nein, mein kommadant," he replied.

Tony laughed. Then, he wiped his brow. "I guess we'll have to work through the Austrian police. I'll send them a list of questions."

Tony placed the file folder on Rieder on the side of his desk atop that of Sebastian. "The third person who wrote for the Schubert program is Thaddeus Cochrane. I haven't had a chance to look into his background at all. According to the letter he wrote to Dr. Hoffman, he didn't know how to use the program. He returned it without using it." He turned towards Debbie. "That's right, isn't it?"

"Yeah," Debbie responded. "He said he was a computer illiterate. Didn't even own one. Sounds like a computer phobic." She laughed. "I know people like that." Touching Harry's arm, she said, "People Harry's age."

"Ouch," Harry muttered.

"Or even older," Debbie added, laughing.

"Thank you," Harry said with a pained look.

Tony smiled. "What else did he say in his letter? Go over it again."

Debbie replied, "He seemed very sympathetic to Dr. Hoffman. He said that he knew what it was like to have one's work--I guess disparaged would be the right word--by one's colleagues. He was particularly hard on Sebastian. He said he'd like to shake him by his long hair or ears for the things he said about Dr. Hoffman."

Tony chuckled as he edged back in his chair. "So he didn't use her program and seemed on friendly terms with Dr. Hoffman." He shook his head. "We'll check him out, of course, but it doesn't sound like there's much there."

Tony opened the manila folder, again and withdrew the final sheet of yellow paper. "L. C. Houston," he muttered. "I've only had time to make a cursory check. Her first name, by the way, is Lucretia and her middle initial stands for either Christina or Carcioni, her maiden name. She is, indeed, a practicing analyst--a lay analyst, not a doctor--in New York City. Very fancy, address on Park Avenue. She does hold a masters degree from Princeton in music, as she claims. By the way, she's loaded. She's married to B. Kent Houston, one of those Texas multi-millionaires--his family owns a string of oil refineries." He shrugged. "We don't know if she has any kind of motive or even if she knows Griffith or Wolfson. We'll have to talk to her." He looked at Harry expectantly.

Harry nodded. "I'll take the train to New York as soon as I can. But it will be a few days. I want to keep an eye on Stephanie, of course, and I have to clear off a backlog of work on my desk." He paused. "If it's urgent, maybe you should ask someone in the New York Police Department to talk to her."

Tony shook his head. "No. You have an intimate knowledge of the case." He smiled. "Besides, you have a way of coming up with things that is—simply amazing--and--I wouldn't want to lose that. Take your time, Harry. Two or three days is fine."

Harry smiled at the compliment and then a quizzical expression slowly formed on his face. "The name Carcioni rings a bell. There was a guy-- must have been 15 or 20 years ago. He was deported. Yes. Tony Carrcioni. Was he Mafiosi?" He looked at Tony. "Didn't they use the RICO law on him? Took everything he had. Down to his last nickel." Harry raised his eyebrows. "Do you think?"

Tony finished the sentence. "That L. C. Houston is a relative?" He smiled. "I doubt it, but, I'll check" He mused. "Tony C.--yeah." His smile broadened. " Harry, you got a memory like an elephant."

Harry laughed. "And about as much grace."

Debbie and Stephanie both grinned.

Tony rubbed his glasses as if he felt a little weary. "That leaves us with four people that warrant our immediate attention: Rieder, Sebastian, Queen and Huston. I'll get back to Vienna about Rieder and look up Queen. Debbie will interview Sebastian and Harry, Huston. And we'll take it from there."

Harry nodded. Then, he inquired, "How about the search of the passenger list of the airline that Stephanie took from Vienna?"

Tony shook his head. He looked chagrined. "Sorry. Nothing to report yet. I gave the assignment to Sergeant Rice. He hasn't been in the office the last few days."

Harry smiled. "Willie Rice?"

Tony nodded. "Willie."

Harry chuckled. "Same old Willie. We used to call him slow-footed Willie. He was pulling that kind of stuff when I was a cub reporter. How did he ever make Sergeant?"

Tony laughed. "Harry, I better not comment on that one." He paused. "We really need the information. I'll get someone else to do it." He clapped his hands together. "I guess that's it, then. I'll talk to Claire. If everything is okay, we'll see you folks tonight."

When his office was clear, Tony leaned back in his swivel chair. Slowly, he turned his chair, first to one side and then to the other. He took his glasses off, placed them on the desk, and rubbed his eyes. He shook his head. It was a hell of a case, he thought. Four people dead. Maybe, they were all murdered. It could be a serial killer. He wasn't sure, but it looked that way. And one of the chief suspects was in Austria.

Tony sighed. He wasn't going to fly to Austria if he could help it. He simply didn't have the time. There was too much work piled on his desk and he had to supervise another homicide investigation. It was the brutal robbery and murder of a seventy-year-old widow named Janice Thompson whom all the children in the neighborhood called "Grandma." The people in the community were incensed about the killing and were screaming for an arrest. And well they should, Tony thought.

If he couldn't go to Vienna, Tony mused, then he had better send those questions off to the Austrian police--questions to ask Rieder. Tony fumbled through the scattered papers on his desk, picked up a yellow tablet and began to jot down questions. An hour later, he turned on his computer and e-mailed a cover letter and his questions to the chief of police in Vienna.

Harry had just finished cleaning the dinner dishes when the doorbell rang. He and Stephanie had supped on a salmon Harry had cooked with hollandaise sauce, along with asparagus and a tomato laden salad. Not a bad dinner, Harry thought, as he walked toward the door. "Password and countersign," he called out like a soldier patrolling a high security radar station.

The voice on the other side of the door replied, "Boola boola--what else?"

Harry laughed. "What else," he repeated. He opened the door, welcoming Tony dressed in slacks and a floral patterned sport shirt and Claire who wore a deep blue summer frock. "You look terrific," he said as he embraced her, and in truth, she did. Tall, bronze and beautiful, Claire had earned the money for her college education at Barnard College in New York by modeling for fashion magazines and in the ensuing years had lost little of her looks.

She asked Harry, "What's the password and countersign routine? I know you guys are a couple of clowns when you get together--but this is new, isn't it?"

"Didn't Tony tell you?"

"Tell me what?"

"Someone may be gunning for Stephanie." He motioned Stephanie out of the kitchenette where she had been making coffee. As she moved forward,

Harry made the introduction. "Claire O'Meara, this is my niece, Stephanie Ellison, excellent musician and fair-to-middling coffee maker."

Stephanie asked, "What's wrong with my coffee?"

"Don't mind him, Stephanie," Claire said, "He's a damn gourmet." She laughed. "If he wasn't such a wonderful cook, he couldn't get away with it. He's been pillaring me about my coffee for twenty years." She paused and smiled. "But he still drinks it." She turned towards Harry. "Is someone really gunning for Stephanie?"

"We're not sure, Claire. We're just being cautious. She's spending her time with me at my office until Debbie gets back from Los Angeles. Hopefully tomorrow night."

Claire nodded. "I'll be glad when Debbie is back."

Harry assented. "Stephanie will be safer then."

Claire turned towards Stephanie. "Hey, that coffee smells good. In spite of what that perfectionist says. Let's go get some." When the two women walked into the kitchenette, Harry and Tony ambled over to the chessboard and took their seats. The match resumed. They played slowly and methodically, each hoping the other might make an error. Neither did. They played for forty minutes until the women emerged from the kitchenette and walked over to the piano bench. Stephanie turned around, looking at Harry. She asked, "Would music bother you?"

Harry looked at Tony. "I think we should call this game a draw," he said. "What do you think?"

Tony pondered for a few seconds. "Makes sense," he replied. "Besides, music sounds good."

Harry waved his hand. "Go ahead." While Harry carefully placed the chess pieces back into a handsome wooden box, Stephanie and Claire rummaged through the now open piano bench looking for music. They found a book of songs from Broadway Musicals, songs of George Gershwin, Jerome Kern, Richard Rodgers, Cole Porter, Irving Berlin, Stephen Sondheim, and Andrew Lloyd-Weber.

"Hey, this is a find," Claire exclaimed with pleasure in both her eyes and voice. She turned toward Stephanie. "You play and I'll sing along--or you sing too."

Stephanie smiled. "I'll just play for awhile, but now and then I'll join in with some harmony."

Claire put her hand on Stephanie's shoulder and said, "That will be nice." She turned towards Harry and Tony. "You guys want to sing?"

Tony said, "I'd rather listen to you. I'll pass."

Claire asked, "How about you, Harry?"

"You know I have a voice like a frog. Even if one of you lovely ladies deigned to kiss me and turn me into a prince, I'd still sound like a frog."

Claire laughed. Harry went on. "You have a lovely voice, Claire. Go on and sing." And sing she did. Claire, who had sung in church choirs since the age of seven, had a fine Mezzo voice and when Stephanie, who was gifted with perfect pitch, joined her in harmony, it sounded as if the two had been singing together for years. They sang: *Where and When*; *Embraceable You*; *The Girl that I Marry*; *Younger than Springtime*, *Send in the Clowns*, *Memory*, and *The Music of the Night*. The men sat back quietly, sipped coffee and brandy and loved every minute of it.

When the performance was over, Harry and Tony applauded warmly. The women joined them for coffee and brandy and they talked quietly until it was approaching midnight. After Tony and Claire took their leave and Stephanie retired to the guest bedroom, Harry gingerly placed a heavy broom against the front door knob so that it would fall to the floor with a thud in the event someone tried to open the door from the outside. Finally, he went to his bedroom, leaving the door open a crack. He checked Debbie's revolver, put it on the night stand beside the bed, patted it twice, and then drifted off to sleep.

Chapter 14

On the following morning, Tony visited the site of the Janice Thompson murder--a poorly lit side street about fifty yards from a convenience store operated by a recent emigrant family from Korea. With the aid of a translator, Tony spoke with a frightened young woman who managed the store. She said that she had heard a scream. A customer, a young black man, had run outside, discovered the body and dialed 911. She said the man was sobbing. He had known the victim well. Later, she identified the body as that of the woman who had just purchased bread, milk and cat food from her--moments before the murder. She could add nothing further.

When Tony finished talking with her, he met with the lead investigator, Lieutenant Sam Orleans. Orleans informed him that the crime lab was now busy going over the evidence and would be analyzing blood samples to try to identify the killer. If any of the blood samples were different from that of the victim, they would be sent out for DNA analysis. Meanwhile, his officers were conducting house-to-house interviews in the neighborhood. Tony nodded approvingly and suggested that they consider offering a reward for information leading to the arrest of the killer.

Around noon, Tony stopped at a fast food restaurant, where he grabbed a tuna sandwich and coffee, and then returned to his office. As was his habit, he checked his e-mail. He was pleasantly surprised. There was a message from Vienna. He thought it was probably an acknowledgment of his request to question Leopold Rieder. No, there was a document attached. He scanned it. It was a transcript of an interrogation. Tony smiled. Boy, that was fast work, he thought. He wished he could move that quickly.

He read the message:

Dear Captain O'Meara,

Thank you for your request for information on Leopold Rieder. Professor Rieder was in our offices this morning for interrogation on another matter. When your report reached us, it was convenient to ask him your questions. We included a few of our own questions as follow-ups. The transcript of the interview is attached. If we can be of any further assistance, please let us know.

Tony grinned, and then examined the transcript:

Q. Professor Rieder, were you acquainted with the late Professor Edward Todd Griffith?

A. Yes.

Q. Tell us about your relationship?

A. Well, we were colleagues. We did not, of course, teach in the same university, but we were both musicologists with an interest in early 19th Century music. We were both recognized authorities on Franz Schubert.

Q. Were you and Professor Griffith trying to organize a symposium together?

A. Yes. We were trying to bring some of the world's leading musical scholars together to discuss Schubert's music. Griffith and I corresponded about it. The symposium was my idea, but he was eager to collaborate. I put considerable time and effort into the planning of the symposium. Griffith agreed to see to the funding. My role was to do the conceptual work and arrange for the participants. As I indicated, I put in a great deal of effort on it, but as it turned out, Griffith was unable to secure the funding. Ultimately, it was deemed advisable to abandon the project.

Q. When the project was aborted, was there any unpleasantness?

A. Of course not. We're both distinguished scholars.

(Our follow-up questions):

Q. No unpleasantness at all?

A. Well, obviously I was disappointed. He had some criticism of my plans for the symposium and I thought he had not been sufficiently energetic in his pursuit of funding sources.

Q. Were any angry words exchanged?

A. Of course not.

Tony smiled. He thought that the man doth protest too much. He resumed reading.

Q. Did you visit the United States about a year-and-a-half ago, in December?

A. December? Yes.

Q. What was your destination?

A. Washington, D.C.

Q. While you were in the United States, did you do any traveling?

A. A little. Not much.

Q. Where did you travel?

A. I rented a car and drove north.

Q. Did you go to New England?

A. I may have. I don't remember exactly everywhere I went.

(Our follow-up questions):

Q. You don't remember whether you went to New England? How is that?

A. It was awhile ago. I mean, it's a strange country. I'm not sure. I don't know.

Q. Did you talk to Professor Griffith while you were in the United States?

A. No. I mean, yes. We talked on the phone.

Q. What did you talk about?

A. I don't remember.

Q. Did you see him during your trip?

A. No. No, I didn't. Absolutely not.

Q. (Our probe): You're certain?

A. No. I mean, yes, I'm certain.

Q. Did you ever receive a copy of Dr. Johanna Hoffman's computer program for analyzing Franz Schubert's music?

A. Yes.

Q. What did you use it for?

A. I wanted to compare Schubert's work as a student with the work of his maturity.

Q. Were you skilled enough with computers to use the program?

A. No. I had an assistant to help me, Peter Weber. Peter's a music student. He's very good with computers.

Q. Do you think it would be possible to use Dr. Hoffman's computer program on Schubert to compose music that would very closely resemble Schubert? Something that was indistinguishable from Schubert?

A. Absolutely not. It's impossible. It can't be done.

Q. Suppose the person who tried doing this was a skilled composer?

A. No. No. Well, maybe.

Q. Professor, were you trained in musical composition?

A. Of course.

Q. Have you ever composed any music?

A. No. No. A few student pieces. Really, nothing.

Q. Do you know any students who are very gifted in musical composition?

A. Of course. There are three or four brilliant students here.

(Our question):

Q. Is Peter Weber among them?

A. No. No. Absolutely not. Not Peter.

Thank you, that's all Professor Rieder.

Tony relaxed in his chair. He thought about what he had read. Picking up the transcript, he read it through again. Then, he eased out of his chair, opened the door to his office, and strolled down the corridor to the fax machine. He had to wait for a moment, because a new recruit, a young Hispanic woman with a pleasant smile, was using the machine. When she finished, he faxed a copy of the transcript to Harry at his office. For awhile, Tony loitered near the bulletin board that hung on the wall across from the fax machine. He perused the announcements and notices on the board to see if there were anything that would affect him. It was all routine stuff. He smiled the faintest of smiles, returned to his office and telephoned Harry.

Harry was in the office and answered the phone. Tony was brief. "I just faxed you something. I think you'll find it interesting. Get back to me when you've had a chance to read it."

Harry assented. He glanced at his fax machine in the corner of the room. For a few seconds his eyes dwelled on Stephanie, who entered his peripheral vision. She was seated on a small vinyl-covered chair, editing her dissertation. Harry walked over to the fax machine to retrieve the transcript that Tony had sent. For a moment he stood silently, studying the transcript. Then, he walked over to Stephanie, who was engrossed in her thoughts, a study in concentration. Harry nudged her shoulder. Stephanie looked up and smiled. "Get a load of this," Harry said, "and tell me what you think."

Harry backed away and waited patiently while Stephanie read. When she put the transcript on her lap, Harry asked, "Sound like the Leopold Rieder you know?"

Stephanie shook her head. "Not a bit, Uncle Harry. He seems so tense. I remember him being so careful and composed. He would state his thoughts very precisely, almost pedantically." She shook her head again. "He's come unraveled."

"He's shaky, all right," Harry agreed. "I'm going to call Tony."

Harry dialed Tony's number. "It's interesting, all right," Harry said. "Stephanie thinks he's come unraveled. Rieder's not at all like he was when she saw him in Vienna."

"Yeah. He's nervous as hell."

Harry mused, "Could be the pressure he's been feeling on the ski resort scam. Interrogations can do that. Still, I don't buy what he's saying. I think he's holding something back. He says he can't remember if he went to New England. Baloney! Sounds like a convenient case of amnesia to me."

"I don't believe that either, Harry. I'm going to call the FBI and the passport office of the State Department to see if we can find out where he went."

"Good! While you're at it, try checking the car rental agencies. Maybe, they have a mileage record."

"Yeah. I'll do that."

"What do you think of checking into Peter Weber and maybe the other students he talked about?"

"Not yet, Harry. It's premature. If it turns out that Rieder went to New England, I'll move on it.

"Sounds good. Fast work, Tony."

"Give the credit to the folks in Vienna."

Harry hung up the telephone. Turning towards Stephanie, he said, "We're making progress." He paused. "I wonder what Debbie will find in California?"

Stephanie smiled. "I bet you miss her already."

Harry grinned. "How did you guess?"

"I got eyes, don't I?"

"Yeah, I miss her."

Stephanie looked at Harry. "I like Debbie, Harry. I like her a lot."

Harry nodded. Stephanie continued. "She's a lot of fun. Easy to get along with." Stephanie hesitated. She raised her eyebrows. "Not at all like your ex."

"Yvonne?" Harry scratched his head. "She was a pretty angry woman, Stephanie. But I can't blame Yvonne entirely. After all, she lived with me for seven years."

Stephanie laughed. "You're not that hard to get along with, Harry."

"I've improved. I've been trying hard. But I can be boorish, and you know that. When I get that way I can run on and on like a bad play. Debbie, bless her heart, is a very tolerant person. She just laughs at my excesses."

"Yvonne wasn't so tolerant."

"Hell, no. She had a temper. We were both pretty abrasive when we married, a couple of brash kids form the big city. We managed to keep things under wraps for a while." He laughed. "Maybe it was passion or good sex. But then the fights started." Harry smiled. "They got pretty bad."

Stephanie asked, "Did you ever hit her, Harry?"

"No. I would never hit a woman. We grew up with a code. Men didn't do things like that. But she socked me a couple of times. Once she gave me a bruise under the eye." Harry pointed to his right eye. "I didn't duck fast enough."

Stephanie laughed. "Do you ever hear from her?"

"No. Not in years."

"Didn't she write to you when you were in the hospital in Lebanon? It was all over the papers. I remember the headline: 'American Journalist Car-bombed in Lebanon.' You were front page news."

"Some news," Harry quipped. "Oh, she knew about it, all right. My daughter wrote me a nice letter. You know, Stephanie, when I was in the hospital in Beirut, while I was waiting to see whether they could repair my leg, I used to fantasize what she would put on a postcard if she wrote one--which of course, she never did. Here's what I came up with:

'Dear Harry,

Heard that you survived the bomb blast in Lebanon. Better luck next time. Yvonne.'

Stephanie laughed. "That's wicked, Harry."

Harry grinned sheepishly. "I know. But as I said, I've improved."

"Harry," Stephanie said slowly, "I have no right to ask you this--but I will anyway. Are you and Debbie going to get married?"

"No, young lady, you don't have any right to ask me that. But since you are my favorite niece..."

"Your only niece," she interrupted.

"Right, only and favorite. The answer is, it is Debbie's decision. It's her call. I think she'd be an idiot to marry me when she could get a good looking young man, but if she wants me, she's got me, and she knows it. The offer's on the table. Enough said?"

"Enough." She lowered her eyes and returned to her manuscript.

Debbie paid her taxi fare, checked the address from her notebook, and then entered the building on Wilshire Boulevard where Sebastian had his business office. This was only the second time she had been in Los Angeles and the first time was just driving through with her parents years ago. She felt a little like a tourist and wished she had a day or two to see more of the city and its environs, particularly Hollywood. She had always loved movies and it would be a delight to visit the sites where all those memorable movies were made.

She spied a bronze plaque in the lobby listing the occupants of the building. Sebastian, Inc. was located in a suite on the second floor encompassing rooms 203 through 208. Walking briskly up a flight of stairs, Debbie soon found herself standing before the door of room 203. Her face flushed and her pulse jumped a few beats as she pictured in her mind the moment of meeting Sebastian. Then, she smiled at her excitement and chastised herself. "Debbie Simmons, when are you ever going to get over being a teenager?" She opened the door and entered into a spacious room. The receptionist, a dark-haired woman in her early twenties, wearing tinted glasses and large ruby earrings, sat behind a slim teak desk. She was reading *People Magazine*. A huge blow-up of a photograph of an earth-day concert Sebastian had given in New York's Central Park filled the wall to Debbie's right. On the opposite wall hung several portraits of men dressed in Nineteenth Century finery. Debbie wondered who they were. As she approached the receptionist, she displayed her badge, and said smartly, "Sergeant Simmons of the Metropolitan District of Columbia Police to see Mr. Sebastian. I have an appointment."

The receptionist gave her an almost disdainful glance before looking at the appointment book on the desk. "I see," she replied. "He's terribly busy, you know. But he should be free in about fifteen minutes. Have a seat." The receptionist returned to her magazine. Ignoring the chill from the receptionist, Debbie turned and walked toward a long green couch that stood under the row of portraits. As she drew near, she stopped and studied one of the portraits. The sensitive face with its prominent nose and long wavy brown hair seemed familiar. It was Frederick Chopin. Debbie turned around. She asked, "Is that Chopin?"

The receptionist looked up from her magazine long enough to nod. Debbie asked, "Who are the other people?"

The receptionist looked up again and replied, "The one on the right is Berlioz, the other two are Lord Byron and Robert Browning."

When the receptionist's face disappeared behind the magazine, Debbie sat down on the couch. She felt a little travel weary. The couch was very comfortable. She stretched her body like a cat and relaxed. She took a few deep breaths. Then, she thought about the portraits. Sebastian really went in for romantics. Part of his self image she imagined, or perhaps his public persona. She lapsed into daydreaming about Harry and recalled the story he had told her about Berlioz's overwhelming passion for an Irish actress named Harriet Smithson and their turbulent relationship. She smiled. Harry was no passionate romantic. She wondered if Sebastian was.

In a few minutes, she was ushered into Sebastian's office. The room was smaller than the outer room. The left wall was covered by a huge mural of giant redwoods. The right wall contained a small tapestry with names sewn into it. Sebastian was seated behind a desk whose surface was bare except for a large photograph of Sebastian standing next to handsome woman set in a silver frame and a foot long miniature piano that appeared accurate in every detail. As Debbie approached the desk, she noticed that there was a note scrawled on the photograph. She glanced at it. "To Sebastian--with exquisite memories, love Margaret." Debbie smiled, and wondered who Margaret was.

Dressed in a silver colored silken shirt and tight dark trousers, Sebastian arose from his chair behind the desk and extended his hand. It was large and strong, yet delicate. Debbie took his hand, gazed into his deep blue eyes and sighed. He looked every bit as good as he did on the T.V. screen. He had a beautiful face. And what a smile! Like his handshake, it radiated warmth.

With some effort, Debbie composed herself and introduced herself. "I'm Sergeant Simmons of the Washington D.C. Metropolitan Police Department and I'm here to make a few routine inquiries relating to the death of Dr. Johanna Hoffman."

Sebastian nodded. "Captain O'Meara explained that to me. I told him that I didn't think I knew anything that might be useful, but I would be glad to talk with you."

Debbie said "Thank you," and sat down in a comfortable leather chair that faced Sebastian's desk. She smiled and began, "Mr. Sebastian..."

Sebastian interrupted her and said warmly, "Sebastian--please--just Sebastian."

"All right. Sebastian. In a murder investigation, we have to follow up all leads, no matter how remote."

Sebastian nodded. "I understand."

"Some months ago, you were interviewed in a late night television show. I didn't see it, but I must tell you I am one of your fans."

Sebastian smiled. "I'm glad," he said.

"Well, anyway," Debbie continued, "they tell me you said some very unpleasant things about Dr. Hoffman's work. What was that all about?"

Sebastian sighed. "It was a damn stupid thing for me to do. I regret it. I've taken a lot of heat for that." He paused. "I'd better explain. I was stoned that night. I'm not sure what the drug was. My guess it was PCP. I didn't take it voluntarily. I found out later that a friend of mine--a practical joker--slipped it into my coffee. He cheerfully admitted it. He thought it was a cute thing to do." He muttered under his breath, "The son of a bitch."

Debbie waited a few seconds before asking, "Have you ever used drugs, Sebastian?"

He nodded vigorously. "Oh, yeah. It's public knowledge. Back when I was in college. marijuana and hallucinogens, acid, 'shrooms'--you know, magic mushrooms, and peyote. I was with a group of kids--both young men and women who were really messing up."

"What made you stop?"

Sebastian lowered his eyes. "One of the guys, Peter Bradley--he was an exchange student from London--had a horrible trip after using acid. Fell backwards down a flight of concrete stairs. Suffered an injury to his spinal cord. He's been paralyzed from the neck down ever since."

"I'm sorry," Debbie said. Her tone was sympathetic.

Sebastian nodded. "I haven't used drugs since." He looked at Debbie. "You may know that I've been heavily involved in the campaigns to make marijuana available for medical use. You know, for glaucoma and for cancer patients. But that's an entirely different matter. I don't use illegal drugs and nothing could persuade me to do so."

His voice had the ring of a deeply felt conviction. This time, it was Debbie's turn to smile and respond warmly, "I'm glad," she said. Debbie paused and considered. Then, she said, "Let's talk some more about Dr. Hoffman. What were your differences with Dr. Hoffman?"

Sebastian leaned back in his chair. "Actually," he began, "I never met Dr. Hoffman. In fact, I've never really known any musicologists other than the professors I had in college. We don't really live in the same world. We don't think the same way. They look into a composer's life and times trying to better understand his music. I'm a performer. You can approach performing using the scholarship of a musicologist. It's perfectly legitimate. But I don't. I let the music speak directly to me without any intellectual filters and I play what I see and feel. I believe that music should breathe. There should be freedom with the tonalities. It's a point of view I've been pushing very hard in interviews and lectures. There are people in the musical establishment who don't care for my approach at all, but my audiences love it. And those are the people I care about."

"And Dr. Hoffman?" Debbie persisted.

"About a year ago, I think it was--I received a letter." Sebastian scratched his chin. "I forgot the guy's name who sent it. He was a professor, I think. Anyway, the letter was brief stating that I might be interested in citing an article that was enclosed in my public appearances. The article was Dr. Hoffman's description of her computer program for analyzing musical compositions. Well, when I read the article, I saw red. I threw it into the wastepaper basket. It irritated me to no end. Music is meant to be played, not dissected. But then I reflected. The guy had a point. I could use Hoffman's computer program as a foil in making my own point. And I have done so on many occasions, and I'm afraid, rather derisively. Now that's she'd dead, I feel very bad about it. I ill used her. No doubt about it."

Debbie considered. "Would it be fair to say that you would not have talked about Dr. Hoffman's work if you had not received that letter?"

Sebastian's reply was quick and decisive. "Oh, yeah. Chances are that I would have never known about it. We don't move in the same circles. I never read that journal." He added, "I don't read much at all these days, except ecology."

"You can't remember who sent you the letter?"

Sebastian shook his head. Then, he said, "No, but maybe I can find out. We may still have it."

He called on the intercom, "Celeste, could you find the file that contains Dr. Johanna Hoffman's article? See if there is a letter in it--by some chance." He shrugged his shoulders. "We'll see," he said.

They waited for five minutes, talking mostly about Sebastian's recent concert tour in Poland and the Czech Republic. Then, the receptionist knocked lightly on the door, entered the room and handed Sebastian a manila file. When Sebastian opened the file, he exclaimed "Voila!" He took a cursory glance at the letter to refresh his memory, smiled, and handed it to Debbie.

Debbie inspected the letter. It was very brief:

I have taken the liberty of enclosing a paper by Dr. Johanna Hoffman. I think you will find it interesting as the approach to understanding music described in the paper seems antithetical to what you are espousing and may serve as a useful point of reference in your discourses about music in the public forum.

The letter was signed Thaddeus Cochrane, Former Professor of Music.

Debbie's eyes dilated when she read the signature. "Well, well," she muttered to herself. Turning to Sebastian, she inquired, "May I have a copy?"

Sebastian nodded, buzzed Celeste and Debbie soon stuffed a copy of the letter into her briefcase. She asked, "Have you ever met Mr. Cochrane?"

Sebastian shook his head. "No, but the name is vaguely familiar." He looked quizzical. "Didn't he write a book?"

Debbie nodded. "I haven't read it. It's a scholarly book on Schubert, I believe. Debbie paused and looked at her notebook. "Sebastian," she said, raising her eyes to meet his, "There are a few other names I'd like to ask you about. Did you ever meet Leopold Rieder?"

Sebastian looked puzzled. Then, he smiled. "I know who you mean now. He wrote a book on Schubert. My sister in Toronto sent it to me as a Christmas present a few years ago. I looked at it but never read it. No, I've never met the man."

"How about Aaron Wolfson? Did you ever meet him?"

Sebastian shook his head. "Of course, I've heard of him. He has a big reputation. But, I've never met him."

"Let's try another name. Edward Todd Griffith?"

"He was a music critic. He was very good. I used to read him. Didn't he die recently?"

Debbie nodded. "About a year ago. Did you happen to know him?"

Sebastian shook his head. "No. I would have remembered meeting him. I would have enjoyed that."

"Two final names. Did you ever meet a man named Oliver Queen?"

Sebastian pondered. "No, not that I remember."

"How about Lucretia Huston?"

"No. I don't believe so."

"I have just one more question, Sebastian. It's completely routine. I'm asking it to everybody I'm interviewing about Dr. Hoffman. Do you remember where you were on the day of August 30?"

Sebastian laughed. "Is that the day Dr. Hoffman was killed?"

"Um hum."

"I think I was in Mexico City, but I better check my calendar." He picked up his appointment calendar and thumbed through it. "Yeah," he muttered. "I was in Mexico City. In fact, I was on stage giving a concert at the University at eight o'clock." He handed Debbie the appointment book. What time was Dr. Hoffman killed?"

Debbie smiled. "About the time you were taking your second bow."

Sebastian laughed. He asked, "Is that all, Officer Simmons?"

"Um hum."

"Well," he said, looking into her large brown eyes, "In that case, would you have dinner with me this evening?"

"Oh, my," she said, sighing. "I wish I could. But I have to be in Washington this evening. I really do."

"Duty?"

"Right. Duty." Debbie sighed again, and then sang a line from Gilbert and Sullivan's *Pirates of Penzance*. "When constabulary duties to be done, to be done."

Sebastian joined in to complete the verse, singing in a mellow baritone, "A policeman's lot is not a happy one, happy one."

Debbie smiled. Sebastian added mournfully, "Constabulary duty does not include dinner?"

Shaking her head, Debbie said, "Rain check?"

Sebastian smiled. "Rain check."

When Debbie returned to Washington, Stephanie was already in bed. Harry was sitting in his easy chair sipping some coffee. "Hi Kitten," he greeted her, "How did it go?"

"Interesting," she replied.

"Tired?"

"Yeah. Kind of."

"Let's go to bed. We can talk there."

Debbie left her overnight case by the door. She quickly stepped out of her clothes and in moments lay in Harry's arms.

Harry rubbed her shoulders and her back for awhile. Then, hesitantly, he asked, "What did you think of Sebastian?"

"He's very nice," she replied, smiling. "He's very witty. She looked into Harry's eyes in the semi-darkness. "I hate to tell you this, Harry, but I think you'd like him."

"I might at that, so long as he doesn't make a pass at you."

"Well," she said coyly, "he did ask me out for dinner."

"Oh?" Harry said in a rising crescendo. Then, he added, "Why didn't you go?"

"I had a better offer," she said quietly, then kissed him passionately.

He pressed her body against his own. "You are something else," he said with admiration.

In the stillness of the night they lay together. "I'll try not to wake you in the morning," Harry said. "You'll need the sleep."

"You're a nice man, Ellison. Hey," she added, "I got something to tell you before I drift off to sleep. Guess who made Sebastian aware of Dr. Hoffman's computer programs for analyzing music? Guess who sent Dr. Hoffman's article to Sebastian?"

"Rieder?"

"Guess again."

"I have no idea."

"Thaddeus Cochrane."

"You gotta be kidding," Harry's voice spoke disbelief. "Wasn't he the guy who wrote the letter to Dr. Hoffman threatening to emasculate Sebastian--or something like that---for the way he was ridiculing her?"

"He's the one. I think he said, 'shaking him by the ears or long hair.'"

"And you tell me he's the one who sent Sebastian the article in the first place."

"Um hum."

"Duplicitous bastard, isn't he?"

"Looks that way, Harry. You know who he reminds me of?"

"Who?"

"You remember last winter when you and I--we read *Othello* together--playing all the parts?"

"It was a cold, snowy night."

"Yeah. You talked me into it. I would never have done anything so insane. But I'm glad you did. It was a lot of fun. Remember Iago?"

"Sure. He of the incriminating handkerchief. Or was it a scarf?"

"A handkerchief. Anyway, Cochrane has something of that sneaky conniver in him."

"He does, My Love. We'll bump him up on the list of suspects. Sleep well."

Chapter 15

On the following afternoon, Tony telephoned Harry at his office. "I managed to locate Oliver Queen," he said. "It wasn't difficult. He's playing in a jazz quartet at The Blue Note."

I know the place," Harry said. "It's in Georgetown, near Wisconsin and M."

"Right. They're performing tonight. I thought I'd drive over there tonight when I'm off duty, listen to the music and have an informal talk with Queen during the break."

"Want company?"

"Sure."

"Should I bring the girls?"

Tony hesitated. "Better not. Particularly if Queen is involved. Stephanie should keep a low profile."

"You're right. And Debbie should stay with her."

"I'll pick you up around eight thirty."

"Fine. See you then."

They sat down at a small table near the back of the room. The room was nearly filled with customers; it was a young crowd, college students and young men and women in their twenties. They sat crowded around small tables, for the most part drinking beer and wine, and listening to the sounds of the jazz quartet playing the strains of an arrangement of Duke Ellington's *Mood Indigo*. There was only a discrete murmur from the crowd as almost everyone was tuned into the music. The musicians were an ill-assorted group to look at, but the sounds of their instruments blended beautifully as if the musicians had played together for years. The music, itself, had a cool, restrained feel to it. The pianist, a black woman dressed in bright African colors, played very well. The young man who played the bass was also black. His hair had a wave in it. He flashed a smile as he played. The drummer was a tall woman with long red hair that fell to her shoulders. Harry tried to remember the last time he had seen a red headed lady drummer. He shook his head. Never! And the tenor sax. That was Oliver Queen.

You listened to Oliver Queen's playing more than you looked at him. For in truth, Queen was not much to look at. He was short, slim, with brown hair that seemed to be receding in spite of the fact he looked to be no more than twenty-five. There was nothing about him you could pin down except possibly his expression or lack of it. His face revealed a vacant, almost desperate look. He seemed to be attending to nothing except his music. But that was undeniably beautiful. If there were no emotion in his expression, there certainly was in his music. He poured his heart into it.

They had been listening for about twenty minutes when Tony looked at his watch. He signaled the waiter. After ordering two more beers, Tony handed the waiter a note. "As soon as the musicians take their break," he asked, "please give this to the saxophone player." The waiter nodded and walked off.

Harry asked, "What was in the note?"

"I asked Queen if he would stop by during the break. I told him I was a police officer and he might be able to help us on a case."

Harry nodded. "You didn't mention Dr. Hoffman?"

"No, not yet."

The waiter returned with the beers. Moments later the musicians took their break and presently Oliver Queen walked over to the table and stood before them. Tony introduced himself, and then Harry, and Queen sat down.

The musician said nothing, waiting instead for Tony to explain the situation.

"We're investigating a homicide," Tony began. "A music scholar named Johanna Hoffman."

Queen's blank expression gave way to a glimmer of recognition. "Yeah, I read about her in the papers. I know her slightly." He paused. "Wasn't it a mugging? Someone trying to rob her? I think that's what the paper said, or it might have been the T.V. news."

Tony nodded. "Could have been a mugging. But we're not sure."

Queen asked, "How did you know I knew Dr. Hoffman?"

"We found a letter of yours in her correspondence."

The young man smiled. "Sure. I wrote her when I was in Sykesville."

"That's right. Could you tell us about how you came to know her?"

Queen settled back in his chair. "I was a student at Julliard. My instrument was the clarinet. I also played tenor sax. At the time I was interested in both classical music and jazz. Now, it's just jazz. I took a year at the Berkeley School of Music in Boston--they teach modern music there--then transferred to Julliard."

Tony nodded. Queen continued. "Dr. Hoffman was over at Columbia. She gave a lecture at Julliard on her researches with her computer program." He looked inquiringly, first at Tony, and then at Harry. "Did you know about her work?"

Both men nodded. "Well, I was really interested. You see, I've always been good at math and love computers. That's how I make my living. Now, don't get me wrong--I love playing jazz. But that's a tough way to make a living."

"You're very good," Harry said.

"Yeah, I like to think so. But it doesn't always pay the rent."

Harry smiled. "Did you talk to Dr. Hoffman?"

"Yeah. I went over to her office. Nice lady. But my girlfriend at the time--Paula--said she was a really strict teacher. Expected you to work your tail off and no nonsense. But Paula said she wasn't mean. Just tough. Well, she was very cordial to me. I made an appointment to see her. I told her I wanted to try out her technique--that I was interested in computers, you know. I asked her to suggest a program. She said her Schubert program was one of the best and to try that. She made me a copy of her disk and gave me a manual of her coding procedures. I took them with me."

Tony asked, "Did you use them?"

Queen smiled. "Sure, it was really neat. I wrote the opening of a quintet for clarinet and strings in the style of Schubert. It sounded a lot like Schubert. I showed it to my composition teacher, Dr. Vassa. He was very impressed. He asked me if he could send a copy to his old colleague, Thaddeus Cochrane. Cochrane is a Schubert scholar who used to teach at Julliard."

Tony asked, "Did you know Cochrane?"

"No. He left Julliard long before I got there. I read his book, though. He really knows his stuff."

Harry was curious. He inquired, "Did Cochrane reply?"

"Not to me. He wrote a thank you note to Vassa. Vassa showed it to me. It was short but courteous. He said what I did was 'interesting.'"

Harry asked, "Do you still have a copy of your quintet?"

"It was only part of the first movement," Queen replied defensively. He thought for a moment. "You know, it could be at my mother's place. She lives near Baltimore. When I went into the hospital, most of my stuff was stored at my mother's."

"If you can find it, send me a copy," Tony said.

Queen asked "Is it important?"

Tony shrugged. "I couldn't say at this point. But we're trying to look at everything."

"Okay. I'm driving up there on Sunday. I'll look for it."

Tony nodded. "Thanks," he said. Then, he asked, "Did you talk to Dr. Hoffman again--after you saw her in her office?"

"Let me think. I remember I saw her in the library at Columbia. It was about a month before I went into the hospital. We just said hello."

Harry asked, "Did you know she was coming to Washington?"

"I had no idea. I wrote her from the hospital thanking her for letting me use the Schubert program and that was the last contact I had with her."

Queen looked over his shoulder. The musicians were returning from the break. "I have to go," he said.

"I understand," Tony replied. "Could you drop by and see me tomorrow afternoon? There are a few more questions I'd like to ask you."

Queen nodded. "Sure."

Tony handed Queen his card. "How about around 2:30?"

"Okay."

Queen arose from his chair and rejoined the jazz quartet.

Queen arrived at Tony's office a few minutes after two. Harry was seated in one of the well-worn chairs to the side of Tony's desk. If Queen had any questions about Harry's presence at the interview, he did not ask them. After last night, he appeared to take Harry's being there for granted. Tony offered Queen a cup of coffee, which the young man accepted. He drank it black without sugar.

Tony asked, "Can you remember anything else about Dr. Hoffman--anything at all?"

Queen shook his head. "No. I didn't see that much of her."

"Did your girlfriend Paula tell you anything more about her?"

Queen scratched his nose. "Yeah. I guess she did." He smiled sheepishly. "Paula liked to talk."

Harry thought of his ex-wife and grinned.

Tony asked, "Can you remember anything else that she said about Dr. Hoffman?"

"Well, as I said, she was a no-nonsense-type teacher. You know how some students try to inveigle higher grades out of their teachers--'can you give me extra credit if I make a poster?' You know, that junior high school, Mickey-Mouse stuff. You had to work in Hoffman's class. Paula said she worked her ass off and barely got a C."

Harry smiled. He thought of Stephanie who got an A+ in Hoffman's course. He asked, "Was Paula a good student?"

"Comme ci, comme ca. Like me."

Harry asked, "What happened to you and Paula?"

"I was having these emotional swings. They must have scared the hell out of her. She couldn't take it. She told me flat out that she didn't want to go through life with that kind of baggage."

"She could have been more understanding," Harry ventured. "After all, it was an illness."

Queen nodded. "Yeah. She could have. But I can see what she was thinking."

Harry asked, "Did it hit you pretty hard when you broke up?"

Queen sighed, "You can say that again. I fell to pieces. Ended up in Sykesville. They say I was suicidal."

Harry nodded. "What did they do for you there?"

"Tried to stabilize my mood first. They said I had bipolar disorder. Put me on Lithium." Queen shrugged. "I hated it. So they tried a plain antidepressant. I was able to tolerate it better and it helped. Then, I was in group therapy for awhile. I don't think it helped at all. When I got out of the hospital, I went into individual therapy. A psychologist. She's very good. She helped me straighten myself out." Queen smiled. "I figured I'd better get a full-time job in networking and play jazz at night. It's worked out pretty well."

Harry asked, "What happened to Paula?"

"Funny thing you should ask. I heard from her this morning. She sent me an e-mail. She had gotten herself engaged and was supposed to get married next week. Then, she broke it off, just like that. She told him she was still in love with me." Queen smiled. "She wants to get back together."

Harry grinned. "Good luck!"

Queen returned the grin. "Thanks. We're going to need it."

Tony asked, "Mr. Queen, did you ever happen to know a music critic by the name of Edward Todd Griffith?"

"Yeah. I didn't really know him, though. I spoke to him once. He's dead, isn't he?"

"He is," Tony replied. "How did you happen to speak to him?"

Queen smiled faintly. "It seems everybody you're asking me about is dead." He paused. "He came to Julliard to give the Wentworth Lecture. It was right before I broke up with Paula." Queen scratched his chin, and then lapsed into a vacant expression. "He was a very entertaining speaker. Told lots of stories about the great composers--Beethoven, Wagner, Verdi--and about conductors and performers he knew. Afterwards, there was a reception. I talked with him."

Harry asked, "What kind of a mood was he in?"

"He seemed to be enjoying himself. He was very lively."

"Did he look at all depressed?"

Queen shook his head. "Not that I could see. I was the one who was depressed, not Griffith."

Harry thought back to Dr. McGregor. The doctor seemed to be the only person who thought Griffith was depressed. Yet his opinion had carried. Harry asked, "Did you ever meet the pianist Sebastian?"

"Sebastian?" Queen's eyes popped. His cheeks colored. "Hell, no. He's not in my league. Man, I'm a struggling musician if there ever was one. Sebastian's big time!"

Harry asked, "What do you think of his playing?"

"Plays with real feeling. I like it." He paused. "Paula really goes for him. She's nuts about him. She even thinks that outfit he wears is cool." Queen broke out with a sudden laugh. "If you ask me, I think he looks like a clown. But he sure can play. And he's the one making the money, not me." He shook his head. There was sullenness in his voice. "I work two jobs."

Harry asked, "Money's been a problem for you?"

"Sure. It is for most musicians. Writers and artists, too. Most of us don't make a living at it."

Harry inquired, "If you had lots of money, what would you do?"

"Play man. Play every night. Sleep during the day, come alive at night. That's what I'd do. Me and my sax and a few good musicians. Have a club of my own, maybe. How sweet it would be."

"Sounds nice," Harry reflected.

"Yeah," Queen replied in a long drawn out, breathy whisper.

Tony smiled, and then asked, "Have you ever met a music scholar by the name of Leopold Rieder?"

"Rieder. Oh God, no! I never want to. I had to read his damn book; it was required reading in my survey course on Western Music. Maybe it was the translation. I don't know. But it was so damn pedantic. What a bore." He shook his head. "Makes me sick in the stomach just thinking about struggling through it. All those wasted evenings."

Tony reiterated, "You never met him?"

"No. I would have thrown his book at him if I had."

Harry smiled. "I get your meaning." He added, "Did you ever do any composing yourself?

Queen settled himself. "Sure. I've written music. Lots of student pieces in the classic tradition. I was pretty good at it. Mostly short pieces. Like the opening of the quintet. And I've published a number of jazz compositions." He smiled. "Some have been recorded." His smile deepened. "I enjoy writing music."

Tony said, "I'd like to hear one of the records."

"I'll send one to you. Along with that score you want--if I can find it."

"I'd appreciate that," Tony said. He looked at his watch. "I think that will be all for today, Mr. Queen. If we have any additional questions--there may be a few--we'll be in touch with you." Tony arose from his chair and smiled. "We appreciate your cooperation."

Queen nodded and said, "Sure."

After Queen left the office, Tony asked, "What did you think?"

Harry shrugged. "I don't know. He's an enigma." Harry shifted his weight in his chair. "Let me run a few traditional questions by you, Tony. First, did he have the opportunity to commit the murders?"

Tony pondered. "I'm not completely sure, Harry, but it looks that way. It should be possible to pin down what Queen was doing at the time Hoffman was killed. The other killings? Probably not, but we'll look into it." Tony's expression showed concern. "Harry, I think the guy's mental condition is fragile. If he's not involved in this business, I don't want to do anything that will push him back into the hospital. I'll have to handle him with kid gloves."

"No polygraph tests," Harry quipped.

Tony smiled. "No way." Raising his eyebrows, he said, "At least, no time soon."

"Okay. Here's traditional question number two: Did Queen have a motive?"

"Yeah. He could use a few hundred thousand dollars. He's working two jobs now and that night club is a wonderful fantasy."

"Could he do the forgery? Does he have the skill?"

"I don't know enough to judge that, Harry. Stephanie probably could. But from what Queen says, Harry, he's already done it in a small way. That quintet, simulating Schubert. It was good enough to send to Thaddeus Cochrane. He must be talented and he knows how to use Hoffman's program. That's for sure."

Harry nodded. "I agree with you on all points. He could be involved in this." Harry leaned back in his chair. "Still, there are a couple of things that I find troubling. If Queen is involved, why would he be so up-front telling us that he had already done--what amounts to a fabrication of Schubert? I would think he wouldn't say anything about it, or at least try to downplay it."

"Yeah. That struck me as odd, too. He could be clever as hell. By volunteering information, he could be trying to inoculate himself from what we might discover later."

Harry grinned. "That would be a neat trick." He paused, again shifting his weight. "Why don't you get a comfortable chair in here, Tony? If I have to sit in this museum piece much longer, I'll end up with an ergonomic injury."

Tony laughed. "I've had a request for new furniture for seven years. The wheels of the City Government turn slowly."

"I'd write my Senator if we had one in this town. I have another problem about Queen. He's not that well organized. Whoever is running this show is a master planner, operating with a tight squad of confederates. Queen strikes me as disorganized and something of a loner."

"He could be conning us. But he sure comes over that way." Tony hesitated. "Do you think he could kill somebody, Harry? What's your gut feeling?"

"I think he could. I don't see him acting in a premeditated way, though I suppose that's possible. Tony, I sense a lot of anger under that skin of his. I think he could explode like a volcano, and could become violent. You could ask the doctor at Sykesville about that."

Tony pondered, "That's a good idea. I'll give the hospital a call later and then we'll look into his whereabouts during the murders. I'll try to be discrete."

Nodding, Harry arose to his feet. He glanced at the chair wryly and launched a mock kick in its direction. Tony laughed. "Speaking of hostility," he said.

Harry grinned. "Ain't it the truth?" He saluted and said, "If Queen confesses, I'll be in my office."

Tony returned the salute and Harry left the small office, walked through the building and then to his car. He still had to make a living and a half-finished column lay dormant in his computer. He drove through the afternoon Washington traffic, turning WETA on the radio to listen to classical music. The *Romeo and Juliet Overture* of Tchaikovsky played through his stereo. The music triggered thoughts about the passions of romance. He wondered about the stormy relationship between Queen and Paula. Then, his thoughts turned to Debbie. He smiled involuntarily. You didn't need storms to have passion. Passion and quiet could mix delightfully. Just not at the same time.

He pulled into the underground parking space in the building that housed his office, and took the elevator to the third floor. Soon, he was sitting before his computer, trying to finish his column on student demonstrations at the World Bank protesting the way decisions were made in global economic matters. They wanted more input from environmentalists, labor leaders, and groups of ordinary citizens. Harry thought that the students had a point, even if radical elements had tried to turn the event into an ugly push and shove match with the police. Still, it was a delicate column to write. He wanted to present his arguments without making the people on both sides mad. When he finally finished, he grinned. He had walked a political tightrope like an acrobat. Maybe he should fashion a new career as a diplomat. He shook his head and burst into laughter. At times he showed as much diplomatic skill as the proverbial bull in a china shop.

The women were preparing dinner tonight, so he relaxed in his office for awhile. He yawned, feeling a little sleepy. Then he dozed off for a half-hour. The loud ring of his telephone jolted him into alertness. It was Tony. He was quick to the point.

"Found out a few things about Queen. Thought I'd brief you before you went home."

"That's fast," Harry remarked.

"Just wanted to impress you. Usually we're slow as hell around here."

"I know," Harry groaned.

"I talked to his doctor at Sykesville. He was a little reluctant to talk, but I finally persuaded him it was serious business. You are right, Harry. He is given to fits of violence."

"I'll be damned. That's twice I've been right this year. I forgot what the other thing was."

Tony laughed. "I don't think Queen killed Dr. Hoffman, though. His quartet was playing that night at the Blue Note. It's possible he could have gotten to her during the break, but it would have taken some fancy footwork. It looks like someone else killed Hoffman. Queen could have been involved, but he didn't do the deed."

"Interesting. It'll give us something to chew on. Thanks."

When Harry returned to the apartment, he saw that the dinner table had been set. Everything looked unusually neat. The plates shone, the wineglasses sparkled, the silverware and napkins were carefully arranged. Harry smiled. "By God," he thought, "Maybe I should stay out more often!"

The meal, sautéed trout with black walnuts, wild rice, fresh peas, and a tossed salad, was prepared to perfection. Harry was effusive in his praise. "Damn. I didn't know you two could cook that well. That was superb!"

The two women beamed. "Praise from the master," Stephanie volunteered.

"What a life of luxury," Harry mused, stretching his arms. "Two beautiful women looking after me. I feel like a Sultan."

"We'll get you a turban so you'll look the part," Debbie said with laughter shining in her brown eyes.

"I'd look like hell in a turban," Harry replied.

Debbie took an appraising look at him. "I think you're right. No, Harry, no turban. No magic rings or lamps. Back to the hot and steamy kitchen for you."

"Paradise lost," Harry said mournfully.

Debbie leaned over, kissing him delicately on the forehead. "And regained," she said.

Harry grinned. "That it is."

"Harry," Debbie began, "I've been wondering how the interrogation of Oliver Queen went."

Harry reached for his coffee. "He's a strange cat," Harry replied. "Sometimes he seems like a real nice young man--and at other times, you get the feeling he could tear your head off." Harry sighed. "He's a struggling musician in a tough, competitive business. And his psyche is fragile to begin with. He can go off the deep end. But he didn't kill Dr. Hoffman. His quartet was performing when she was killed."

Stephanie asked, "Does that mean that Queen is eliminated as a suspect?"

"Oh, no, Stephanie, far from it. He could be involved in this business up to his neck. Not only can he compose music, he's already turned out part of a quintet using Dr. Hoffman's Schubert program. And it's apparently a good job of mimicking Schubert."

"Well," Debbie said smiling, "this is getting interesting."

"Yeah. He's going to look for the manuscript of the quintet this weekend. If he can find it, he'll send it to Tony. Then, Stephanie, you will get a crack at it. I'd like your opinion as to whether the same person who composed the other manuscripts--the alleged Schubert scores--also composed this one."

Stephanie's eyes widened. "If they were," she said slowly, "that would implicate Queen."

"Exactly."

Debbie asked, "Do you think there's any chance that Queen could be working with Rieder? They both need money. Queen can compose and Rieder could tell whether the score could pass muster. In fact, they might have thought that since Stephanie visited Rieder in Vienna, Stephanie would suggest that Rieder serve as the person to authenticate the score. That could have been the reason to get her involved."

Harry thought for a moment. "Rieder and Queen would be one hell of an odd couple," he observed. But, Debbie, you have a real neat idea there. It would be a damned clever thing to do." Harry shook his head. "I wouldn't rule anything out at this point. This case is a muddle." He smiled. "Say, you kids made a great dinner. I feel unbelievably lazy and satisfied. Want some help in cleaning up?"

"Your day off, Uncle Harry," Stephanie responded. "Just relax."

Harry smiled. "I will." He edged away from the table, slumped into his easy chair and sipped some bourbon. He arose only long enough to walk to the stereo and put on a recording of Schubert's Trout Quintet. What could be more appropriate?

Chapter 16

On Monday afternoon, Tony was shuffling through the hopelessly disorganized papers on his desk when he was buzzed on the intercom. "Mr. Queen wants to see you, Captain. He's here with a young woman."

Tony's expression brightened. This was unexpected. "Please send them in," he replied.

Oliver Queen looked in better spirits than he had during the previous visit. The woman who stood at his side was in her twenties. She had very dark eyes and blonde hair. They didn't quite go together, Tony thought. She was a good six inches taller than Queen and weighed at least 30 pounds more. The woman seemed to dwarf the slightly built Queen. Queen introduced the woman as Paula Kartolis. Tony extended his hand to the woman and smiled. "Mr. Queen mentioned you after our visit to the Blue Note. I'm a jazz fan and I liked the quartet a lot." Tony gestured with his right hand. "Please sit down."

Paula sat down and smiled. "The quartet is very good," she said. "Oliver plays beautifully, doesn't he? He almost lays his soul out there when he plays."

Tony offered his agreement. "He does."

Queen sat next to Paula. "I have the score you wanted, Captain," he said, "and a CD that contains two of my songs."

"That's very kind of you to bring them, Mr. Queen. I appreciate it."

"I had a little trouble finding the score. It was packed away in cardboard boxes. I couldn't locate it. But my mom found it."

"Glad to have it, and so promptly."

Queen inquired, "Have you found out anything about Dr. Hoffman's murder?"

"We're working hard on it, Mr. Queen. We're pursuing a number of leads."

"She was my teacher," Paula volunteered. "I can't say she was a favorite of mine. In the classroom, she was a bit like Captain Bligh in *Mutiny on the Bounty*. Just one assignment after another. You'd think that was the only course we had to take. She wore us out. But my God! Somebody killing her. That's horrible. That poor woman. I hope you catch him and he gets what's coming to him."

Tony replied, "We'll catch him, Ms. Kartolis." He paused, "Or her." Tony studied her and then Queen. "We have some good leads. You've been very helpful. Thank you so much for coming."

Tony shook hands with both Queen and Paula. As soon as they left the office, he telephoned Harry. "Queen came by with his score," he said.

"Great!" Harry replied. "I'll pick it up in an hour. Let's see what Stephanie thinks of it."

Tony made a copy of the score for Harry and put the original into his folder on Oliver Queen. In a few minutes, Harry arrived and with the copy of the score in hand, was soon in his car making his way through the heavy afternoon traffic toward the apartment. He was eager to get the manuscript into Stephanie's hands and the drive was frustratingly slow. At times he thought he might do better on a bicycle, weaving in and out of traffic. It was an absurd idea, but Harry liked absurd ideas and the thought kept him amused until he arrived home. He found Stephanie as eager as he was to begin. She had copies of the earlier manuscripts placed prominently on the piano and could hardly wait to compare Queen's music with the manuscripts left for her in the Library of Congress.

"We'll leave you absolutely alone while you work," Harry said. "I'll be in the kitchen preparing lunch. I'll take my sous-chef with me." He reached for Debbie's hand.

"I've been promoted," she said. "Sous-chef. Wow!"

They went into the kitchen and began dicing onions, mincing garlic cloves, grating carrots and zucchini and crushing thyme, all in preparation for cooking a large pot of fresh garden soup that along with garlic bread would serve for lunch.

While the chef and sous-chef were busy fixing lunch, Stephanie played sections of Queen's music on the piano. Then, she would stop for awhile and consider. The spell of quiet was then broken by a rendition of fragments of the earlier scores. Then, silence reigned again. Presently, Stephanie appeared in the kitchen, edging herself into the crowded space where she could fully sniff the aroma of the soup. "M-m-m," she said. "That smells good."

Harry nodded. "We shall see if it tastes as good as it smells. Taking a break, Stephanie?"

"No, Uncle Harry. I'm all through. It was an easy call. Queen didn't write the earlier scores. His composition is very different."

Harry shrugged. Stephanie asked, "Are you disappointed?"

"Sure. I was hoping we could tie somebody into this business and wrap it up. It was our first real chance."

Stephanie nodded. "Yeah. I guess it was."

"What made you so sure so quickly that Queen didn't write the earlier score?"

"It was obvious. Queen's technique wasn't polished. It was a student's work. I could see that at once. The technique in the earlier manuscripts was impeccable." Stephanie paused. "At the same time, Queen's composition shows a freshness of musical invention. You don't hear Schubert in the score as much as you hear Queen. Uncle Harry, Queen is gifted. When he becomes more secure in his grasp of musical composition, he could write some very interesting, even lovely music. As I said before, the first set of compositions is lacking in musical ideas. It's technically brilliant, but it's labored and even a little dull. It tries to be Schubert, but I'm now positive it isn't".

Debbie asked, "Now that Queen is out, what next, Harry?"

Harry smiled. "Soup," he replied tersely.

Harry spent the late part of the afternoon in his office. He telephoned Tony relating Stephanie's opinions about the manuscripts. Tony accepted the judgment, but said he would still try to check out Queen's whereabouts during the other killings. "It doesn't look like he was the killer, but we have to check everything out as far as possible."

Harry asked, "Who's our best bet now?"

"Rieder, I guess. But it's too early to say. It could be someone else, maybe Sebastian, maybe L. C. Huston, maybe someone we haven't thought of."

"I'd still put my money on Rieder," Harry replied.

"So would I, Harry. But I wouldn't give odds."

When Harry hung up, he leaned back in his chair and began to think through the case. After awhile, he threw up his hands, concluding that there was a lot they needed to know. If Rieder were the killer, well and good.

They would probably have to lean on him to make him crack. He already appeared to be cracking, so it might not take much more pressure. But if, as Tony suggested, it could be someone else, then the next step was to talk to L. C. Huston, and that was his responsibility. He would go to New York in the morning.

In the evening, Harry, Debbie, and Stephanie watched a concert on PBS. The orchestra played the Beethoven Seventh Symphony, the conductor taking the last movement at what Harry thought was breakneck speed.

"Much too quick," opined Harry.

"Just right," Stephanie retorted. "It should be a fast tempo."

While they argued about the merits of the performance, Debbie smiled and picked up the newspaper to read. The advertisements featured sales on attractive swimsuits. Her mind took flight. When this business was over, wouldn't it be nice if she and Harry could fly away to the Caribbean and relax on the beaches? The orchestra began to play Ibert's *Ports of Call*. Debbie took this as a propitious omen.

In the darkened bedroom, they lay together, their hands clasped. "I have something to tell you," Harry said. "I'm catching the early train to New York. I'll try not to awaken you in the morning."

Debbie murmured, "As I said, you're a nice man, Mr. Ellison." She wrapped her arms closely around him and for a moment savored the feelings of closeness. Then, she asked, "You're going to see L. C. Huston?"

"Yeah."

"You have an appointment?"

"No."

"She may be busy."

"She probably is. But she'll see me. I'll lean on her."

Debbie laughed. And with that, he pressed his body firmly against her and kissed her goodnight.

Chapter 17

Harry arrived in New York City around one o'clock. As he walked away from Pennsylvania Station, he telephoned Huston's office on his cell phone. The receptionist informed him that Mrs. Huston's office hours were normally from 9:00 to 4:00 and asked whether he would like to make an appointment. Harry replied, "Not at this time," and set out by a taxi for Chinatown to eat a leisurely lunch. Then, he took a second taxi to the Houston apartment on upper Park Avenue, near 72nd Street, a very fashionable address.

When Harry alighted from the taxi, he gazed at a tall, wide building that covered the entire block. It was impressive. Almost involuntarily, he recalled his student days in New York, way back when, and the cheap apartments he had shared with fellow students on the West side. Those apartment buildings were nothing like this place. He took another look at the building. It looked like it had been constructed in the 1920s when the rich were rich and glitz was glitz.

A uniformed doorman pointed to a well-dressed, well-groomed woman who sat behind a very neat, well organized desk, who at his request phoned the Houston apartment. The woman answering said that Mrs. Houston was not in, but that Mr. Houston was. Harry told the woman behind the desk that he would like to speak to Mr. Huston. She studied him, hesitated, and then passed on his request.

A moment later, Harry heard a man's voice on the intercom. It was a voice with a pronounced drawl. "Mr. Houston," Harry began. "My name is Harry Ellison. I'd like to speak with your wife when she comes in. I'm not a patient of hers, but, it is a rather important matter."

"Ellison?" the voice on the other end replied.

"Yes. Harry Ellison."

"I recognize your voice, Mr. Ellison. I've heard you on PBS and NPR. I have a strong interest in politics and world affairs." There was a brief pause. "What is the important matter?"

Harry deflected the question. "May I come up?"

"Sure. I'd love to meet you. We have a penthouse. It's a duplex. I'll meet you at the door."

"Thanks. I'll be right up."

As he rode up in the elevator, Harry tried to picture in his mind what the wealthy Texan would look like. He imagined a tall, rugged looking man, perhaps wearing a 10-gallon hat. But Houston was nothing of the sort. He was slightly built and looked anything but rugged. His facial expressions suggested a quiet demeanor and the grip of his handshake was mild. He was neatly dressed in an expensive imported suit. As Harry entered the apartment, he cast his eyes about him. The entrance way to the penthouse was spacious, almost the size of a room. And the rooms only became larger as they walked into the interior of the apartment. Houston ushered Harry towards an oversized couch while he sat in a small armchair facing him. As Harry made himself comfortable, his eyes drifted, again, this time around the room. There were paintings on the wall. One of the paintings struck him forcibly, arresting his gaze. It was an unmistakable Renoir, one that was reproduced in the large book of impressionist paintings that lay on the coffee table in his own apartment. He knew the painting well. But, this was no copy. It was the original. There was no doubt about it. The Houstons were loaded.

Harry expected that Houston would ask him, at once, about his reasons for speaking with his wife, but instead asked him about his work as a correspondent in the Middle East and what his views were of the situations in Saudi Arabia and the Arab Emirates. Huston said he was on the Board of a Fortune-500 Corporation that own refineries on the Gulf Coast and needed to keep abreast of developments that might affect the world's supply of oil. It turned out to be a very pleasant conversation and in a while became so engaging that if it were not for Houston pausing to look at his watch and musing, "It's not like Lucretia to be so late--I wonder what's keeping her," Harry might have forgotten the reason for his visit.

Jolted back to the task at hand, Harry smiled, and casually asked, "Where did you meet your wife? In Texas?"

"Oh, no," Houston replied. "At Princeton. We were both graduate students. I was studying economics, she was studying music. Actually, we met at a concert on campus. It was a string quartet." He smiled. "They played works by Haydn and Mozart. We talked during the intermission, and after the concert, we went out for coffee." Houston sighed. "And, we began to see each other"

Harry smiled. "Sounds romantic."

"Yes. It was. Very. Lucretia was a very beautiful woman. She still is." He shrugged. "I think she really wanted to stay in music. But things didn't work out." He shrugged again. "I wanted to study philosophy. Didn't work out, either. Orders from on high."

Harry ventured a guess. "To run the business?"

"Not quite. More like get seriously involved in it. My father was," he grinned "a forceful man." He turned, looked out of the spacious window, and added, "He could have been a character in one of those Victorian novels. His word was law. So, neither Lucretia nor I ended up doing what we really wanted to do. But, we both came out okay. Lucretia is a successful therapist, and I'm happy as a member of the Board and a trustee of our foundation. We support many interesting projects."

The conversation ceased as both men heard the soft click of an opening door. In a moment, a woman entered the room. She had long dark hair, dark penetrating eyes that struck one almost immediately, classic facial features that one would have expected to see on the silver screen and an ample but still trim figure. She must be in her mid-'30s, Harry thought, but still unquestionably a beauty. Yet, as she approached, Harry sensed this was not going to be an easy conversation. Beautiful, yes, but her expression did not convey a trace of warmth. Was he being fair, he wondered? Or was his impression accurate that she was an ice queen. "Lucretia," Houston ventured, "this is Mr. Harry Ellison. We watched him together on PBS. He would like to discuss an important matter with you. I did not inquire about it, of course. I will leave you two here and retire to the library." Lucretia looked puzzled. Houston continued, "I'll ask Helen to bring you your usual drink. Mr. Ellison, would you like a drink?"

"Thanks. I would. Do you have bourbon and ice?"

Houston nodded and walked out of the room. Lucretia sat in the chair vacated by her husband and stared at Harry, sizing him up. Then, she said in a dismissive tone, "Mr. Ellison. I have no idea why you wish to see me. I have no expertise in foreign affairs and have never been to the Middle East."

Harry smiled and responded. "This has nothing to do with foreign affairs. It's about music." And, then, to shake her out of her unreceptive pose, he added, "And murder."

"Murder?"

"Yeah. You've heard about Johanna Hoffman?"

Lucretia gripped the arm of the chair. The tensing of the muscles in her hands was almost palpable. Taking a deep breath, she slowly regained her composure. "Yes, of course," she said. "It was in the paper. There was a big story." Then, casually, almost derisively, she added, "For a day or two."

"Even bigger in Washington where I live. Where the murder happened."

She nodded. "Still, I fail to see what I have to do with it. Or, for that matter, you."

"I got involved because my niece, Stephanie, was a doctoral student of Dr. Hoffman and the lead investigator, Captain Tony O'Meara, is a good friend of mine." He paused, trying to determine whether there was any reaction in Lucretia's facial expression. There was not. It remained fixed, almost frozen.

Harry continued. "Tony authorized me to tell you that the programs Dr. Hoffman developed to analyze musical tendencies may have some bearing on the case. He asked me to talk informally with a few of the people who have used the programs to learn what I could. Harry smiled, hopefully. "May I ask you a few questions?"

Her reply was quick and pointed. "I don't see why I should talk with you about my work. It has nothing, whatever, to do with the murder. Good day, Mr. Ellison."

Harry's smile deepened. "No. You're absolutely right. You don't have to talk with me." Harry shifted his body about as if he were preparing to leave. "I'm sorry. By talking with me informally, Tony was hoping to spare you a visit from the New York Police Department. Lieutenant Alvarez of the Department is involved in the case, and Tony will ask him to see you, or perhaps Alvarez will want you to come to police headquarters." Harry arose. "Have a nice day, Mrs. Houston."

As Harry sauntered nonchalantly toward the entrance way, a voice called out to him. "Mr. Ellison."

Harry turned around. Lucretia spoke. "I think I was too hasty. I would rather not talk to the police. Please sit down."

Harry retraced his steps to the couch. "Thank you, Mrs. Houston," he said. "I think it will be better this way." He smiled. "Tony asked me to talk with the people who wrote Dr. Hoffman for permission to use the Schubert program. I have always loved Schubert's music--particularly his song cycles, so I was happy to do so." He looked directly at Lucretia. "I imagine you must be fond of his music, too."

"Of course."

"Tony showed me a copy of the letter you wrote to Dr. Hoffman. It sounds like a very interesting study you are doing. It is certainly original and very ambitious."

Hoping the compliment would break the ice, Harry looked for a smile on her face. There wasn't a glimmer of one. He continued. "Have you found Hoffman's Schubert program at all helpful?"

Lucretia considered carefully. "Yes. I think so. I see several possible connections between his musical style and my analysis of his personality." She paused and added, "Of course, I will have to verify these conclusions with further evidence."

"Further evidence?"

"Yes. Psychoanalytic confirmations."

Not having the slightest idea what she meant, Harry nodded his head as if he understood fully. He inquired, "How did you learn about Dr. Hoffman's programs?"

Again Lucretia considered carefully before replying. She spoke very deliberately. "My husband and I were watching an interview with Sebastian on television." She looked at Harry. "Have you ever watched his show?"

Harry nodded.

She continued. "During the interview, he made some very critical comments about her work." She paused. "Kent was surprised. Dr. Hoffman had applied to the Houston Foundation and had been awarded a seed grant to pursue her research. Kent said that the outside reviewers who were called in to evaluate her proposal said her work was very creative. Kent normally does not discuss the internal reviews at the foundation with anyone as he is scrupulous about maintaining confidentiality. He said nothing else to me about Dr. Hoffman." She paused, again, and considered. "Nonetheless, I was intrigued by what I heard. When I had the chance, I dropped into the library at Columbia University and read her articles. I agreed with the reviewers at the foundation. Her work was both original and creative."

"So you wrote her a letter."

"Yes."

"Have you ever met her?"

"No. I had hoped to. I was planning on calling her to see if we could get together for lunch. I regret not being able to."

"What do you think of Sebastian?"

There was a hint of a smile in her eyes. "He is an externalization, a personification of Freud's concept of libido. He breathes sex."

Harry thought about Debbie's interview with him and grimaced. He forced the image of Debbie and Sebastian together out of his mind. "So, you have a high regard for Dr. Hoffman's work?"

"Oh, yes. I admire creative people."

Harry reflected for a moment, and then said, "My niece, Stephanie is doing her dissertation on Schubert. She told me that Leopold Rieder is one of the foremost authorities on Schubert. She spent time with him in Vienna. Stephanie told me he wrote a biography of Schubert. I haven't read it yet." He paused. "Have you read it?"

"Yes."

"What did you think of it?"

"He has his facts right. His technical analysis of Schubert's music is sound. After all, he is a well-trained musicologist."

Harry sensed that she was holding back. He smiled. "Did you like the book?"

"No. Not at all." There was another faint signal of emotion in her eyes. Harry waited. She continued. "I found it very superficial. It conveys next-to-nothing of what Schubert was really like. There was no insight into the well-springs of his creativity."

"Sounds like a very timid approach to the subject."

"Absolutely!"

The force of her expression gave Harry the feeling that he may have cracked a little of the ice that shielded Lucretia. He considered for a moment, and then said, "Stephanie mentioned a few of the other well-known Schubert scholars. One of them was a man named..." Harry paused and deliberated, acting as if he had trouble recalling the name. "Cochrane, that's it. Thaddeus Cochrane." Harry smiled as if recalling the name had given him a feeling of satisfaction."

"Oh yes. Thaddeus Cochrane."

"You know him?"

"No. I've heard him lecture about Schubert while he was teaching at Columbia. He had some interesting thoughts about Schubert. He knew Schubert's music cold." She reflected for a moment. "He was an odd sort of a man. Made me wonder about him."

"From a psychoanalytic perspective?"

"That would be speculation. Obviously, I really don't know him at all. It was just an impression"

"Stephanie said he was a recluse."

"So, I've heard."

"The third person she mentioned was a man named Wolfson. He was murdered last year. He taught at Princeton." Harry feigned a look of surprise. "You must have known him."

Lucretia's mask of indifference vanished. Her expression was livid. "I knew him all right. The bastard!"

Taken by surprise, Harry tried to project an expression of calm in his demeanor. But his eyes remained fixed on Lucretia's face where her immobile expression had given way to an expression of rage. And then, almost as suddenly as the rage had surfaced, it disappeared. Harry knew he had struck an emotional chord and he had to play it carefully. He spoke quietly. "It sounds like Wolfson was a big problem for you."

"That is an understatement," she replied with an edge in her voice.

Harry nodded and waited. There was a touch of sadness in her eyes as she continued. "When you have a lifelong dream, and it goes up in smoke, you don't feel very kindly towards the man who destroyed it."

"Your hopes for a career in music?"

She nodded. "Yes. I loved music from the time I was a little girl." She reflected for moment. Her voice mellowed. "My father had a wonderful voice. He used to sing. Every Saturday he would play the opera on radio. It was a ritual." She smiled. "A very pleasant one. I learned some of the arias and used to sing them later. Sometimes, I would sing along with my father. I sang in the church choir. I had a very good voice." Her smile faded. "But, apparently, not good enough."

"Is that what Wolfson told you?"

"Yes. And he said the same thing about my efforts at composition. "A flare for melody. But a serious composer? No." She looked at Harry. "I was getting my master's degree in music, but Wolfson said I was not gifted enough for the doctoral program. He said that there were only a few slots available and he wanted to reserve them for students who were absolutely first-rate."

A second flash of anger--more muted than the first--something like the aftershocks following an earthquake flooded her face. "And he had the clout at the University to enforce his decision." She paused. "And, so, I was through."

Harry shook his head in a gesture of dismay. A feeling of empathy engulfed him. "I can imagine how you felt. I know I would have been very upset and I think I would have been mad as hell."

She nodded. "Yes. I was angry and depressed." She smiled faintly. "But not as angry as Kent. We had been dating for awhile and were getting serious." She reflected. "Kent is a gentle person, levelheaded, not given to expression of anger. But, when I told him what Wolfson had said, he exploded. At the time I had no idea how wealthy he was and how much power he could wield. I am sure he made inquiries. Still, there was nothing even he could do. Wolfson was the rising star in American music. His prestige was enormous and he was untouchable."

"Did you consider going to another university? Indiana has a great reputation in music. Or, a conservatory like Eastman or Juilliard?"

"I thought about it. But only briefly. Anywhere I applied to would have inquired to Wolfson. I don't know how Wolfson acts in everyday life. Maybe, he is more flexible in his give-and-take with people." She shook her head. "But, in music he was a perfectionist, supremely confident in his judgments, and made no effort to tailor them. Not the least bit."

"It must've made him very popular among his colleagues," Harry observed with sarcasm.

Lucretia smiled. "You would think so. But, no. He was widely admired. Both for his musical acumen and his integrity. Most people couldn't get away with the way he acted, but he did. If they had a Mount Rushmore for Twenty First century musical icons, he would be the first person carved in stone."

Harry waited a moment, and then asked, "What did you do, next?"

Lucretia spoke slowly. "I was depressed. I made an appointment with a doctor. He prescribed an antidepressant. It didn't help. It just made me tired. I went to the university counseling center. I saw a psychologist there for 12 sessions. He used cognitive-behavioral therapy--tried to alter the way I was looking at things." She smiled. "I felt a lot better. I really did. But, still, I knew I had to go deeper than that. The therapist agreed and recommended a psychiatrist in New York City, Dr. Mordecai Levy, who he said was a top notch psychoanalyst. I wanted to try him, but I had no way to get to the city and I couldn't afford him." She paused. "I was on a scholarship." She hesitated for a moment and then said, "I told Kent about it." She flashed a grin. "He said he would take care of it. He said if it would make me feel less guilty about the expense, I could wear his ring." She flashed a larger grin. "Mr. Ellison. I felt like Cinderella."

Harry returned the smile. "So, you went to see Dr. Levy."

"Yes. Kent drove me twice a week to New York. Levy is a terrific analyst and a wonderful man. I really began to understand myself for the first time." She paused. "He said I had an unusual capacity for insight both about myself and other people. He suggested that with a career in music no longer possible, I might consider training as a lay analyst. Mr. Ellison, my undergraduate minor was in psychology and I liked it. When Kent and I were married, we moved to New York City, where I took courses at the Psychoanalytic Institute. Dr. Levy, himself, agreed to be my preceptor. Now, I have an office a few blocks away and I have a full load of patients everyday. So things worked out."

Harry nodded. "I'm glad things worked out for you." He hesitated. "You know, of course, about Wolfson's murder?"

"Oh yes. It was all over the papers. I must tell you in all candor I did not shed a tear. Nor did my husband. We hardly discussed it. That part of our lives was over."

Harry arose. "Mrs. Houston, thank you for your cooperation. Oh, just one more thing. Did you happen to know Edward Todd Griffith?"

"You mean the music critic?"

Harry nodded.

"No. I was still an undergraduate when he left New York. I understand he committed suicide. I read his reviews when I was in high school. We were living in Brooklyn at the time. Like Wolfson, Griffith was a bit full of himself. Unlike Wolfson, who I believe didn't hurt people deliberately—in retrospect, I think Wolfson probably did what he did because he saw it as a duty." She grimaced. "Like most perfectionists, he carried it much too far, with"—she choked—"unfortunate consequences. Unlike Wolfson," she repeated herself, "I think Griffith enjoyed tearing people down. He had an acid tongue which he used with relish. I suspect that there was more than a little sadism in his psychological makeup." She smiled faintly. "I am sure he had more than a few enemies who would have helped his suicide along if they had had the chance."

Harry returned the smile and nodded. "Yeah. I can see your point." He paused. "I'll be off, now. I want to assure you that everything you told me will remain confidential. I will tell only Tony and Sergeant Simmons who is working with him on the case. Please give my regards to your husband. I enjoyed talking with him very much."

Lucretia showed him to the door.

Chapter 18

Within seconds of reaching the street Harry flagged a taxi which took him to Pennsylvania Station. An hour later, he boarded the train for Washington. After settling comfortably in his seat, Harry withdrew a small notepad from his coat pocket and began to jot down recollections of his interview with Mrs. Huston. A half an hour later, he closed his eyes and thought about Lucretia. A smile formed on his face. Beautiful she was. Smart, too, no doubt about it. And complicated. Was she ever!

When Harry arrived at his apartment, he found Debbie and Stephanie seated across from one another at a card table that usually stood folded in the hall closet. An open cardboard box with the label *Domino's Pizza* stood on the far side of the table, the inviting aroma of the still warm pizza filling the air. Two glasses nearly filled with beer flanked the pizza, while a deck of playing cards stood nearby. A pile of poker chips covered the table in front of Stephanie while the space in front of Debbie was nearly vacant. Both women waved their arms as Harry walked towards them. Debbie showed her cards. "A pair of kings," she said.

Stephanie smiled. "Three aces," she replied as she dropped the cards on the table.

Debbie shook her head in disbelief.

Harry turned toward his niece. "I didn't know you played poker."

"I didn't. Debbie taught me tonight." She smiled. "It's fun."

Debbie looked at Harry. "She's a natural. She's got a mind like a computer. I'm glad we're using chips, not money. I'd have to get a second job moonlighting." She paused. "Are you hungry, Harry? There are two more slices of pizza left and they're still warm."

Harry nodded. "What's on them?"

"Pepperoni."

"Sounds good to me."

Harry walked into the kitchen and returned shortly with a small plate for the pizza and a glass of beer. Drawing up a hardback chair, he pulled it next to the table, and sat down to watch the poker players. Stephanie won the hand and the next one as well. In mock frustration, Debbie threw up her hands and laughed. "I quit," she said. Her gaze shifted to Harry. "How did New York go?"

"Interestingly," Harry replied. "I'll tell you all about it when we meet with Tony, tomorrow. I just want to think about it for a while." Debbie nodded. Harry let out an involuntary yawn. "I'd better call Tony, now, and arrange a meeting." He arose, left the poker players, and walked to the telephone.

The three had an early breakfast of melons, coffee, and croissants. As Harry cleared the table, he asked Stephanie whether she had work to do on her thesis. "A lot," she replied.

"Well, then, while Debbie and I meet with Tony, would you be comfortable working here?"

"Sure."

"Good. We should be back before lunch. By the way," he added, "keep the door locked and don't open it for anyone." He smiled. "Until you hear the secret knock."

Stephanie smiled. "Secret knock?"

"Sure. The opening to Beethoven's Fifth Symphony." He hummed, "Dot Dot Dot, Daa!"

Stephanie roared with laughter.

Tony was just completing a meeting with Mike Caldwell, a detective from the Montgomery County, Maryland, Police Department about a shooting on upper Georgia Avenue near the border of the District of Columbia and Montgomery County. The shooting had occurred outside a bar on the D. C. side of the line and the chase had spilled across the county line. When Caldwell left, Harry and Debbie joined Tony. Tony poured coffee for them and then looked expectantly at Harry. He echoed Debbie's question to Harry the proceeding night. "How did it go in New York?"

"Fine."

Tony asked, "Did you see Lucretia Houston?"

"Oh, yeah. I saw her. By the way," he interjected. "You were right about the Houstons. They are loaded. The entrance way to their penthouse." He spread out his arms. "It's cavernous. It's bigger than my living room. And, there's a Renoir on one of walls. I'm sure it's an original."

Tony nodded. "I did some more checking, yesterday. Houston is an exceedingly wealthy man."

"Doesn't act like it. He is a very pleasant guy. Extremely well-informed. I had a long chat with him while waiting for Lucretia to return from her office."

"What's Lucretia like?"

"That's a good question, Tony. I can't figure her out. When we met and I told her that I wanted to talk with her about Dr. Hoffman's murder, she froze. She was as cold as an iceberg. She refused to talk with me about the murder and gave me my walking papers. It was only when I casually mentioned that it was either talking informally with me or your calling in the New York Police Department to interview her, that she reluctantly consented to talk with me." Harry smiled. "When I raised the specter of a visit to the police station, she threw in the towel."

Tony nodded. "I think I know why she was so reluctant to talk to you about Dr. Hoffman's murder."

Harry grinned. "I just thought it was my charming personality."

Tony chuckled. "That too, old buddy. But I checked her out further. She is Tony Carcioni's niece."

Harry reacted like he had been hit by a punch in the solar plexus. "I'll be damned."

Tony continued. "Her father, Mario, had nothing to do with the mob. He avoided his brother and his brother's associates like the plague. Mario was squeaky clean. He won a Silver Star in Vietnam for bravery. But, it's pretty hard to live down an uncle like Tony C. no matter what you or your father do in life."

Harry thought for a moment. "Yeah. That helps make sense of her reaction to being questioned about Dr. Hoffman. Lucretia knew she's had contact with two murder victims. And her uncle is Tony C. That would have to raise a red flag when I mentioned Hoffman."

Tony raised his eyebrows. "Two victims?"

Harry nodded. "Hoffman and Wolfson. She never met Dr. Hoffman. She told me she admires her work. But she hated Wolfson with a passion." Harry cleared his throat. "It goes back to her days at Princeton. Wolfson was the reigning deity in the music department. He had a terrific reputation.

Anyway, he turned thumbs down on her life-long dream of becoming an opera singer. He told her that her musical abilities were not first rate. It was crushing. She and her husband-to-be, Kent were both incensed. They both had strong motives to kill him."

Tony asked, "Do you think they might have?"

Harry shook his head. "I honestly don't know. As I said, I can't figure her out. If you can discreetly check out their whereabouts during the Wolfson killing--it might be worth doing." Harry mused. "Even if they have alibis for the time Wolfson was murdered, that would not exonerate them. Being Tony C's niece with her contacts, and his fortune, they could arrange a killing for hire which would be next to impossible to trace."

Debbie ventured, "Sebastian was in Mexico when Hoffman was murdered. But, he could have done the same thing. He is making a ton of money."

Tony nodded. "Yeah. I know." He looked at Debbie. "Debbie, Sebastian is still a suspect. We need to know more about him. Why don't you run a background check on him? The usual things. Something might turn up in his past that may surprise us. And while you are at it, look through the articles in the popular magazines about him. There may be some gossip that's worth pursuing."

Debbie nodded, restraining a smile. She enjoyed those magazines, but she wasn't going to let Harry know it.

Tony looked at Harry. "Did Lucretia say anything else?"

"Yes. I asked her about Rieder. She doesn't think too much of him. I have a feeling she has contempt for the man. Described him as well-trained and all that, but said he takes a superficial approach to Schubert. She thinks he's timid."

Harry looked at his notebook. "She doesn't know Cochrane. She heard him lecture once. She says Cochrane knows Schubert's music cold. Interestingly, she described him as something of a queer duck." He smiled. "I'm half inclined to describe her that way, too. Maybe, it takes one to know one."

Tony laughed. "What conclusions have you reached about Mrs. Houston at this point?"

"She had plenty of reason to kill Wolfson, but none that I can think of to kill either Griffith or Hoffman. Could she have perpetuated the scam? Written the fake Schubert score? Possibly. She has had training in composition and she's very, very bright. But, what would be her motive to do it? I can't see one at this point. There was certainly no financial motive. $300,000 to them is like three cents to me. Still, she is pretty deep, and despite her training as a psychoanalyst, she probably has a lot of resentments. She--and her husband for the matter--could be involved in Wolfson's death." He paused. "Maybe, Wolfson's death is independent of the others. Maybe, we're barking up the wrong tree when we're assuming it's one person we're looking for--a serial killer." He sighed, "I don't know at this point."

"What are you going to do now, Harry?"

"I don't know. I'd like to think about it. I'll get back to you later"

"Okay."

"How about you Tony?"

"I may have to fly to Vienna. Rieder is still far and away numero uno. He has a motive, the opportunity, and an ability to orchestrate the scam."

"Yeah. I agree with you about Rieder." Harry arose from his chair. "I'll call you tomorrow."

Chapter 19

Debbie did not return with Harry to the apartment for lunch as they had originally planned, but spent the afternoon beginning a background check on Sebastian. She made telephone calls to the School of Music at Indiana University where Sebastian had been a student. The reports from his professors in both composition and piano studies were strikingly similar. "Very talented, but difficult to teach. Very much an individualist and a nonconformist." She could believe that after her conversation with him. Then, she did a routine check of police records and found that Sebastian had a clean slate. His early experiences with drugs did not surface. She didn't expect to find much that would suggest that Sebastian had anything to do with Dr. Hoffman's murder and she didn't.

She grinned. The gossip tabloids might be more productive. Then, she had a sudden thought. Her older sister Lorna had a teenage daughter Sarah who was absolutely gah gah about Sebastian. She could be a mine of information. Debbie looked at the clock on the far wall. It was very nearly 4:00 p.m. Sarah should be home from school by now. She dialed Lorna's number in suburban Virginia.

Lorna answered the phone. "Hi Lorna," Debbie began.

"Hi, Deb. How are you?"

"Fine."

"And, you?"

"Just fine. How's Harry?"

"Same as ever."

Lorna pictured Harry in her mind and chuckled. "Mom still pushing you, two, to get married?"

"No. She stopped."

"What happened?"

"Harry and I went to visit her. We spent the weekend with her."

"I can imagine how that went."

Debbie grimaced. "Yeah. Not too swift. But don't blame Harry. He was on his best behavior. I was proud of him. He never uttered a sarcastic remark. Not a one. He did make a few quips that were over Mom's head, but, you know how things are."

"Yes, I know. He certainly isn't Mom's choice."

"You can say that again."

"She wanted you to marry Freddie. Safe, steady, polite, and."

"Boring." Debbie finished Lorna's sentence for her.

Lorna laughed. "Yeah. He certainly was. You never have to worry about being bored with Harry. I like Harry. At times he can be overwhelming. But he sure is fun."

Debbie couldn't resist a smile. "Yeah. He is entertaining." She paused. "Lorna, we got company. Harry's niece, Stephanie is visiting."

"Is she smart like Harry?"

"Yes. She's getting a Ph.D. in music. I like her a lot, Lorna. She's very nice." Debbie laughed. "I taught her how to play poker last night. She cleaned me out."

"Shouldn't teach her bad habits."

"Guess not. Say, is Sarah around?"

"No. She's at cheerleader practice. Won't be back for an hour, at least."

"It's she still wild about Sebastian? Or, has she becomes addicted to a pop star or a rock band?"

Lorna laughed. "It's still Sebastian, I'm afraid. She and her girlfriend, Mary Kay talk about him all the time. I can hear them, now. "He's sweet, awesome, fantastic, over the moon."

Debbie laughed. "I guess it runs in the family. Grandma was nuts about Elvis, and you were wild about the Beatles."

Lorna laughed. "I sure was. I still think they were great."

"So do I."

"Sarah's still fixated on Sebastian. She lives and dies with every show. She knows more about Sebastian's doings than she knows about any of the subjects she studies at school." She paused. "I wish she would spend more time on her geometry homework. She's not doing well at all. I talked with her about it, but she told me not to worry. She said her math teacher, Mr.

Brown, will let her make a poster for extra credit and she's sure to get an A or a B that way."

There was a note of irritation in Debbie's reply. "I wasn't that good at math, either. But, they didn't let us make posters to get a grade when I went to school. We had to learn math." Debbie paused and the tone of her voice lightened. She asked, "How does Sarah pick up the gossip on Sebastian?"

"She used to get it from the tabloids. Now, she just relies on Felicity Fair's blog, 'Celebrity watch.' She has an update on Sebastian every week."

Debbie thought, "Maybe, I can get what I need from Felicity Fair's blog." She changed the subject and asked about Lorna's husband, Jim, who had recently sprained his ankle tripping over a pair of her shoes in the dark. Lorna said that Jim was wearing an ankle brace in his shoe and that the doctor expected him to be fine in a week or two. Debbie said she was glad of that, smiled at the thought of Lorna's booby-trap shoes, and said goodbye.

Switching on the Internet to her usual search engine, Debbie soon found the address for Felicity Fair's website, 'Celebrity Watch'. She clicked on Sebastian and was greeted by a stunning picture of the musician standing by a grand piano clad in his white cape. She thought wistfully that he even looked sexier in the flesh. She could have shared lunch with him and probably his bed as well. Then, she kicked herself for her thoughts. She was not about to cheat on Harry and he wouldn't cheat on her. She laughed. She hoped that was the case. Anyway, he better damn-well not. She turned on the audio to listen to Felicity Fair. Her voice had a sing-song quality to it and she sounded more than a little condescending. A kind of know-it-all quality. What was the word her mother used to describe this? "Catty." That was it. She laughed, again and listened to the latest update on Sebastian.

What is new about America's heart throb? Well, here is something interesting. The off-and-on passionate romance of Sebastian and film star Kitty Rogers is all over. The two of them had a row at you know what Hollywood restaurant which shocked even the sophisticated patrons who lunch there. Was Kitty cheating on Sebastian (unthinkable!) Or was it the other way around? Whatever, watch that temper, Sebastian!

Good news for the legion of Sebastian fans. The threat of a lawsuit against their idol by Johanna Hoffman has now ended. My sources tell me the Columbia professor was about to file a multimillion-dollar damage suit against the reigning prince of music, but her untimely death put an end to the pending litigation. I am sure Sebastian must be mightily relieved to escape from a protracted lawsuit, which would have severely detracted from the image he has so carefully cultivated. I talked to one of Sebastian's most intimate friends who told me that Sebastian deeply regretted the comments he made about Dr. Hoffman on television and was shocked and dismayed by her murder. One of Sebastian's many ex-girlfriends, who I must say bears a grudge against him, has been doing a lot of talking, spreading the downright ugly idea that Sebastian, himself, had something to do with the murder. But as they say, 'Hell has no fury like a woman scorned.'

And here is a final item which is likely to be a disappointment to Sebastian fans, particularly those living in the New York City area. Sebastian will not participate in the gala musical event at Lincoln Center to raise money for AIDS awareness. Sir Charles Southwick who is organizing the event will have nothing to do with Sebastian. Could it be that the fling Lady Southwick had with Sebastian at Tanglewood last summer still rankles the esteemed conductor? Who can blame lady Southwick? Grow up, Charlie. The benefit is for a good cause.

Debbie listened for more, but that was all there was about Sebastian. Still, what she had heard was more than interesting. She printed two copies of the material on Sebastian, attaching one to a note and left it in Tony's mailbox. She put the other copy in her pocketbook. She was anxious to go home and talk with Harry and particularly Stephanie who knew Southwick to see what they made out of it. Her background checks had indicated that Sebastian had training in composition and was talented. The gossip from Felicity Fair was intriguing to say the least. A possible motive for the Hoffman murder jumped out at one and there was a link to Southwick. It was a good afternoon's work. She couldn't resist a broad grin. Picking up her pocketbook, she left the police station.

When Debbie opened the door to the apartment, she was greeted by a wonderful aroma from the kitchen. She stood inside the door for a moment and savored it. She broke into a broad grin. As she stood there, the door to the bedroom opened and Stephanie appeared. Debbie ventured, "It smells good, Stephanie. What is it?"

"Harry's cooking roast duck with his special sauce."

"He does that every once in a while. It's great."

"My dad told me Harry was a great cook. I think that's an understatement."

Debbie replied, "Why do you think I moved in?"

Stephanie laughed. Then, Harry appeared from the kitchen with a white apron tied around his waist. Walking over to Debbie, he kissed her lightly on the lips, and then said, "Just in time for dinner."

"I have a good sense of timing, don't I?"

"Sure do, Kid. When it comes to dinner, it's unerring. Did you find anything in your background check about Sebastian?"

She smiled. "Plenty. But that can wait until after dinner. She sniffed the savory aroma again and said, "Let's eat."

Harry served the roast duck with wild rice, green beans and a tossed salad and opened a bottle of a German Rhine wine. The three ate leisurely, fully enjoying themselves and then, well satisfied, lingered over coffee, fruit, and a plate filled with a variety of cheeses. Only, then, did Stephanie pass around her notes on Sebastian's studies at Indiana, and the hard copy of Felicity Fair's latest news about the pianist.

After reading the material, Harry smiled at Debbie. "Well done," he said. Then, after rereading the notes from Indiana University aloud, he turned to Stephanie, inquiring, "Does this sound like Sebastian could have written the phony score?"

"With Dr. Hoffman's program to assist him, it's certainly possible."

Harry nodded. "Do you know anything about this business between Sebastian and Lady Southwick?"

This time it was Stephanie who broke into a broad grin. "Oh, yeah. A lot"

"I'm all ears, " Harry said.

"Well, I was at Tanglewood when it happened. I had been there once before, a few years earlier when I was an undergraduate. I was playing violin in the student orchestra." She smiled. "It was great fun and I learned a lot.

Two years ago, I returned. This time, I was assisting Sir Charles, who had a lot of conducting responsibilities. I was his go-for. Running errands, checking on things. I was on my feet a lot." She turned toward Debbie and asked, "Do you know much about Tanglewood?"

Debbie shook her head. "I've heard of it. That's about it."

"Well, it's the summer home for the Boston Symphony Orchestra. The Boston Pops plays their, too. And it's a summer training camp for music students. It's up in the Berkshires--beautiful country in Massachusetts.

They tell me it was a summer place for the wealthy at one time. Now, there's the outdoor Music Shed for performances and other buildings. It's grown into an expansive, wonderful setting for music making and study."

She turned towards Harry. "Did you know that they have jazz performances at Tanglewood as well?"

Harry nodded. "Well," she continued, "One night, there was a big, impromptu party, mostly students, but some professional musicians as well. Sir Charles and Lady Southwick were there. Her name is Margaret. Well, Lady Margaret is much younger than Sir Charles--I would say 20 years younger at least. She is very attractive, dresses wonderfully, and she's very spontaneous and outgoing." Stephanie raised her eyebrows. "She's more than a bit of a flirt and." She hesitated. "She drinks too much. Anyway, a jazz combo played at the party. They were great. The kids began to dance. The beer and wine were flowing. It was a wonderful party. Then, suddenly, the jazz band struck up a Charleston tune. The Charleston, of course, was the craze during the 1920s—the roaring '20s. If you have never seen the Charleston, it's a high energy, frenetic dance. Of course, nobody knows how to dance the Charlestown, today, that is almost nobody. But, Lady Margaret does and she began dancing the Charleston by herself and everyone around her applauded. She called out, 'Can anyone do the Charleston with me.?' Sir Charles glumly shook his head. Sir Charles is built more like a pro football linebacker than a dancer and is clumsy on his feet. Then, from across the room slowly moved Sebastian, doing the Charleston. He moved towards her, she saw him and responded by moving towards him."

Stephanie turned toward Harry. "Harry it was like one of those old Fred Astaire, Ginger Rogers movies that Dad has in his DVD collection of classic films. Just like in these movies, the romance was in the dance. It was palpable. The people around them watched. At first they were quiet. They seemed mesmerized and then suddenly they began to cheer. It was infectious. The jazz combo intensified their playing. Everyone was caught up in this scene--except for Sir Charles, who just looked stone-faced."

Harry shook his head. "That must have been something, Stephanie."

Stephanie replied. "It was, Uncle Harry. It really was."

Harry asked, "What was Sebastian doing there?"

"Oh. He gave a recital during the afternoon. By the way, this all happened before Sebastian started his television show. I believe the TV show started that fall. He wasn't a big celebrity, yet."

Suddenly, Debbie remembered the photograph on Sebastian's desk. She recalled the scrawled note, something about sharing exquisite memories. She wondered, was this the same Margaret? She would give odds that it was. Curious, she asked, "What happened after the party? Did Lady Margaret and Sebastian see each other?"

"They sure did. Sir Charles was tied up in rehearsals and they were spotted together often. It was hard to be discreet. There were simply too many people around. I saw them myself in a secluded spot." She laughed. "I was seeing a bassoon player, named Freddie. We were looking for a spot where--uh--we could be alone together. We found one but we weren't alone. There were Sebastian and Lady Margaret locked in an embrace, kissing passionately."

Debbie asked, "Did Southwick find out about them?"

Stephanie nodded. "Sure. Everyone knew about it. Somebody must have told him. Anyway, there was a big explosion. I've heard that Southwick and Sebastian got into a ferocious argument. The story goes that Sebastian had fallen in love with Lady Margaret and had asked her to leave Sir Charles and go back with him to California. Lady Margaret was torn between her attraction to Sebastian and the privileges she enjoyed as Sir Charles' wife. Anyway, the two men ended up shouting at each other--there's no doubt that that happened--I know someone who heard the argument--and Lady Margaret ended up in tears."

Debbie inquired, "How did it end?"

"She didn't go to California with Sebastian. Instead, she took a flight to England the next day to think things over. Eventually, she reconciled with her husband."

"A real soap opera, " Harry observed sarcastically.

Debbie grinned. "He's still carrying a torch for her. He has her picture on his desk, and there are some endearing words scribbled on it."

Harry looked at Stephanie, "Why didn't you tell us about this?"

"It didn't occur to me that this had anything to do with Dr. Hoffman's murder and." She paused. "I still can't see that it does."

Harry reflected. "Maybe, that's true. But, then again, this affair may well have a bearing on the case." He paused. "For one thing, we now know the Sebastian had a plausible motive for killing Dr. Hoffman."

Stephanie responded quickly. "You mean the threat of a lawsuit."

Harry nodded. "Yeah."

Stephanie responded defensively. "I didn't know about the lawsuit, Uncle Harry. Dr. Hoffman didn't tell me."

"That doesn't surprise me, Stephanie. Professors often like to keep some distance from their students. It preserves their role as the authority figure, as the teacher."

Stephanie nodded. "That's right."

Harry's continued. "And, now we also know that Sebastian could have perpetrated the scam--He may have had the talent--and, he had a strong motive to do so."

Stephanie looked quizzical. "Motive? I don't understand."

Debbie smiled. "Embarrassment, Stephanie. When it came out that the score was a fraud, Southwick would have looked like a fool."

"Exactly!" Harry observed. "It would have probably cost him his job as well as his reputation." He added, "What a sweet way to get revenge. Maybe, even Lady Margaret would have dropped him and gone to Sebastian."

Stephanie's eyes dilated as she explored the possibility. "I see what you mean."

"Sebastian would have had to work through a third-party to keep his fingerprints off of the scam, but anyone smart enough to produce the forgery could have arranged that."

"So you think Sebastian was the killer, Uncle Harry?"

Harry rubbed his forehead. "I don't know, Stephanie. There are just too many loose ends. This is like a jigsaw puzzle with missing pieces." He raised his head and faced Debbie. "It's like swiss cheese. When we examine every suspect, there are holes in the case. Either we don't as yet know something that's important or there is nothing there to know."

Debbie asked, "Can you be more specific?"

Harry nodded, "Sure." He thought for a moment, and then said, "Let's start with Sebastian. He's most on our minds tonight. Debbie, you interviewed him. You will be our expert witness about Sebastian."

Debbie smiled. "Okay."

"My first question, "Did Sebastian have the talent to do the scam and the motive to do it?"

"Talent? Possibly. Motive, yes."

"Now, let's consider the victims, one-by-one. Did Sebastian have a motive to kill Dr. Hoffman?"

"Yes."

"How about Griffith? Did Sebastian have a motive to kill him?"

"Not that we know of."

"Wolfson?"

Debbie repeated herself. "Not that we know of."

Harry summarized. "So, you can see that there are lots of holes in the case against Sebastian. Of course, there may be things we don't know as yet which could tighten the case against him." He paused, briefly, and then said, "Okay, let's consider Rieder." He turned toward Stephanie. "Stephanie, you are our expert witness for Rieder. Talent and motive for the scam?"

"Talent? Probably. Motive, definitely."

"Any motive to kill Hoffman?"

She thought for a moment. "No." Then, quickly, she added, as if inspired, "To cover up the scam, maybe."

Harry nodded, approvingly. "How about Griffith or Wolfson? Did he have a motive to kill either of them?"

"I doubt it."

Harry thought for a moment. "Rieder and Griffith were planning a symposium that fell apart. It may be that Rieder was angry at Griffith. But that's a stretch. A big stretch." He paused. "I'll be the witness for Houston. "Talent? Possibly. Motive for the scam? Maybe, she wanted to show up the deities of classical music who rejected her. That's a stretch, too. She did have a strong motive to kill Wolfson. But not the others, except possibly Hoffman as Stephanie suggested as a cover up for the scam." He paused, and said, "Let's consider Queen, briefly. He certainly had a motive. He needed money. And he probably had the talent. He is gifted. But Stephanie has made it clear that he didn't compose the phony score. Someone else did it. And he has an airtight alibi for the time Hoffman was murdered. And he had no motive to kill either Griffith or Wolfson. Besides, he is much too disorganized to design and carry out a scheme as elaborate as this scam was. And Cochrane? We know very little about him. He is a shadowy figure, a bit of an oddball and apparently devious. He may be involved in this business, maybe a bit player, but there is nothing at this point to suggest that he's a serial killer." He turned toward Stephanie. "Do you know whether he has composed any music?"

"I believe he has, although I never heard it performed."

"Interesting. We'll certainly have to look into that. So there's our Swiss cheese." Harry sighed and said, "Let's give it up for tonight and give ourselves a rest."

Stephanie smiled and said, "That sounds good. Anybody for poker?"

Chapter 20

That night Harry had trouble sleeping. He had a succession of dreams, the last one of which was strange and bizarre. He was back in the small town in Illinois, where he was raised and had not visited in decades. In his dream, he was not the child that he was then, but the man he is now. He stood on the vacant lot where he and his childhood friends had played baseball, the same uneven dirt surface that had sent balls hit along the ground over his glove, smacking him in the face. The field was still there, but it was not as he remembered it, a place where children played. Instead the booths, tents, and Ferris wheel of a carnival were set in the field in a helter-skelter fashion. It did not seem altogether strange, however, for there had once been a carnival on the lot, in the year in which Harry and his family had moved to New York City. But, now as Harry strolled along, everything seemed wrong, because there were no customers visible, only two people standing behind booths and an open tent. As Harry approached the first booth, he saw a man standing behind a small table on which stood a row of porcelain dolls. He was fondling the dolls lovingly. Although Harry had never met the man, he knew him instantly. The man had golden locks and was dressed in a white cape. It was Sebastian. Sebastian did not speak, but merely pointed to several plastic rings on the table. Harry knew that he was supposed to toss the rings around a doll in order to win the doll. Harry also sensed that he was supposed to first put a dollar in the small box on the table and then try to encircle a doll with the rings. Harry tried the task again and again but he could not do it. Then, he realized that the rings were too small. It was a con game. Harry looked at Sebastian who only grinned. Harry felt disgusted, turned around, and walked away.

He spied the tent and now took in its colors, a shade of pale green splattered with yellow polka dots. A large painted sign posted in front of the entrance stated, "No one admitted under age 18." As Harry entered the tent, he was greeted by heavy, perfumed smoke. At first, he could hardly see his hand in front of him, but gradually the smoke cleared and then sounds of exotic music filled his ears. Where had he heard these sounds before? Then, suddenly he knew. These were musical sounds he had heard in the cafes in the Near East. Now, the mist cleared and he could see the sensuous movements of a belly dancer. Then, he spied a musician, playing some kind of strange wind instrument. Harry expected the musician to look like the musicians he had seen in Lebanon and Syria but instead what he saw was an American dressed in blue jeans. The half-dreaming musician seemingly lost to the world was Oliver Queen. Astonishment gripped Harry and he left the tent.

Harry walked over to the remaining booth. He saw the figure of a woman standing behind a table, upon which stood a gleaming crystal ball. The woman was dressed in the colorful garments of a gypsy. Then, he saw that the figure was not a live woman, but a life-size porcelain doll. He recognized her. It was L. C. Huston. She looked older and graver than he remembered her, but still beautiful, even in porcelain. Her penetrating eyes, however, were shut tight.

Now, Harry noticed a small box next to the crystal ball. There was a slot on the top of the box, a slot for depositing coins. The saying, "A penny for your thoughts" flashed into his mind. He reached into his pocket, found a shiny penny and deposited it. The eyes of the porcelain figure suddenly opened wide. Harry asked, "What can you tell me about the murders of Hoffman, Wolfson, and Griffith?" ·

"I have already told you all you need to know." The eyes shut tight, and, then suddenly, there was an explosion and Harry woke up in a sweat.

Debbie, who had always been a light sleeper, awoke instantly. She whispered, "What's wrong, Harry?"

"I had the wildest dream," he said, shakily.

"Nightmare?"

"It sure was. There was a bomb blast at the end."

"Like what happened to you in Lebanon?"

"Yes."

"A flashback?"

"No. Not really. The scene was somewhere else."

"Tell me about it."

"Okay."

Harry's memory for the dream was stark, and he related it in every detail. When he had finished, Debbie responded, "Well. That was one hell of a dream."

"Yeah. It was very vivid." Then, he added, "I don't often have nightmares. About the worst dreams I have is wandering through a garden party in my underwear. I'm not even naked."

Debbie chuckled, and ventured, "Maybe, the dream was trying to tell you something."

"Like a psychic dream?"

"Sort of."

"I don't believe in that stuff. It's all hogwash." He paused, reflecting. "Doesn't Lorna believe in psychics?"

"She used to. Anyway, she went to see one. I told her to take off her wedding ring and to dress up fashionably so she wouldn't give the psychic any clues. "Well, the psychic told her she would soon meet the man of her dreams. Of course, Lorna is happily married and wasn't looking for a man, so she gave up psychics."

Harry laughed. Debbie continued, "But, she's still interested in dreams. In fact, she loaned me a book on dreams. You remember last summer when we spent a few days at Ocean City?"

Harry nodded. "Sure," he said.

Debbie continued, "We were lying under the beach umbrella, remember?" Harry nodded. Debbie said, "I was reading while you were watching the girls parading up and down along the beach."

"I was watching the waves. It was very restful."

"Why were you turning your head sideways all the time?"

"Well, umh," Harry grunted.

Debbie laughed. "With what passes for swimsuits these days, I don't blame you. You got quite an eyeful."

Harry chuckled. Debbie stroked the hair on his chest lightly and continued. "It was a really good book. The guy who wrote it had done research on dreams for years. Anyway, he said that one way of analyzing dreams was to look at each scene in the dream separately and see what pops into your head—particularly, real experiences you may have had or ideas which simply come to mind. Then, think about these ideas or experiences and what they mean to you."

Harry thought for a moment. "It sounds plausible. All right, let's try it."

"How about the first scene with Sebastian?"

"Oh yeah, fondling the dolls. Glad one of them didn't look like you. I would have belted him even in the dream."

Debbie laughed. "I guess he does like to play around."

"Mrs. Houston says he breaths sex." He smiled, "And, then, of course, there's Lady Southwick. That sounds like it was a hot affair. And the game he had with his customers to win the dolls. That was rigged. It was phony. Just like the act he does on television. All that intensity. The man's a charlatan."

"This is getting interesting, Harry."

"I agree. You may be onto something."

"How about the second scene with Queen?"

"Queen was in a dreamy state playing exotic music. You know, Debbie, It's sort of the way I see him in real life. Just a bystander in this case."

"And the third scene with L. C. Houston?"

"Now that's a real corker. In the dream she said to me, 'I've told you all you need to know.' Sounds like a line from Keats. You remember, 'Beauty is truth, Truth beauty. That is all ye know on Earth, and all ye need to know.'" Harry paused. "That doesn't get me very far." He pondered. "Well, maybe, a little bit. She is beautiful by any standard, so maybe she is saying, 'I told you the truth.'"

"Then, what did she tell you?"

"She talked about the other suspects and the people who were murdered."

"What did she tell you about the murdered people?"

"Well, she admired Dr. Hoffman and hated Wolfson, which, of course, implicates herself and her husband." Harry stopped short. "Oh, shit!" he exclaimed. "How did I miss it? She told me that Griffith had written devastating reviews about some people and had made himself some bad enemies." Harry wiped the perspiration from his forehead. "And when I visited with Dr. Rubenstein at Yale, he alluded to the same possibility. Of course, I should have looked through Griffith's reviews to identify these people. What an idiot I am! Debbie, you should have gone with Sebastian. At least, he's a good-looking idiot."

Debbie laughed, and then hugged him. "What are you going to do now?"

"Go to New York. I'll call Elliot Byrnes tomorrow. You know that Elliot and I were college roommates and we have remained good friends. Elliot is now the associate editor of the paper that Griffith wrote for. I'll ask Elliot if he can arrange for me to look through Griffith's reviews. Maybe I can learn something."

"Sounds good! When are you going to New York?"

"As soon as I can arrange it with Elliot. I'd like to go the day after tomorrow." Then, he added, "That was a terrific idea of yours, Debbie. Thanks!"

She squeezed his arm. "By the way," he said, "For heaven's sake, don't tell Tony or Stephanie I got the idea from a dream. It will ruin my image as a hard-boiled, no-nonsense, skeptical journalist."

Debbie chuckled. "Don't worry. I wouldn't dream of telling anyone."

Harry laughed. "That's not the best choice of words."

Debbie grinned. "You're right. But, you're not that hard-boiled, Harry. You got a big heart."

"Tell that to my ex."

"What does she know? She's sounds like an over-competitive neurotic."

Harry laughed. "She would say the same thing about me."

Debbie smiled. "Maybe you both are."

"Probably."

Debbie asked demurely, "Want to make love?"

"Sure." Harry leaned over and kissed her passionately.

Chapter 21

Harry called Elliot Byrnes in the morning. Byrnes was more than happy to help and they agreed that Harry would come to New York City the following morning. Harry spent the day doing research for future columns and acting as a watchdog for Stephanie. He was anxious to get to New York and the day could not pass too quickly.

Harry arose early in the morning, tiptoeing through the apartment in an effort not to awaken Debbie and Stephanie. After dressing, he walked over to Pennsylvania Avenue where he spent ten minutes vainly trying to flag down one of the many taxicabs that passed by him. Finally, a taxi stopped. The driver was Ethiopian, a recent émigré with only a fledgling command of English. But he did know where Union Station was and threaded his way through the early morning traffic in the heart of the Nation's Capitol with the skill of a NASCAR driver. Harry was all admiration.

The train ride to New York City was uneventful. Harry whiled away the travel time reading *Time*, *U.S. News and World Report*, and *Newsweek* to see what his fellow pundits were writing. When he finally put the magazines down, he smiled. It was the same drivel he was writing. Whoever named columnists "talking heads," and "the chattering class" was being charitable. Maybe, they should all go back to making an honest living as reporters.

When Harry walked into the midtown Manhattan offices of the newspaper, he checked in with his old friend, Associate Editor Elliott Byrnes. Byrnes was a throwback to an ancient breed of newspapermen, who, if provided with green eye shades and cigars, would fit in comfortably in the cast of Hecht's and MacArthur's vintage play *The Front Page*. The associate editor was up to his neck in sorting out the morning problems and could only spare a smile, a grunt and a handshake for Harry. However, he was able to page a young intern who upon arriving at the editor's office was told, "This is Harry Ellison, an old buddy. He needs some help looking through past issues. Help him any way you can." The young man nodded and off they went.

The intern's name was Jim Rafferty. He was twenty-four, sandy haired, had a disarming, almost boyish smile and was eager to work. He reminded Harry of himself many years ago.

They settled themselves in a quiet office which contained a large wooden table and comfortable leather chairs. Harry outlined the task. "We're going to look through the music reviews of a former music critic of the paper, Edward Todd Griffith. He was a legend in his day. He died under mysterious circumstances about a year ago. What I need is a list of people whom he wrote lousy reviews about--real scorchers."

Rafferty raised his eyebrows. "You think--maybe..."

Harry nodded. "Yeah," he said. "I think. Oh, by the way, keep an eye out for columns that Griffith might have written about several people. The first is an Austrian professor. His name is Leopold Rieder. The second is a pianist who calls himself 'Sebastian.'"

Rafferty raised his eyebrows again. "You mean the guy with the long blonde hair who comes onto the stage wearing a white cape? I saw him on television."

Harry nodded. "That's the guy. With that getup, you'd think he was a professional wrestler."

Rafferty laughed. Harry continued. "It's all show business, of course. But he plays decently. Actually, quite well. Early reviews about him might be under the name of Bjorn Sabatini."

"Anyone else?"

"Yeah. Three more names. A guy named Oliver Queen. I don't expect we'll find anything there but we might as well look. There's also a musicologist by the name of Thaddeus Cochrane and a one time music student named Lucretia. C. Huston. You should also check her under her maiden mane which was Lucretia Carcioni."

Rafferty summarized his assignment. "Anyone who got burned by Griffith, and keep an eye out for Rieder, Sebastian, Queen, Cochrane, and Huston or Carcioni."

"Right!"

The young man nodded. Harry began whistling a tune from the Disney classic film *Snow White*, "Hi Ho, Hi Ho, It's Off to Work We Go," and off to work they went.

The task proved easier than Harry had imagined, for the caustic wit of Edward Todd Griffith, like an arsenal of deadly weapons, was stockpiled more than used. Slowly the two of them went through the weeks, the months, the years of Griffith's tenure as the newspaper's music critic. Slowly a list of names emerged, a Russian pianist, "who had mangled Beethoven's Fourth Piano Concerto beyond any hope of recognition," a conductor whose rendition of Mozart "sounded at times like the Mickey Mouse Club Anthem," and a tenor whose singing in Tosca "would stir up the hounds in a dog pound." As Harry entered the names on his list of suspects, he wondered how difficult it would be to check out the whereabouts of these maligned musicians.

They worked steadily through the afternoon taking only a short break for coffee and a Danish. It was close to three o'clock when Harry uncovered a brief notice about Bjorn Sabatini. He read the notice aloud. "We should also note the Town Hall debut of a young pianist, Bjorn Sabatini. A recent graduate of Indiana University, Sabatini plays with considerable force and gusto. Technically, he has more work to do before rising to the first rank of pianists, but one cannot but be impressed by his spirited playing. He is a talent worth watching."

Harry put the review aside. "A nice review for a young artist," he mused. "Nothing in this to cause hard feelings. No reason for a grudge."

Rafferty nodded. "I agree," he said. They resumed their search. Nothing emerged about Oliver Queen or L. C. Huston, but that was not surprising. What was surprising to Harry was that there was not a word about Leopold Rieder. Harry had a gut feeling that Rieder was involved in this business and if that was the case, something disparaging should show up in one of Griffith's columns. However, as they moved further and further through the years toward the beginning of Griffith's tenure as a music critic, there was nothing. Harry was beginning to wonder whether he was barking up the wrong tree when Rafferty suddenly shouted, "Eureka!"

Harry reacted excitedly. He asked, "Is it Rieder?"

"No, Mr. Ellison. Look at this!" Rafferty thrust an article into Harry's hands entitled, "Cochrane's First Symphony: A Bust by Any Other Name."

Harry read the review aloud. "Thaddeus Cochrane, by any measure, is already a distinguished musical scholar. His book on Franz Schubert is justly considered one of the finest books available on the subject. But, unfortunately, a scholar does not a composer make. His first symphony, premiered under the baton of Charles Southwick, the noted British conductor who soon may be in line for the post in New York, was an abysmal piece of music. While technically sound, the symphony lacked any interesting musical ideas. It was a dreary, intellectual exercise combining the worst excesses of contemporary music without a spark of creativity. The score reminds one of the story of three monkeys sitting behind a typewriter, randomly pushing keys while a patient observer waits to see whether one of the monkeys might eventually end up typing *Hamlet*. Cochrane's score sounds like it was fashioned in just such a manner. It was pointless and boring. Bad as the symphony is, it was made worse by an inept performance. For all of his musical acumen, Southwick seemed to have no idea what he was doing with the music. His tempos were erratic and his phrasing unintelligible. All in all, it was a dismal evening. Cochrane's first symphony should be his last!"

"Whew!" Harry muttered. "What a hatchet job! Cochrane has ample reason to be unhappy with Dr. Griffith and Sir Charles Southwick as well." Harry grinned. "What an interesting tie-in!"

Harry took off his glasses and rubbed his eyes. He tried to imagine how he would feel if he had received a scathing review like that--say, for a book he was planning to write on the Middle East. He knew that he would be mad as hell, and Harry had the skin of a rhinoceros. What if Cochrane had a thin skin? What if he couldn't stand criticism? Harry pictured in his mind the musical scholar living in a perpetual burn, brooding, nursing resentments. If this were the case, there's no telling what he might do.

Harry smiled faintly. Their persistence was paying off. What they had uncovered was tantalizing. But he knew that there was more work to do, more reviews to look through. Harry put his glasses back on. He pushed aside Griffith's review of Cochrane's Symphony, shoving it to the edge of the table and he and Rafferty returned to their task. They spent the remainder of the afternoon carefully sifting through Griffith's reviews until at long last they reached the bottom of the pile. When they were through, Harry counted their gleanings; eighteen scorching reviews published during the critic's tenure at the newspaper. Eighteen names that he or the police would have to check out.

Harry yawned, arose from the chair, and stretched. While Rafferty looked fresh, he was feeling tired. He sat down again and reread the Cochrane review. If anything, the review seemed more devastating than upon first reading. Closing his eyes, he once more reflected about Cochrane's possible involvement in the string of murders. He knew that only Cochrane, the Austrian scholar Leopold Rieder, Oliver Queen, L. C. Huston, and Sebastian had access to Dr. Hoffman's computer program for Schubert, and Rafferty and he had drawn a blank in looking for Rieder and Queen's names in the newspaper's files, and there was nothing in the reviews to point to Sebastian's involvement in the murders. While there was not a fragment of hard evidence against Cochrane, he was at the nexus of too many currents not to bear serious scrutiny.

In the evening, Harry shared a booth in a deli with Jim Rafferty. Over a thick corn beef sandwich and a glass of ale, Harry perused a dossier that Rafferty had pieced together on Cochrane. Thadeus Adams Cochrane was born in Boston of old New England aristocracy. His ancestors arrived in Boston in the Seventeenth Century and had accumulated a fortune in trade between the American colonies and England. Like his father and grandfather before him, Thaddeus had been educated at Harvard. After brief stints in the family shipping business, he renounced business in favor of music. He studied music at Oberlin Conservatory, and then returned to Harvard for a Ph.D. He joined the faculty at Julliard where he wrote widely acclaimed books on Schubert and Brahms. At Julliard he turned his attention to composition, publishing three short works, variations on themes of Mozart, Beethoven and Schubert. At the age of forty, he composed his most ambitious work, his first symphony which received its premiere in New York a year later. Shortly after the presentation of this work, Cochrane abruptly resigned from the faculty at Julliard and returned to New England, where he currently resides. Cochrane is independently wealthy being the beneficiary of a large family trust. He never married.

Harry mused, "Looks like his musical career ended abruptly when Griffith shot down his symphony. Quit teaching, quit writing, quit composing--looks like he quit everything."

"You think he killed Griffith?"

"I have no idea at this point. He certainly had the motive. Probably the opportunity. We'll be looking into it--and several other killings as well. This has the makings of a big news story. Keep it under your vest for the time being. We'll get you involved when the time comes." Harry smiled. "Meanwhile, thanks for your help." Harry arose from his chair, extending his hand. "I'll be in touch."

Chapter 22

When Harry left Jim Rafferty, he felt tired. An adrenalin surge which had propelled him throughout the long day had faded and fatigue had set in. He decided against making an evening trip to Washington. Instead, he telephoned a hotel reservation service and within the hour found himself stretched out on a comfortable queen sized bed facing an unlit television set and a table set with shrimp and crackers, and a tall glass half filled with bourbon and ice. A nice view came with the expensive tab for the hotel room: New York City in all of her nighttime finery, with lights stretching as far as the eye could see.

For awhile, Harry just relaxed. The bourbon tasted good and he enjoyed the pleasant sensations from the alcohol. Then, he stirred himself enough to telephone Debbie and tell her that he would return home sometime tomorrow afternoon.

Rising from the bed to collect the remainder of his drink, he thought about the television set. Why not? Maybe there would be a rerun of an old movie. Wouldn't it be nice to watch a classic Humphrey Bogart film?

Harry grabbed the remote control and began pushing the button while his eyes followed a succession of situation comedies, medical dramas, a New York Yankees' baseball game in which the Yankees were far ahead, a show about the South American rain forest and an old film about an alcoholic trumpet player that starred Kirk Douglas and Doris Day. It wasn't a bad film, but for some reason he couldn't get interested. He turned off the television set and swallowed the last drops of his drink.

He closed his eyes and thought about going to sleep. But now, he no longer felt sleepy. He checked his watch. It was only a quarter 'til nine. Without making any effort, his mind began to drift over the contours of the case he had become inadvertently involved in. For awhile, he thought about Thaddeus Cochrane and wondered whether he might be the person behind the murders. Then he shook his head. "Don't jump to conclusions yet, Ellison," he told himself. "Better go over the whole business from beginning to end and see if you missed something."

And so, his mind retraced the sequence of events beginning with Stephanie's telephone call on that warm June evening. Visual images and memories of conversations flowed through his mind as if they were fragments of a database called up by a computer program. His mind eventually focused on the victims. Particularly Griffith, Hoffman and Wolfson. Hoffman's murder seemed most comprehensible; she knew too much. The killer had to get rid of her to cover his or her trail. For Griffith, he now had the outlines of a plausible theory, although there were pieces still to be filled in. But Wolfson? Why was he killed? Only L. C. Huston and her husband Kent had motives to kill Wolfson and their grievances had nothing to do with either Griffith or Hoffman. How did Wolfson fit in with the other victims?

As he thought about Wolfson, the puzzle only deepened. He simply needed to know more about the man and his relationships both to the other murder victims and to the suspects, particularly Cochrane. And the best way to seek answers was to talk to Wolfson's widow.

Harry glanced again at his watch. It was now shortly after 10 o'clock. Could he call her at this hour? Could he even find her telephone number? It's worth a try, he thought. He dialed information. He was in luck; there was a telephone listing for Aaron and Ruth Wolfson in Princeton, New Jersey. Mrs. Wolfson had kept the telephone listing in both their names.

He dialed the number. A woman with a low, throaty voice answered the telephone. Harry inquired, "Is this Mrs. Wolfson?"

"Yes."

"Sorry to call you at such a late hour."

"It's all right," she said.

"My name is Harry Ellison. I'm a journalist. I wonder if I could come see you, perhaps tomorrow. I would like to ask you a few things about your late husband"

"Ellison?" Mrs. Wolfson paused. "Your voice sounds very familiar. I know," she said with a glow of recognition, "You're on the Sunday morning talk shows."

"That's me all right."

"Well, it's nice to meet you Mr. Ellison," she said cheerfully. "My son David is a news junkie. He's interested in politics and international affairs.

We watch the programs together every Sunday morning. He's a fan of yours."

"You've made my day, Mrs. Wolfson."

She laughed. Then, she asked, "What do you want to know about Aaron?"

"It's a long story, Mrs. Wolfson. My niece Stephanie was a friend and student of Johanna Hoffman..."

"Poor Johanna," Mrs. Wolfson interrupted. "Wasn't that awful?"

"Yeah. It was a terrible business. We think--and I'm working with the police on this--that there just might be some connection with your husband's death. Could I come to see you tomorrow and talk about it?"

"Aaron's death?" There was a quizzical note in her voice. She hesitated. "All right," she said. "When?"

"Around noon?"

"Fine."

Mrs. Wolfson gave him the directions which Harry dutifully jotted down on a small note pad.

In the morning he would rent a car and drive to Princeton.

It turned out to be a pleasant day for a drive. The sky was bright blue and clear. The glare of the sun was intense enough to cause Harry to don his sunglasses. As he drove along the New Jersey Turnpike, he thought of Princeton. He had never been there, but thoughts of F. Scott Fitzgerald, J. Robert Oppenheimer, Woodrow Wilson and Albert Einstein, luminaries of the University, filled his mind as his car approached his destination. He checked his watch to see if he had time to explore the campus before keeping his appointment. He shook his head. No, it was almost noon. He would save his touring for another time.

The directions to the Wolfson home were easy to follow and Mrs. Wolfson, a tall, dark-haired woman of about forty, greeted him at the door. She was dressed in tan colored slacks, a loose fitting blue blouse, and sandals. Standing next to her was a lanky boy of 15. Like Mrs. Wolfson, he had dark hair. But unlike his mother, whose hair was cut short, his was long and wavy.

Mrs. Wolfson introduced Harry to her son David. Harry followed them into a comfortable living room whose centerpiece was a vintage Steinway grand piano. Harry seated himself on a large couch that was fronted by an elegant marble top table on which stood a dark vase filled with yellow roses.

The couch was placed to look upon a cubist painting of a guitar on the near wall. Harry thought it looked like a Braque.

While Mrs. Wolfson went into the kitchen to make coffee, Harry and David talked about what it was like being a columnist and television commentator. Harry rarely thought of himself as a celebrity, but it gave him a warm feeling to be treated as one, even if it was for five minutes--ten less than Andy Warhol's criterion. When Mrs. Wolfson returned, David excused himself, and the two settled down to conversing over coffee.

"You have a rare kid there," Harry began. "I haven't seen a teenager in a long time who was interested in international affairs. Usually it's sports, clothes, cars and, of course, the opposite sex."

Mrs. Wolfson smiled. "I think it's living in a university town. But David's interested in all the other things, too, and he plays the piano very well."

Harry nodded. "He gives me hope." He paused and rubbed his glasses. A quizzical look formed in his eyes, as if he were uncertain how to begin the interview. Finally, he asked, "Did your husband happen to know an Austrian musicologist by the name of Rieder?"

"Sure," Mrs. Wolfson replied quickly. "Leopold and Irmgard are very close friends. We date back a long way. Irmgard was matron of honor at our wedding."

"I had no idea," Harry replied, smiling. Then, he paused and asked, "Do you happen to know anything about the trouble Leopold's in now?"

Mrs. Wolfson gave a disparaging shake of her head. "Do I ever," she said. "Irmgard has been writing me long letters about it. Leopold is a wonderful scholar, but he's an absolute boob about practical things. He had a very comfortable situation. He had inherited some money, his books had sold well and he had a really good position at the University. For years he let Irmgard run the house and family finances and everything was fine. Then, one day he met this...," she hesitated for a second, "this guy at a musical soiree who went by the name of Otto von Metternich."

Harry frowned, "Metternich...?"

Mrs. Wolfson interrupted. "Yeah, Metternich. He claimed to be a descendent of the illustrious Austrian statesman who almost ran Europe single-handedly after the Napoleonic wars."

"I'll be damned," Harry reacted. "Was this modern day Metternich for real?"

Mrs. Wolfson laughed. "Well, sort of. Since the debacle over the ski resort, Irmgard has had some investigations done on his background. He is related to the famous Metternich, though he's far from a direct descendant. When he was a young man he changed his name to Metternich--I can't recall what it was previously. Irmgard would know. Well, anyway, Otto and Leopold became great friends. They went to the opera together, to horse shows--even did some gambling in which Leopold won some money. I suspect Otto arranged for Leopold to win. When they were together, Otto would fill Leopold's head with stories of the old Austrian empire. He claimed that his great grandfather--not the original Metternich, of course--was an intimate of the Emperor Franz Joseph and that he knew the Strauss family, Johann, Josef and Edward. He was a charming bastard and he dazzled not only Leopold but others as well. When he set up the ski resort, he had no shortage of investors. He collected millions and it's probably in an unmarked Swiss bank account. The police are looking for him, but I bet they never find him. He's most likely living in Argentina wearing a beard."

Harry laughed. "Hell of a scam. What was Leopold's role in it?"

"Leopold was the front man. He had an impeccable reputation as one of Austria's foremost scholars." She sighed. "Now he's lost that and all his money too. His son has set up a legal defense fund to try to keep him out of prison." She looked downcast. "And maybe, even worse, psychologically, he's come apart at the seams. Irmgard says he's an emotional basket case. He can't concentrate, can't sleep. He rants and raves at himself for his own stupidity, then crawls into a shell like a tortoise. Irmgard is really worried about him."

Harry nodded sympathetically, and then hesitantly asked, "Do you believe that Leopold would be capable of violent acts, if he saw it was a way to restore his financial position?"

"No," Mrs. Wolfson replied. "Far from it. He's a very timid man. I can't imagine him having anything to do with violence."

Harry paused for a moment, reflecting. Then, he said, "I'd like to ask you about a music student who was here some years ago. She was studying voice. She wanted to be an opera singer. Perhaps, you remember her. Her maiden name was Carcioni, Lucretia Carcioni."

Mrs. Wolfson smiled. "Oh, yes. I remember her very well. You see, at the time I had a job here as an accompanist. I accompanied singers on the piano and also worked with instrumentalists." Her smile faded into a look of chagrin. "Lucretia was a bitter-sweet story--I'm afraid more bitter than sweet. Lucretia wanted so much to be an opera singer. We worked together for many hours along with her vocal coach." She sighed. "But you need a great voice to be an opera singer. That is a gift of God. I knew deep down that she wasn't going to make it. No matter how hard she worked. Aaron-- he was not my husband, yet--told her so. Aaron doesn't like to tell students that they are not going to make it. I know it upsets him. So he tends to be brief and frank to get it over with as quickly as possible. To others it may seem almost blunt and uncaring. But this is not really the case. Anyway, Lucretia took it hard. I was very worried about her. I was afraid she might." She did not finish the thought she started, but began again. "I was glad to see she went to the counseling center for help."

She paused. "Mr. Ellison," she said with intensity, "I know what she was going through. Once, I had dreams of becoming a concert pianist. But there's only so much room at the top for concert careers. There are some household names that are big draws. You know who they are. Then, it falls off rapidly. I entered a pianist competition and soon learned that I wasn't going to be one of those big names. I consider myself very fortunate to have found the job at Princeton as an accompanist. And I loved what I was doing, working with the students. It was wonderful." She smiled. "And, of course, I met my husband, here. We had a good marriage."

Harry said, "I heard he was a brilliant man."

"Oh, yes. He was indeed."

Harry ventured, "I heard he was a perfectionist."

She smiled, "He was. Certainly with music. He always strove for the ideal."

"How about in his daily life?"

"Sometimes. But, not usually with me. Unlike some people who have this problem, he realized that he had these tendencies and tried to control them. He usually did. But, sometimes we did have a flare up." She smiled. "He'd always bring me a bouquet of flowers, afterwards with an apology. With David, he expected a lot. But David was like his father. He is very, very smart and a self starter. He doesn't need pushing. So Aaron and David got along just fine."

Harry nodded. "I can see that he is intellectually curious."

"Oh yes, just like his father."

Harry nodded. "I'd like to ask you about one more person your husband might have known. His name is Thaddeus Cochrane."

Mrs. Wolfson nodded her head. "Aaron knew Cochrane, though not all that well. I met him once myself. Cochrane had driven down from Massachusetts to see Aaron. They spent the afternoon at Aaron's office at the University, then returned here for dinner."

"About when was the meeting?"

"Two summers ago. I think in June."

"Did Aaron tell you what the meeting was about?"

Mrs. Wolfson shook her head. "No, he didn't. But from what he said-- more throw-away remarks than anything else, I had the feeling the meeting didn't go very well at all. He seemed annoyed at what happened. He was quite irritable the next couple of days. I remember that very well."

"Do you have any idea why?"

Again, she shook her head. "No, not really. He was upset by the meeting. But that's all I can say."

"What were your impressions of Cochrane?"

Mrs. Wolfson thought for a moment, considering her answer carefully. "Well, for one thing, he was a fastidious dresser. The professors around here--particularly my husband's friends in the arts--are pretty casual in the way they dress. But not Thaddeus Cochrane. He wore a really expensive suit and it was perfectly tailored. He seems to care a good deal about the appearance he presents. Then, his manners are unusual. Very courtly. Almost Victorian. He can be very charming. Still," she shrugged, "I didn't like him at all. There's something about him that left me cold."

"Interesting," Harry pondered. "What do you think it was that made you feel that way?"

"That's a tough question. And you must bear in mind that was a first impression. If I knew him better, perhaps I would change my mind. But despite his courtly manners, he struck me as anything but a warm person. Maybe it's his eyes. At times he had an icy cold stare. Again, I could be reading too much into those few hours. But he made me uncomfortable. That is for sure." Suddenly she laughed. "My Uncle Bernie—he died a few years ago—he was in World War II. He was in Patton's Third Army that marched across France. He used to have a saying, 'I'd hate to have that guy in a fox hole with me.'" She looked at Harry. "That's the way I felt about him."

"You wouldn't trust him?"

Mrs. Wolfson smiled. "Not for a minute." She paused. "Mr. Ellison, how does all this relate to my husband's death?"

Harry sighed. "I'm not sure yet, Mrs. Wolfson. But it's beginning to look like the person who killed your husband also killed Dr. Hoffman, and probably two other people as well."

Mrs. Wolfson gasped. "A serial killer?"

"Something like that, only the killings aren't random."

She exclaimed, "But why?"

"I think I know the reason, but I can't prove it. Not yet, anyway."

"He sounds very dangerous."

He sighed again. "Exceedingly."

Concern filled her face. "Does he know you're looking for him?"

Harry flashed a smile. "Oh, yeah. He knows that I'm looking for the killer. But I don't think he knows that I suspect him. At least I hope not. If he does, I'll have to start doing things differently. I'll have to become much more careful."

There was intensity in Mrs. Wolfson's expression. "Please be careful, Mr. Ellison."

"Thank you. I will. But I have a guardian angel looking after me. The lady in my life. She's a cop. And she's a crack shot." Harry smiled. "As long as I don't stray too far from her, I'll be fine."

He cast his eyes at the piano. Rising to his feet, he walked over to the instrument and looked at it. "It's a beautiful piano," he observed.

Mrs. Wolfson replied, "Thank you. Do you play?"

Harry shrugged. "Only by ear. I played the cello when I was a kid. It was such a cumbersome instrument that I gave it up in favor of baseball."

Mrs. Wolfson laughed. Harry said, "I know you play"

"Yes. I love the piano."

Harry smiled. "Who are your favorite composers for the piano?"

"Chopin and Schumann."

"I like that. Do you know Chopin's Ballade Number Two? It's a favorite of mine."

"It's a favorite of mine, too. Would you like me to play it?"

"It would be a salve to a road-weary journalist."

Mrs. Wolfson sat down at the piano and without notes played the haunting Chopin piece. Harry sank into the couch, closed his eyes and drank in the beautiful music. When she had finished, Harry said, "That was wonderful. Thank you so much."

He rose to his feet, shook her hand, and said quietly, "When things break on this case, I'll call you."

She nodded. "Be careful, Mr. Ellison, please."

"Yeah," he replied almost wistfully. I'll try to be."

Chapter 23

It was a hot, humid afternoon. Because of the very high temperature, power had been cut throughout the city to prevent an overload of the entire electrical system, so by 3 p.m., air conditioning was more of an illusion than a reality. Harry and Tony were in shirt sleeves as they sat across from each other in Tony's office. As they sipped lukewarm coffee, Harry voiced the thought that a cold beer would be more in keeping with the weather. "Wouldn't it, though," Tony agreed. "Where are the ladies?" he asked.

Harry glanced at the large clock on the wall. "They're late," he mused. "Debbie's usually punctual. She's very efficient about doing things. Stephanie takes after her mother."

"Not very efficient?"

"No. Her mother's people are artists and musicians. Very talented, gifted people. But I don't think anyone in the family has ever owned a watch."

Tony sighed. "Nice work if you can get it."

There was a rap on the door. It was Debbie and Stephanie. Debbie carried a brown paper bag from which she distributed straws and four plastic cups filled with ice tea.

"The ice man cometh," Harry said gleefully.

"Ice woman," corrected Debbie.

Harry laughed. "Ice woman? No way. Would I live with a woman who wasn't passionate and tender hearted?"

"I like the description," Debbie replied smiling. "But I'm glad you didn't add hot blooded. Hot blooded is a lousy recipe for a police woman. It'll get you killed."

Harry nodded. "You're cool in a crunch, Debbie."

"That she is," Tony concurred, smiling faintly. "That's why way-back-when, I assigned her to protect your posterior, Old Chum."

"Don't I know it," Harry agreed.

Tony sipped the ice tea. He sighed. "This is good." He cleared his throat. "Okay, folks, let's get down to business. We've been running checks on Oliver Queen. It looks more and more like he's in the clear. We were able to verify that he was at his mother's house during the week of the Wolfson murder. We were also able to verify that he was here in Washington at the time of the break-in at Dr. Hoffman's office and the murder of the security guard. We have two witnesses for that. I'm putting Queen in the inactive file." Tony looked at Stephanie. "No big surprise there after what Stephanie told us about the scores." Tony looked at Harry. "What did you come up with in New York? Debbie told me that you were looking through Griffith's reviews."

"Well, Harry began, "I have a list of eighteen people--musicians who received abysmal reviews from Edward Todd Griffith during his stint as music critic at the paper. I think you'll have to run at least a routine check on these people to eliminate them from any connection with Griffith's death." Harry handed the list of names to Tony, who perused the list and nodded. When he had Tony's attention once more, Harry grinned in the manner of a cat that had swallowed the canary. "Now, Tony, here's the good stuff... what I think is the motive that could underlie the killings." He handed the copy of Griffith's review of Cochrane's symphony to Tony. "Read this," he said. "It sizzles. It really sizzles!"

Tony read the review aloud. Then he wiped the sweat off his forehead. He shook his head and said, "Wow!" He passed the review to Debbie, who in turn passed it to Stephanie.

Harry waited for Stephanie to look at the review before speaking. His mood was reflective. "You know when I went to New York, Rieder was my chief suspect. I think you had the same feeling, Tony. Everything pointed to Rieder. Cochrane was still only an afterthought, although I was beginning to pay more attention to him after Debbie's interview with Sebastian. Now, we can't dismiss Rieder as a suspect--it's still possible that he is connected to this business in some way, but from what Mrs. Wolfson told me in Princeton, Rieder doesn't sound like a murderer. She's known him for years and says he's timid."

Tony asked, "You went to Princeton?"

"Yeah," Harry replied. "I thought I'd stop in and see Mrs. Wolfson on the way home. Very nice woman. Has a nice boy, too. A teenager. As I was saying, I went to New York, focused on Rieder, but so many threads are beginning to connect Cochrane to this business that I'd be surprised if he's not deeply involved in it. Up to his neck, as we used to say."

Harry leaned forward in his chair and spoke more intensely. "I'm not ready to say Cochrane murdered Professor Griffith, but he sure had a reason for a grudge. He had plenty of reason to be angry with Southwick, too. Hoffman's murder could be an attempt to cover his tracks. I'm not sure how Wolfson's murder fits in with this scenario, but I'd be surprised if it isn't related. According to Mrs. Wolfson, Cochrane came to see Wolfson at Princeton. The meeting did not go well, although she doesn't know what it was all about. Debbie said from the first that some kind of con game was going on. I think she's right and Southwick is the pigeon."

Debbie observed, "He took Southwick for $300,000.00."

"Yeah," Harry replied. "Three hundred grand. That's a bundle, but I don't think that's the reason he's doing this. The man is rich. He inherited both banking and shipping money. He doesn't need money."

Tony asked, "What is he looking for, Harry?"

"If I'm right," Harry replied, "it's revenge. Debbie and I were toying with a similar idea the other night. Only, we thought it was Sebastian who was looking for revenge. You see, we thought Sebastian might have orchestrated the scam as a way of getting back at Southwick. We learned from Stephanie that Sebastian had carried on a torrid love affair with Southwick's wife, Lady Margaret. Sebastian wanted Margaret to leave her husband and come to him. Margaret was ambivalent but decided to stay with Southwick. The scam would have destroyed Southwick which would have given Sebastian his jollies and Margaret might be there for the picking.

While we were close to figuring out the right motive, we had the wrong person. It wasn't Sebastian who acted out of revenge. It was Cochrane. Cochrane wanted to get back at Griffith. Cochrane's career was demolished by Griffith's review. I suspect that his musical career was all that he ever cared about. He murdered Griffith and now is set to destroy Southwick's reputation. Southwick would be a laughing stock. Can't you see the headlines in the papers? 'Southwick Duped! Famed Conductor's Ballyhooed Premier of the Completed Unfinished Symphony is a Forgery.' Not only a forgery but a computer-derived forgery. It will be the biggest musical joke since Mozart composed a piece by that name over two hundred years ago. I can see Cochrane doubled over on the floor laughing with glee."

"You make him sound like some kind of nut," Tony observed.

"He's demented all right. He could be paranoid. But he's a clever, calculating bastard and dangerous as hell. And the problem is we haven't got a thing on him that will stick. It's all supposition."

Tony sighed. "Thank you for the reality check. You're right, unfortunately. We haven't got a shred of evidence. Nothing we could take to a grand jury. Not even for fraud at this point, much less for murder. We'll have to keep at it until we really get something on him."

There was silence in the room. Then, Harry looked at Tony. "We still have some unfinished business which we ought to tie up. Has Alverez sent you the list of phone calls that Dr. Hoffman made?"

Tony shook his head. "I put in a call yesterday. He's out on a murder-suicide investigation. I'm hoping he calls in the morning."

"What about the passenger list for the flight Stephanie was on?"

"I took the assignment away from Willie Rice. He's still out sick. I gave it to Mike Jordan."

"Jordan? Don't know him."

"He's new. I like him. Debbie's met him. Local kid. Grew up in a real hot spot in the Northeast section of town. Drugs, gangs, shootings. He survived it all. Put himself through college. Had a year of law school at Howard before he decided he wanted to join the force." Tony paused. "I'll see if he's around."

Jordan was paged and soon appeared. He was tall, well over six feet, and slender, almost thin. In his right hand was a manila folder.

After Tony introduced Harry and Stephanie, he asked Jordan, "What did you find?"

"It turned out to be pretty easy, Captain," he replied. "Almost all the passengers on the flight were in packaged tours arranged by a travel agency in Vienna. The passengers were Austrians on their way to see the U.S.--Washington, D.C., New York City and San Francisco, ending at Los Angeles. Their last stop was Disneyland."

Harry laughed. "The Austrians gave us Mozart, Schubert and Strauss, and we give them Donald Duck and Mickey Mouse."

Tony smiled. "I imagine all of those people were booked on the flight for months."

Jordan nodded. "Three months in advance. They couldn't have been tracking Ms. Ellison. They wouldn't have known she would be in Vienna when they signed up for the flight."

Tony inquired, "How many people on the flight were not in the tour groups?"

"Just six. One was a British woman, a Mrs. Olivia James. She was on her way to Toronto. I checked her out. She was in the airport for less than an hour, just long enough to change planes. All of the other passengers were Americans."

Jordan turned toward Stephanie, smiling. "One of the five was Ms. Ellison." Returning his gaze to Tony, he continued. "Three of the remaining four were members of the same family, the Oskar Pilsons. They live in Minneapolis. Mr. and Mrs. Pilson own a small bakery. It's called the Alpine Bakery. They've run it for twenty years. They were visiting Mrs. Pilson's cousin who lives in a town about 60 miles from Vienna."

Harry asked, "Who is the third member of the Pilson family?"

"Their daughter, Lisabeth. She's fifteen, a high school student in Minneapolis."

Tony asked, "Do the Pilsons have any police record?"

Jordan shook his head. "None. They sound like solid citizens to me. Very respectable."

"Yeah, Harry replied, "We could strike out on this. Who was the last American?"

"A guy named Jonathan Starke." Jordan grinned. "This one could be interesting. He's a shadowy figure. He's supposed to be an independent businessman but no one seems to know what business he's in. He has no criminal record, or any other kind of record, for that matter. Tracking him down is like tracking down an undocumented alien. No trails."

"This is interesting," Tony mused. "Where does Starke live?"

"Salem, Massachusetts."

In a flash of an instant, Tony and Harry looked at each other. Both of their eyes widened, their expressions conveying amazement.

Debbie caught the sudden change in the atmosphere. She tugged at Harry's arm. "What's it all about, Harry?"

Harry's voice sounded a little shaky. "You remember the letter Cochrane sent Dr. Hoffman?"

"The letter?" Suddenly she exclaimed, "Oh, my God! It came from Salem."

"Yeah," Harry muttered. "Salem."

Recovering somewhat from the shock, Tony asked Jordan, "Do you have Starke's address?"

Jordan withdrew a sheet of yellow paper from the folder on which was scribbled a number of addresses. "This one," he said pointing to the address at the bottom of the list.

Tony looked at the address. Harry inquired, "Is it Cochrane's?"

Tony shrugged, "Don't remember. Got to find that letter. It's somewhere on this desk." Tony scrambled through piles of notes, memos and folders, all the time muttering to himself. "Claire says I ought to get better organized. I've been resisting the idea, but I have to admit now she's right." Then his voice exclaimed, "Gotcha!"

He turned towards Harry. "It's Cochrane's place all right. Same address."

Harry felt a surge of electricity. He thought out loud. "Could Starke and Cochrane be one and the same?"

Tony asked Jordan, "How old is Starke?"

Jordan looked through the folder. "He's listed at twenty-eight."

Tony shook his head. "Cochrane's in his fifties. Different people, same house."

Harry asked, "Any chance of getting a picture of Mr. Starke? I just may have seen him before."

Tony inquired, "You want a photo?"

"It's a good place to start."

Tony thought out loud. "I suppose we could try the passport office. I imagine they keep copies, though I'm not sure. Even if they do, there are privacy regulations. We'd have to make a legal case and that could take some time."

"We could take a picture ourselves," Harry suggested.

Tony shook his head. "We have to be very careful in the way we approach this. We don't want to give Cochrane the slightest hint that we suspect him. Not at this point. Let me make some discrete inquiries. Then, we'll talk about how to proceed."

Harry nodded. "Fine. I'll wait to hear from you." Harry looked at the clock. "I hate to go out into the heat," he said, "but I have a few things to do." He looked at Debbie and Stephanie. "Okay, kiddies, let's go home and have a beer. A nice, ice cold beer."

Tony sighed, muttering under his breath.

Tony's phone call came at one o'clock the following afternoon. Harry was in the kitchen, stirring the food he was cooking slowly in a large crock pot--rice, peas, celery stalks, tomatoes, onions, garlic, green peppers, shelled shrimp and chicken breasts--a Jambalaya in the making. Stephanie answered the phone, and then beckoned Harry to the receiver with a wave. "Tried to get you at your office," Tony explained, "but they said you didn't come in today."

"I turned in my column last night," Harry replied. Decided to stay home today. I've been cooking some Jambalaya for lunch." Harry sniffed. "Smells terrific."

"Um," Tony replied, "Love that dish. Can I talk myself into being a luncheon guest? Besides, I want to talk some more about Cochrane."

"Sure. We're eating in about half an hour. Can you make it?"

"I'll be there."

The food was on the table when Tony arrived--Jambalaya, a large tossed salad, freshly baked rolls with Rhine wine or beer to drink. Tony slipped into a chair beside Debbie while Stephanie and Harry sat across from him. He sighed as he inhaled the aroma of the Jambalaya. "Does this beat my brown-bag special!"

"Enjoy," Harry said, and they all did.

When he finished his second helping of the Jambalaya, Tony leaned back in his chair. "I finally heard from Lieutenant Alvarez," he said. "Dr. Hoffman made two long distance calls the night before she left for Washington. Nothing out of the country. The first was to the hotel here for a room reservation. The second was to the home of--guess who--Thaddeus Cochrane, in Salem, Massachusetts."

Harry grinned. "So he knew of her travel plans. The circumstantial evidence is piling up."

"Yeah. But we need more though, before making a move. I was interested in your statement that you say you may have seen Starke before."

"Possibly. My guess is that the group carrying out this scam is a tightly-knit one. Probably only a few players. When Stephanie and I went to the restaurant to meet with the Austrian lady, there was a chauffeur who picked up the money. I made a point to get a good look at him. If we could get a photograph of Starke, I think I could tell if it were the same person."

"Good. We could tie Starke directly to the swindle. That would really help."

Harry asked, "How do we get a picture?"

"Not easily," Tony replied. "I made some discrete inquiries. My source who is in the real estate business tells me that Cochrane lives in a big isolated house outside of Salem. He built the house after he left Julliard. The house is very traditional, with a widow's walk overlooking a rocky cliff leading to the sea. Cochrane owns a big piece of land surrounding the house. His property is fenced off by a white wooden fence. It would be hard to get close to the house to take pictures without trespassing."

"I bet he keeps a pack of hounds," Debbie remarked.

Tony smiled. "I hate to tell you this, but my source tells me he does keep a kennel of German Shepherds."

Debbie shrugged. "I'm not volunteering for the picture-taking."

"Don't worry," Tony replied. "Can't have anyone who even looks like a police officer go near the place. If Cochrane is as paranoid as Harry thinks, he'd smell 'em out. You are definitely out of this one and so is Harry."

"Tony's right," Harry agreed. "But I know someone who will do just fine. He's a bright young chap I met in New York. He works for the newspaper and helped me sort through Griffith's reviews. I can see him now with a van, tripod and camera taking pictures for a photographic essay of 'The Historic Town of Salem.' There is a big story in it for him and his cover would be perfect. If Cochrane checks him out, he'd find he's legit. And sooner or later, he'll get a picture of Starke."

Chapter 24

Jim Rafferty always wanted to be a journalist from the day he began writing for his high school newspaper, *The Roosevelt Reporter*, but he had never quite imagined himself doing undercover work for what might turn out to be a very big story. But there he was, planting the tripod he had borrowed from a photographer friend on the sidewalks of Salem, focusing his camera on the town's historic sites, snapping pictures, and looking very much the part of a photojournalist. To establish his cover, he paid an initial call at the Salem Visitor's Center, which was operated by the National Park Service. Here he explained what he was doing and received a host of tips from the staff on sites to photograph. And then he and his camera were seen everywhere. He photographed exhibits within the Peabody Essex Museum and included a nice shot of the outside of the building with its one-time title, *East India Marine Hall* still engraved near the top. He took pictures of people strolling on Derby Square, and interviewed them about life in Salem. He photographed the old red brick Town Hall and the House of Seven Gables immortalized in Nathaniel Hawthorne's novel. Near this ancient, strange-looking structure, he took pictures of an 18th-Century granite sea wall and the accompanying seaside gardens. Venturing into the Witch Dungeon Museum, he took still shots of a re-enactment of a Salem witch trial. In between these highly visible activities on the streets of Salem, he spent time in the town's most popular restaurant and bar, sipping ale and talking freely with all comers, soliciting information about interesting places to photograph.

In a few days, he made his presence sufficiently known that his cover of "doing a photographic essay on Salem" was more than credible. When he mentioned to people in the restaurant that he wanted to photograph some of the houses in the outlying areas, he received suggestions aplenty, including several that he might photograph the Cochrane estate. One of these suggestions came from a tall, white-haired man with ruddy cheeks named Harvey Austen. Austen, a retired postman who had spent much of his life trotting the pavements of Salem through fierce winter storms, was now quite content to spend the afternoons drinking beer and chatting the time away with anyone who would listen. Austen described the Cochrane home as recently built by New England standards, but traditional in design and very nicely done. He described Cochrane as "old family, something of a loner, but very courteous." Austen also mentioned the other people who lived there, Mr. Starke whom he had never really spoken to--he seemed to fade into the background when Austen came by, a lady who came from Austria--she spoke with a German accent--she was pleasant and friendly-- and a girl who was nice and pretty and went to school in Salem. "Never had too much to say to Mr. Cochrane, or for that matter, Mr. Starke. But the Austrian lady and the child always had a friendly hello for me. I think the Cochrane estate would make a great picture for you. That is, if Cochrane will let you inside. You never know. He's a very private person." Jim said he just might go over to the Cochrane estate and take a look-see.

The Cochrane estate was located very close to the shore. The house itself was large and stately, situated on elevated ground with an imposing widow's walk that looked far out to sea. The wooden platform was perched high above a rocky shoreline where the waves pounded at high tide. The grounds were large. A well kept garden with rows of red and white flowers bordered the house. Further out there was an expanse of thick, low cut grass, which gave way to wild flowers reaching to the borders of the estate which was marked by a freshly painted white picket fence. A gravel driveway traversed the distance from the road to the house.

As Jim surveyed the estate, he noticed a girl and two large German shepherds near the house. She was playing with the dogs. When the girl spied the station wagon, she trotted over with the dogs running ahead of her. The girl looked as though she might be eleven or twelve years old. She was dressed in jeans and wore a Boston Red Sox baseball cap on her head. Her complexion was rosy and she looked as healthy as she did pretty.

The dogs barked loudly. Jim called out, "What are their names?"

The girl answered, "Ludwig and Franz."

"They're musical, eh?"

The girl smiled. Jim spoke to the dogs, "Hi, Ludwig, hi Franz. I'm a friend. My name's Jim, though you can call me Wolfgang if you like."

The girl laughed. "You're funny," she said. "Look. They quit barking."

"Dogs like me for some reason. I always had a dog when I was a kid."

"You're a photographer, aren't you?"

Jim smiled. "Yeah."

"You're taking pictures of the historic spots in Salem for a magazine article."

"Hey. You know a lot about me. How did you find that out?"

The girl smiled. "Oh, my grandma told me. She goes to town every day to do the shopping. She says everybody's talking about you." She smiled. "She says they want to be mentioned in your article."

Jim laughed. "I wouldn't be surprised. Now I'm looking at the countryside nearby Salem. Your former postman, Mr. Austen, suggested I should look at your place. It's very nice. I wonder if I could take pictures of your house."

"Thank you," she said. "I suppose you could take a picture of the outside. But you can't go inside. Uncle Thaddeus--he isn't really my uncle, but I call him that. He'd have to give you permission to go inside. He's out of town with Mr. Starke."

"When's he coming back?"

She shook her head. "I don't know. They've been traveling a lot lately."

Jim shrugged. "Maybe, I'll see them sometime later if I'm still in Salem. How about I take a picture of the outside of the house now, and how about one of you with Ludwig and Franz?"

The girl giggled. "Sure, they'll like that."

In the afternoon, Jim telephoned Harry at his office. He related the conversation he had with the girl. Then, he asked, "What do I do now?"

Harry pondered. "Fax the pictures of the house and the girl to my office."

"Okay."

"Can you hang around another day or two? Maybe, Starke will show up."

"Sure. I like it here. It's like a vacation."

"Good. I'll fix it with the boss and call you tonight."

Harry returned from the office after dinner. Stephanie was playing a Chopin etude on the piano while Debbie was relaxing on the couch sipping a light beer.

"Hey, I got something to show you," Harry said as he walked over to the couch. "A picture of Cochrane's house and a girl who lives there."

Debbie asked, "Anything on Starke?"

"Not yet. But take a look-see. Pretty nifty place he lives in."

Harry handed Debbie the photograph of Cochrane's house. Debbie looked at the picture. "Yeah. Real nice. But I bet it's spooky in a storm, isolated out there."

Harry smiled. "Yeah. The house is right on the ocean. Can you imagine what it must be like when a storm blows up the coast? Think of the raw power of the waves lashing the rocks and the rain and the wind. Harry laughed. "You know, Debbie, I think Cochrane would love every minute of it. Probably make him feel alive."

Debbie shook her head and sighed. She did not say anything. Harry's musings had made her more anxious than she cared to admit. Cochrane sounded demented. Someday Harry might encounter Cochrane and the thought unsettled her. Involuntarily, she clasped his arm. Harry did not pick up on these feelings. Instead, he put the second photograph, the one of the girl and her dogs, into Debbie's free hand. "Take a look at this," he said.

Debbie stared at the photograph. Her mouth opened widely. She dropped the picture into her lap. "It's her!" she exclaimed. "That girl who was in the Library of Congress. The one who left the manuscript for Stephanie and then dashed out to the limousine."

"Are you sure?"

"I'm sure, all right. She's dressed differently, but I'd know her anywhere."

"Good! Good!" Harry exclaimed. "I was hoping that would be the case." He gritted his teeth in a gesture of confrontation. "Thaddeus Cochrane has made a big mistake. We can now tie him to the forgery. Now, let us see if we can tie him to the murders."

Chapter 25

Debbie and Stephanie had gone to a movie near Dupont Circle. Harry waited in his apartment for Tony who had called earlier from the office, saying he would like to stop by to discuss the Hoffman case. Tony said he would be by at 8:00 and he was punctual as always. When Tony settled on the couch, he pulled out a notepad and said, "Harry, I heard from the FBI. They've been able to trace Rieder's movements. Rieder was in Connecticut."

Harry loosed astonished. He blurted out, "No kidding?"

"He was there, alright." Tony smiled, "but it doesn't change anything, fortunately. He got to New Haven, two days after Griffith's death. So, he's in the clear."

"Thank Heaven for small favors."

"Yeah. That would have really complicated things."

"Do you have any idea why he didn't tell that to the Austrian Police?"

"Just a guess. We'll find out in time."

"What's your guess?"

Tony smiled. "Rieder knew Griffith and Wolfson quite well and Hoffman to some extent. They are all dead. He must have suspected something. I think Wolfson told him about Cochrane's phony manuscript as well. When we started asking him about Hoffman's programs and his whereabouts at the time of Griffith's death, he may have thought he was under suspicion, which of course, he was. He was already on edge and panicked."

"Sounds plausible," Harry observed. "As you say, we'll find out in time."

"Rieder seems clear as far as direct involvement in Griffith's death. I doubt that he had anything to do with it. Rieder's not our problem. But Cochrane sure is, Harry. And it's getting to be a bigger problem every day. The clock is running against us. It's only two weeks to Southwick's concert. If we can't get something on Cochrane before then, we'll have to tell Southwick to call if off. We can't let him go ahead with the concert knowing what we know."

Harry agreed. "No, we can't let it go forward."

Tony continued, "If the concert is called off, Cochrane may conclude that we're on to his game. He might dig in his heels, destroying whatever evidence there is that could incriminate him. Without such evidence, we may never get a conviction for the murders."

"Yeah. That could happen all right," Harry mused. His expression took on a speculative look. "Tony, I think he's more likely to hide the evidence than destroy it. I imagine it took a huge amount of work to fabricate a believable Schubert symphony. If I read him right, he's got a big ego. I doubt that he could ever bring himself to destroy his work. In a sense, this is his life's work."

Tony nodded. "Could be. But hide it or destroy it, it might not make any difference. If he gets suspicious, we won't find anything. What I'm driving at is we just can't sit tight on this. We may have to flush him out. And we only have two weeks to do it."

Harry removed his glasses and placed them on the coffee table. He asked, "How do you propose to flush him out?"

Tony spoke hesitantly. "We might--and I put this as a hypothetical--get a search warrant. Then, conduct a surprise raid on his home in Salem and hope to find evidence of the work he did on the symphony. Of course, we would be looking for evidence of fraud."

Harry shrugged. "Let me play devil's advocate. What if the evidence is not in the house, and I suspect he's much too smart to keep it there at this point--then where are you?"

Tony laughed. "Dead in the water."

"It's a gamble," Harry said. "Maybe you'll just have to take it. Maybe not. Let me run another idea by you that might work better. It appeals to my sense of the dramatic."

Tony sighed. "I'm not sure I'm going to like this. But go ahead."

"Imagine a dress rehearsal of the completed Schubert symphony. Picture this. There is Sir Charles Southwick waving his baton." Harry moved his right arm expansively. "There is the orchestra playing away, and there in the audience are a few invited guests: Sir Charles' wife, Lady Margaret; a few friends of his from the New York music establishment; our good friend and quarry, Thaddeus Cochrane; budding musician Stephanie Ellison--and her half-assed celebrity uncle."

Tony smiled and nodded.

"Now, the rehearsal is over. There is a little get-together in which Uncle quietly buttonholes quarry and starts telling him that he thinks the symphony is phony and that he plans to break the story a few days before the concert in his nationally syndicated column."

Tony rubbed his chin. "Interesting. Go on."

"Now, imagine how friend Cochrane will react."

Tony considered. "He's got to be terribly upset, Harry. If our theory is correct, he's been spending years planning this supreme moment of revenge. Now, with a stroke of the pen, you threaten to take it away from him. I think he'd be panicky."

Harry nodded. "Right. And to up the ante, I could casually mention that I've figured out how the score was fashioned...though," Harry grinned, "I don't yet know who did it."

Tony sighed. "Oh, boy."

Harry asked, "How do you think he'll react to that?"

"You know the answer to that as well as I do. The same way he reacted to Dr. Hoffman's telephone call. He'll try to kill you."

"Exactly."

Tony's facial muscles tightened. "He may have killed four people already. What makes you so eager to be number five. You got a death wish, Harry?"

Harry smiled faintly. "Not that I know of."

"I'm not so sure about that, Harry. You nearly had your leg blown off in Lebanon. And that business in the mountains of Virginia. That was a close call. That night still gives me the creeps."

"I've been in some tight spots, Tony. But your guys can be in tight spots anytime."

"We're professionals, Harry."

"True," Harry replied.

"You know, Harry, I think you love excitement. I know you rise to a challenge. Is it something between you and Cochrane? Has he got under your skin and you want at him?"

Harry laughed. "You should have been a shrink, Tony. Sure, I want at him. He's messed up Stephanie's life and now he's messing up mine as well.

I'd like to clobber him. Only it won't come down to that. It will be a battle of wits."

Tony smiled faintly. "You'd like that even better."

Harry nodded. "Um hum" He studied Tony. "I don't think your psychoanalysis changes anything. We have to flush Cochrane out. I think my plan has the best chance of working. Maybe the only chance."

Tony was silent for a moment. Reluctantly he said, "I agree." He looked Harry squarely in the eyes. "If we do this crazy thing, I'm going to lay down some strict conditions."

"Fair enough."

"First, there will be a window of opportunity for Cochrane to strike- -from the time of the dress rehearsal to the time your column is supposed to appear. During that time we will have every movement of yours outside your apartment under surveillance. You will have to notify me each time you're going out."

"Understood."

"Now, there will be two men trailing you, both in plain clothes. One of the men will have the responsibility of apprehending Cochrane, Starke, or whoever else it is that makes the attempt on you."

"What about the other policeman?"

"He'll have the job of protecting you. You'll recognize him. African-American, wears glasses, dresses conservatively and roots for his alma mater when they play the big game with Harvard."

Harry laughed. "Et tu Tony? Everybody wants to get into the act."

Tony smiled. "Can't let anything happen to you, Harry. Claire would kill me. Especially after that anniversary present you sent us. What a beautiful painting! She still talks about it."

"I'm glad you'll be there, Tony. I really am."

Tony nodded, and then inquired, "Who calls Southwick to arrange things?"

"I'll do it--tomorrow. I'll have to come up with some kind of cock and bull explanation--something short of the whole truth at this point. I don't want to change his behavior in any way during the rehearsal. We can't have him tip off Cochrane by his actions."

"When are you going to tell him the whole story?"

"Don't know yet. Sometime before the concert. He's going to have to know."

"I agree. By the way, stop in the office tomorrow. Bring Stephanie too. We're fitting both of you with body armor."

Harry grimaced. "Hell, I'm already a little heavy. I'll look like a truck wearing that! Cochrane will spot it in a minute. He'll know we're on to him."

Tony considered. "Yeah. Maybe you're right. But, I want Stephanie to wear it."

"Agreed. By the way, did you ever play in one of those big games with Harvard?"

"Once. During my sophomore year. I was in the game for fifteen minutes. Caught a pass for twelve yards going over the middle. Some guy in a red uniform that I didn't see hit me so hard that I was knocked silly. They had to call time out and help me to the bench." Tony smiled. "But I held onto the football!"

Chapter 26

Harry called Sir Charles Southwick in the morning. The conductor was surprised at Harry's request to stage a special rehearsal for his opening program. "Out of the question," was his tart reply. However, when Harry explained that there was a chance the affair could lead to a break in the Hoffman murder investigation and possibly the Wolfson case as well, Sir Charles' curiosity was instantly aroused. Harry did his best to fend off the conductor's persistent questions, but only succeeded with a promise to tell Sir Charles the full story one week after the rehearsal. The conductor was satisfied and agreed to Harry's request.

The special rehearsal was scheduled to take place in four days. Because of the short notice, invitations to the select lists of guests were made by telephone rather than by engraved cards. Everyone invited accepted. A preview performance of the completed Schubert masterpiece was not to be missed. Harry breathed a sigh of relief when the only acceptance that really mattered--that of Thaddeus Cochrane--was duly received.

Harry, Stephanie and Debbie planned to drive to New York the night before the rehearsal. Debbie would be attending the rehearsal as Harry's guest. On the day before leaving for New York, Harry drove to his office. In spite of his deepening involvement in the Hoffman murder investigation, he still had to complete his biweekly column.

For an hour he sat at his desk with an old ballpoint pen and a lined yellow pad composing an essay on changing directions in American foreign policy. He smiled as he read through the completed column. Not bad, he thought, for an old crime reporter.

The phone rang. It was Sam Harris, a producer for C.B.S. Could Harry be available for a roundtable discussion this Sunday? Harry begged off. It was no time to make commitments. Harry arose and prepared to leave when the phone rang again. He thought about ignoring it, but finally picked it up. It was Jim Rafferty calling from Salem. "I got a picture of Starke," he said. "I don't think he saw me take it. He was driving with Cochrane in a convertible. I was parked along the road. It's a good picture. Not even a blur."

"Terrific. Can you fax it?"

"Sure. Won't take long. Then, I got to run to New York."

Harry sat down again, waiting eagerly for the picture of Starke. As Jim promised, it did not take long. Harry had a feeling he would recognize the face. And he did!

He called Tony immediately. "It's all coming together nicely," he said. "As I suspected, Starke is the guy who chauffeured the woman in the restaurant--the one Stephanie and I gave the money to. And the woman herself? I'll bet the mortgage she's the child's grandma. I'm not sure how much she and the child know what's going on, but it looks like one big happy family of swindlers."

When Harry hung up the phone, he felt both satisfaction and a deepening sense of anxiety. He felt satisfied because he had formed a nearly complete explanation for the series of killings and bizarre events. He felt anxious because he knew that they might not yet have enough evidence on Cochrane to get a conviction. The circumstantial evidence against Cochrane was piling up, but unless they discovered more concrete evidence such as Cochrane's composition records, it might be difficult to prove that Cochrane had actually forged the score. Cochrane could claim that he had discovered the manuscript during his researches in Austria. He could even say that in his expert opinion--and he was one of the prominent authorities on Schubert--the manuscript appeared to be genuine. He could explain away the $300,000 by saying that he planned to use the money to establish a scholarship fund or a fellowship for musical research. It would not be beyond the man. He had plenty of chutzpah. If it proved difficult to convict Cochrane for forgery, it might be almost impossible to do so for murder. There were no witnesses to tie him to the killings. To make matters worse, if they failed to prove the case, Cochrane and Starke would be on the loose. Cochrane had a long and unforgiving memory and could seek revenge on Stephanie, Debbie and Harry himself. The Salem pair had four killings behind them, an unhappily successful track record. Harry knew that this was a contest he had to win or he would be spending the rest of his life looking over his shoulder.

Chapter 27

The twelve invited guests were seated together in the front row of an otherwise deserted Avery Fisher Hall at Lincoln Center. Sir Charles Southwick had taken the orchestra through two works which would also appear on the program, Rossini's Overture to the Barber of Seville and Mozart's Symphony Number 39. The orchestra played the Rossini with gusto and brilliant sound and the Mozart with sensitivity and sparkle. The small audience applauded enthusiastically. Now came the event everyone was waiting for--the heralded realization of Schubert's masterpiece, the Unfinished Symphony in B Minor.

As Sir Charles raised the baton, Harry whispered to Debbie. "When they begin the third movement, keep an eye on Cochrane." Then, almost in a soliloquy, he muttered to himself the words that Hamlet uttered when he set out to gauge his uncle's reactions to his carefully contrived play of murder: "The play's the thing wherin I'll catch the conscience of the king."

The symphony opened with its slow somber theme, only to be quickly followed with the familiar burst of melody that so characterized Schubert. The orchestra played well and Harry found himself caught up in the music as much as the grave matters at hand. Now, the second movement began with its slow, lovely themes, working them through as only a great master could do. When the last sounds of the movement subsided, it was time for the moment of truth. Harry nudged Debbie and they both turned their attention toward Thaddeus Cochrane.

He was a lean figure of a man with neatly combed sandy hair punctuated by a few streaks of gray. His eyes were deeply set and had a fixed quality about them, as if he were staring even when he was not. He sported a short, carefully trimmed beard. He was dressed in an expensive Italian-made suit.

Harry watched Cochrane intently as the first notes of the Scherzo movement began. Cochrane's expression was intent, as if his mind were turning over every note. Then, Harry noticed a slight tremor in Cochrane's left hand. As the music progressed, the tremor became more pronounced. Finally, Cochrane became aware of it and placed his hand in the pocket of his trousers.

Harry turned his attention away from Cochrane and listened to the music. The Scherzo sounded like Schubert, though there was nothing very imaginative about it. The final movement had the driving quality that Harry enjoyed in Schubert, but once again the thematic content seemed almost pedestrian. Schubert's gift of melodic invention wasn't there. The fall off in quality between the first two movements of the symphony and the new movements was unmistakable.

As the audience applauded, Harry turned toward Stephanie. He asked, "What do you think?"

Stephanie shook her head. "It's a good try. The orchestration is vintage Schubert and there are some other things which sound so much like Schubert it's uncanny. But Schubert never lacked for fresh musical ideas. This doesn't have them. The composer is a wonderful technician, but nothing else. It's a fake. I no longer have any doubts."

Harry nodded. "That's what I thought." He turned toward Debbie. She put her hand on his coat sleeve.

She whispered, "Did you see that tremor in his hand?"

Harry nodded. "Oh, yeah. He was shaking like a leaf."

Debbie asked, "What does it mean?"

Harry shrugged. "I'm not sure. I'd have to ask a shrink." He smiled, thinking of. Lucretia Huston and her prescient comments about Cochrane. "May be hyper excitement," he said.

The reception following the rehearsal was held in a room not far from the recital hall. Sir Charles' wife Lady Margaret was hostess. Harry spent a few minutes chatting with her, picked up a glass of white wine and a plate of cheese, and then buttonholed Thaddeus Cochrane in the corner of the room.

"Thaddeus Cochrane, isn't it?"

Cochrane replied, "Yes. How did you know?"

"Remembered your picture from the jacket of your book, *Schubert's Life and Music*. Fine book. Best thing on Schubert since Deutsch."

Cochrane smiled. "Kind of you to say so. Didn't know you were a Schubert aficionado, Mr. uh--"

"Ellison," Harry said smiling, playing out the charade, for Cochrane knew exactly who he was. "Harry Ellison."

"The columnist?"

"Yes."

"So you like Schubert?"

"Oh, very much. Always have. I've gotten particularly interested in Schubert's work since my niece, Stephanie...she's standing over there with Sir Charles...started her dissertation on him."

"Stephanie Ellison? The name is familiar. Wasn't she one of poor Dr. Hoffman's students?"

"Yes, poor Dr. Hoffman," Harry echoed. "Great loss to music."

Cochrane nodded. "Sad," he said. His face was blank, without expression.

Harry asked, "What did you think of the realization of the symphony--the last two movements?"

Cochrane hesitated. "Very interesting," he said noncommittally.

"I agree," Harry replied.

"You do?"

"Yes. Very interesting. Beautiful job."

Cochrane smiled.

"A beautiful job. But not by Schubert. It's a beautiful job by someone faking Schubert. The whole thing is a fraud, a colossal fraud."

Cochrane's hand began to shake. He blurted out, "How do you know?"

"It's dull. Lacks any fresh musical ideas. Schubert would never have turned out such pedestrian stuff. You're a renowned Schubert scholar, Professor Cochrane. Don't you agree?"

"Well, it's certainly not the best Schubert I've ever heard."

"Not the best?" Harry's tone became derisive. "Maybe the worst. Probably some second rate composer--some hack--put it together."

Cochrane's hand continued to tremble. "If you're right," he said, "and I'm not conceding that--how in the world could someone have so closely followed Schubert's thinking and musical technique? The technique is clearly Schubert's. I'd stake my reputation on that."

Harry grinned. "Absolutely," he replied. "Technically it's perfect." Harry sipped some of the wine. "I know exactly how it was done. It was very, very clever. But I have no idea at this point who did it."

Cochrane stared fixedly at Harry, as if he were trying to assess his words. "You say you know how it was done--but you don't know who did it?"

"Not yet."

Cochrane asked stiffly, "What do you propose to do with your theories, Mr. Ellison?"

"Publish them, of course. In my next column. It will come out shortly before the concert."

"Before the concert?"

"Yeah. That will give Sir Charles a chance to cast the whole thing in a different light. He'll be able to back away from the initial hullabaloo. You know, he could say something like it was an interesting modern realization of Schubert's Symphony by an unknown composer, instead of implying it's the real thing. It will be very awkward for him after that press conference but if he handles it skillfully--and Sir Charles is a master of the press conference--it should save his career. Don't you think so, Dr. Cochrane?"

Cochrane paused. "I suspect it would save his career." He looked at Harry. He smiled faintly. "You have some interesting ideas, Mr. Ellison. Very interesting. I'd like to think about them. Perhaps, we could get together before you finish writing your column to discuss them further. Perhaps, with my knowledge of Schubert, I could be of some material help to you."

Harry grinned. "I'd love that." He handed Cochrane his card. "Call me. Call me any time."

Chapter 28

Two days following the rehearsal at Lincoln Center, Harry was seated at his desk in his office when he received a telephone call from Cochrane. "I've been thinking about your forthcoming article," Cochrane began. "I think you're on to something. The more I've considered the score, the more I'm inclined to concur with your view."

Harry replied, "That's reassuring, professor."

Cochrane continued. "I have some archival materials in my collection that will buttress your position considerably. We really should get together soon, but unfortunately, I can't travel for awhile. An old injury is acting up in my leg. Is there a chance you could come up here tomorrow or the next day and perhaps spend the afternoon or even the evening at my place on the ocean? It would be my pleasure."

It was an unexpected proposition. Harry had to improvise. "Sounds like a very good idea, Dr. Cochrane. I do have some appointments scheduled over the next two days." Harry suddenly felt inspired, and gilded the lily. "At the White House," he added. "I'll see if I can rearrange my schedule. It could be difficult, but I'll see what I can do. I'll call you tonight."

Harry, Debbie and Tony sat on the couch in Harry's apartment huddled over Jim Rafferty's pictures of the Cochrane estate. Tony spoke glumly, "I don't see how it can work, Harry. Sure, you can go in wired up with a bug. I like that part of it. On his own ground, he is more likely to spill the beans and we can record it. That's great. But what happens when they pull a gun on you--and they will. How are we going to protect you? If you came in with someone, Cochrane would know it was a cop. He'd clam up."

Harry nodded. "I agree."

"If you went alone, it could turn into a hostage situation. Those are always tricky. And if Cochrane is the homicidal nut we think he is, the outcome would be unpredictable, to say the least. Better find some other place to meet him. Some place that's more open."

Debbie suggested, "How about a restaurant?"

Tony considered, "That might work. I wonder if there is a nice inn around there. One of those charming New England places with a fireplace and a cozy corner for a quiet conversation."

"Just me, my lobster and my recording device," Harry quipped.

Tony smiled. "Got another idea?"

"Nope. But, what if Cochrane won't buy it? Suppose he insists that I come to his lair so he can dispose of me in the style to which he has become accustomed?"

"You won't go. Tell him you don't have time or something. You'll think of a good excuse. But going to Cochrane's place is out." Tony stared at Harry. "No way--chum."

Harry smiled. "Okay, Tony. I got the message. Now, if we go with Debbie's idea, who's going to be doing what?"

Tony considered. "We'll get a local policeman stationed in the restaurant," he said. "If it comes down to it, I'll buy him a lobster dinner myself. I'll be waiting in an unmarked car nearby listening to what your bug picks up."

Harry suggested, "Why not use Jim Rafferty's van? Everybody's used to seeing him around Salem. You could be sitting in his car fooling around with the equipment while he's taking pictures on the street."

Tony nodded. "I like that."

Debbie asked, "What about me?"

"Cochrane knows you," Harry replied. "He undoubtedly knows that you're a policewoman. If you go to Salem, you'll have to keep out of sight."

"That can be arranged," Tony said. "She can stay with the local police and coordinate things with them if and when we make an arrest."

"Fair enough," Debbie replied. She turned, looking at Harry. She touched his arm. "I'd rather be closer to you so I could keep an eye on things."

Harry smiled. "I know." He sighed. "Now, I'll see whether I can con Cochrane into dinner at Ye Old New England Inn or whatever you come up with."

Harry spent the rest of the afternoon trying to think of a credible reason for not going to Cochrane's home. He conjured up a few scenarios but nothing seemed convincing. Finally, he hit upon the idea of telling Cochrane that he was writing a romantic novel and had planned to write a scene that took place in an old fashioned New England Inn. As he didn't get up that way very often, it would be a "lovely opportunity" to fill up his notebook with impressions. He had heard there was just such a place near Salem called *The Sailor's Cove* and could Cochrane meet him there tomorrow night for drinks and dinner?

Harry rehearsed the speech twice, grimaced, and then called Cochrane. Cochrane hesitated, before replying. "Certainly."

Harry breathed a sigh of relief. Maybe this harebrained scheme would work after all. He shrugged. Then again, he thought, everything could go wrong. It was a roll of the dice.

Harry, Tony and Debbie left Stephanie in the care of Claire, and then took the shuttle to Boston. Waiting for them at the airport was Jim Rafferty. His van, loaded with photographic equipment, was ready to go. They entered the van and the four drove off. Following Tony's directions, Jim drove to a deserted spot on a country road. Here Tony unpacked a suitcase filled with electronic equipment, sensitive listening and recording devices borrowed from the F.B.I. After Tony had set up the equipment and tested and retested it, Jim restarted the van and soon they turned onto the road that led to Salem.

The late afternoon sky darkened and their drive was punctuated by brief rain showers. As they approached Salem, a fine mist had settled in the air. A perfect setting, Harry thought to himself glumly. Next we'll have a dense fog. However, when Harry looked to the right, he could see the clouds breaking. And then, the sun emerged almost magically. Harry smiled. He wished he believed in omens. The burst of sunshine would be a good one.

Jim brought the van to a stop one block past the police station. Quickly, Debbie alighted from the van and walked briskly to the building. Moments later Harry did the same as Tony and then Debbie kept him in sight. Finally, when Tony left the van, Jim drove away with instructions to return in an hour.

Harry, Tony and Debbie spent the hour going over the details of the operation with Officer Kevin Kelly, who would be stationed inside the inn. Kelly, a short, stocky man with a tinge of red hair, would ostensibly be enjoying an evening meal. However, his real assignment was to keep an eye on Harry. Like Harry, Kelly was wired with a listening device; however, he was instructed not to switch it on unless there was an emergency. Jim Rafferty's van would be parked outside the restaurant at about 5:30 p.m. Rafferty would be on the street setting up his camera for taking pictures of the inn, while Tony would man the communications equipment inside the van. Debbie would remain at police headquarters, in radio contact with Tony.

While their positions were set up like a battle plan, there was no guarantee of success. It was now strictly up to Harry to force Cochrane's hand. Cochrane was cunning, maybe insane, and it was Harry's task to draw him out. And, Harry was eager to get on with it.

At 6 p.m., Harry telephoned the inn to confirm his reservation. He was told that a table in a quiet corner of the inn would be held for himself and Professor Cochrane. Now, there was nothing to do but wait.

Harry thought of all the times in his life he had waited for important events...the hours before his marriage--the one that had failed; those hours waiting for the birth of his daughter, who now lived in Big Sur, California and called him only at Christmas; the vigil before his father's death so many years ago. Many things had turned out badly, he thought. But not everything, he smiled. He thought of Debbie and a light filled his eyes. He was a pretty lucky guy after all. And, maybe, he would be lucky tonight.

At 6:30 Harry parked a rented car in the large parking lot behind the inn. As he entered the inn, he glanced about the room. A model of a clipper ship standing upon a wooden table near the entrance immediately caught his eye. It was beautifully constructed with sails and rigging carefully fashioned to the last detail. The tables in the inn were spread apart, giving the customers both elbow room and privacy and the chairs, covered in deep red, were large and well padded. The inn was about half filled with customers. Harry immediately recognized one of them, a man who was meticulously buttering a large rum bun while occasionally glancing at an open, oversized menu. It was Officer Kelly.

The Maitre d', a lean gray haired man with a pleasant smile, ushered Harry to his table, a quiet spot not far from the unlit fireplace. While the placement of the chairs at the table afforded little view of the room, it was perfect for two people who wanted to be alone; in happier circumstances, a romantic rendezvous for lovers or, as was the case tonight, a tête-à-tête with a killer. Harry chatted briefly with the waiter. The conversation served as the final test for the listening device.

Cochrane was punctual. At precisely seven o'clock he entered the inn, spotted Harry and walked briskly over to join him. If Cochrane had a bad leg, it had marvelous healing powers. Harry smiled. He hadn't been invited to the White House either.

Cochrane was carefully groomed, his sandy hair neatly combed. He wore a grey tailored suit. He carried a black leather briefcase.

"Good of you to come, Mr. Ellison," he said as he extended his hand to Harry.

"My pleasure," Harry replied, rising from his chair, smiling, and trying to appear as self-assured as a used car salesman.

Cochrane took a seat and they ordered drinks, Harry a martini, Cochrane, white wine. They chatted for a few minutes about the inn, other restaurants in Salem, and the pleasures of sailing in the bay. Then, Cochrane ventured into the business at hand. "Mr. Ellison, you mentioned in New York that you know how the symphony was--shall we say--forged. I must admit that I've been very curious. How could it have been done so well?"

Harry smiled. "That was the easiest part to figure out. Are you familiar with the late Johanna Hoffman's paper, 'A Computer Program for the Statistical Analyses of Symphonic Scores?'"

Cochrane's finger began to shake. "Certainly," he said. "Dr. Hoffman was a good friend of mine. She showed me an early version of the paper. I told her that it would be very controversial and that she should expect a great deal of criticism which unfortunately proved to be true."

"So I've heard. Still, the program provides a perfect model for anyone wanting to mimic Schubert or any of the other composers that she had developed programs for."

Cochrane frowned. "Oh, come now, Mr. Ellison. You don't really believe that just anybody could use her program and write a Schubert symphony."

"Certainly not, Professor Cochrane. I didn't mean to imply that anybody could do it. Far from it. The number of people who could do it is actually quite small. But someone, for example, that was trained in musical composition in a conservatory like Julliard or Oberlin or a fine school like Harvard--now that would be a different story, Professor."

Cochrane stared at Harry. His eyes seemed to burn. He cleared his throat. "I notice that you mentioned Oberlin and Harvard--my own alma maters. Surely, you're not suggesting that I had anything to do with this detestable business. I don't know anything about computers. I find the whole idea of working with computers baffling."

Harry smiled. He sipped his martini. "I wasn't suggesting anything, Dr. Cochrane. Only that anyone with thorough training in composition, and of course musical talent, could effectively use Hoffman's program. But just to illustrate my point, let's use you as an example. Consider your background. Given a knowledge of Schubert's tendencies, wouldn't you have more than enough skill to fashion a replica of Schubert's work? As I remember, you were a composer of considerable note."

Cochrane cleared his throat again. "Well, I did write a few things."

"Sure. It wouldn't be too difficult for a man of your talent to dash off some Schubert-like passages. However, to fabricate an entire movement of a symphony might take months or even years of hard work and revision. It would be a formidable challenge even for a skilled composer like yourself."

"I see what you mean."

Harry smiled. "But, of course, you don't know anything about computers. I'm sure there's not even a computer in the house."

Cochrane's hand began to shake slightly. "No. We don't own a computer."

"Of course not. But you can see how a person with such a profound knowledge of Schubert and compositional talent would be a logical suspect... that is, if you were computer literate."

Harry waited for a comment but there was none. He took another sip of his martini. "Of course, other distinguished Schubert scholars would be high on the list of candidates; for example, there's Herr Rieder in Vienna."

Cochrane nodded. "Yes. Rieder knows Schubert's works intimately."

Harry responded dismissively, "A scholar, yes. A composer, no. Not Rieder. I checked him out. He's never published a line of music in his life. Unlike you--a doer, an artist--Rieder's just a bookworm. Just doesn't have the talent, poor fellow."

Harry looked at Cochrane. His lips were tightly drawn. His stare was intense. "Well," Harry continued. "Johanna Hoffman certainly had the capability, but alas." He shook his head forlornly. "And Aaron Wolfson had the capability, but alas, he too was erased from my list of possibilities. And I'm told that even Edward Todd Griffith dabbled enough in composition to have done the deed. Poor fellow." Harry looked deeply into Cochrane's eyes. "You knew them all, didn't you?"

Cochrane spoke slowly, "Yes, I knew them all."

"What did you think of Griffith?"

Cochrane did not answer. Harry fingered the olive at the bottom of his glass. "Remember those choice lines he wrote about your symphony? Should I quote them?"

Cochrane's hand shook wildly. He knocked over his wine glass. Harry only smiled. He asked, "Does Mr. Starke know anything about computers?"

"Damn you," Cochrane sputtered. There was rage in his voice. "You know too much."

Harry only grinned.

"Too damned much," Cochrane repeated sullenly. He gazed at his watch. "So, you're interested in Mr. Starke." Cochrane smiled, for at that very moment, Mr. Starke entered the room. With a movement as quick as a cat, he was behind Officer Kelly who was studying Harry intensely. A swift, sure blow from the butt of a revolver leveled the policeman and he collapsed unconscious into his chair. Hearing the scream of a customer, Harry whirled around, only to see Starke's gun pointed at his head.

"You're coming with us, Mr. Ellison," Cochrane said confidently.

"Move!" It was Starke's voice, blunt and menacing.

Reluctantly, Harry slowly rose to his feet. The customers were in shock, glued to their chairs. "Stay put," Starke called out, as he walked toward the entrance, his gun nudged firmly against Harry's backbone, Cochrane following behind. They walked quickly to the black limousine and sped off into the night.

Chapter 29

The limousine sped away from the parking lot of the restaurant. The three men sat in the front seat. Starke was driving. Harry sat beside him. Cochrane was to Harry's right, pressing a revolver against Harry's side.

"Where to?" Starke asked.

"North. Let's see if we can get out of here."

Starke nodded and hit the accelerator. They had gone only a few miles when a road block loomed ahead. Starke muttered under this breath and hit the brakes. Then expertly, he wheeled the car across the dividing line onto the adjoining shoulder, completing a u-turn, and sped off back toward the inn.

"We're not going to be able to get out," he said. "What do you want me to do?"

"Drive back to the house. We'll use Ellison as a hostage. Try to bargain."

Starke shook his head. "We'll be trapped."

The siren of a police cruiser was now audible on the road behind them. Cochrane asked, "Do you have a better idea?"

"Not now."

Starke pushed the accelerator. The limousine hurtled along at 80 miles per hour, and then swerved onto the side road that led to Cochrane's estate. There was a police cruiser parked near the gate. A lone deputy sheriff stood in front of the gate guarding it. Starke didn't hesitate. He drove the limousine headlong towards the deputy sheriff who jumped out of the way, barely escaping the onrush of the automobile. The limousine smashed through the wooden gate, splintering it into large white fragments. Starke drove the car to the front entrance of the house. He turned off the engine and the three men alighted, Cochrane now pressing the revolver against Harry's spine. Starke unlocked the front door. The three men entered a spacious living room. A built-up fireplace dominated the far wall. A large portrait of Thaddeus Cochrane dressed in full academic regalia hung on the near wall. In the middle of the room stood a couch covered with blue slipcovers. A glass-top coffee table stood in front of the couch and facing the couch and the portrait of Cochrane were three vintage Queen Anne chairs.

Starke asked, "Where's Anna?"

"Upstairs in bed. She's still not feeling well."

"And the child?"

"She's spending the night with a schoolmate in town."

Starke nodded. "So there's just the three of us. What do we do now?"

Cochrane sighed. "We might as well make ourselves comfortable. They'll be here soon enough. Take a chair, Mr. Ellison."

Harry sat in one of the Queen Anne chairs.

"Care for a drink, Mr. Starke?"

Starke shook his head.

"Mr. Ellison?"

"No thanks, Dr. Cochrane. I suddenly lost my appetite. I don't think I could eat or drink anything."

Cochrane smiled faintly. "Think I might poison you?"

"The thought has crossed my mind. You've done it before."

"Oh, Griffith." Cochrane's voice was disdainful. "He had it coming."

Harry's eyes twinkled. "How did you manage it?"

"It wasn't difficult. Would you like Mr. Starke and I to give you a demonstration?"

"No," Harry said. "I can think of a half a dozen ways myself. Holding a gun on a person makes all things possible."

"You are a bit of a philosopher, Mr. Ellison. But as I said, it wasn't difficult."

"Why did you do it? Was it just the review? It was clearly an unfair, overstated piece. But why did you do it?"

Cochrane walked over to the coffee table. A decanter of red wine stood on the table surrounded by five elegantly shaped wine glasses. He filled a glass. "Excellent claret," he said. "You're sure you won't reconsider and join me?"

"No thanks." Harry returned to his question. "Why was it necessary to kill? You're a very clever man, Cochrane. You could have found some other way to exact your revenge."

"Oh, indeed, I had no intention of killing anybody, not even Griffith; I had something much sweeter in mind. When I completed my first version of the B Minor Symphony, I sent it to Griffith with a note stating that I had picked it up during my travels in Austria and wanted his opinion on it. I really had an ingenious story worked out about how I found the manuscript. I hoped he would buy into it and put his seal of approval on it. Then, when the music was performed and I let it be known that I had really composed the music." Cochrane smiled and chuckled, "and to guild the lily, with the aid of a computer." He laughed, "How sweet that would have been." He looked at Harry. "You guessed right, Mr. Ellison. Both Mr. Starke and I are highly conversant with computers. My poor-mouthing didn't fool you for a minute, did it?"

"You don't give yourself enough credit, Cochrane. You fooled us all for awhile."

Cochrane smiled. "Well now," as Sir Charles is fond of saying, "It would have been so sweet. I'd have made a bloody fool out of Griffith just like I would have made out of Sir Charles next week." Suddenly, his voice became menacing. "If you hadn't interfered."

Harry shrugged. "I didn't interfere. You were the one who brought Stephanie into this thing. If not for that, I would have never become involved."

Cochrane's anger cooled almost as quickly as it had been aroused. "You're right about that."

"Why Stephanie?"

"I needed someone to bait the trap for Southwick. I tried to use Wolfson, earlier. But it didn't work."

"What happened with Wolfson?"

Cochrane cleared his throat. "After my misadventure with Griffith, I finished a second version of the symphony. I thought it was much improved. But, I wanted to try it on someone who was a first rate Schubert scholar before springing it on Southwick."

"Good plan," Harry remarked. "What went wrong?"

Cochrane clenched his glass of claret tightly. "Everything. Wolfson saw through it immediately. Said it was--to use his words--'phony as a three dollar bill.' That might have been the end of it as far as Wolfson was concerned. I had no desire to harm him, but he got curiouser and curiouser--to quote Alice in that delightful book. So much so, that I couldn't take a chance that he wouldn't expose me. Like the proverbial curious cat, he paid the price."

"And Stephanie?"

Cochrane released his grip on the wine glass. He rubbed his forehead. "Well, I set back to work on the score with a vengeance. I went back and forth from Johanna's program to my score, always edging closer to my goal—making my score a near perfect fit to the Schubert model. I worked tirelessly, sometimes, night and day. Mr. Starke will testify to that."

Harry looked at Starke, whose face was immobile.

"This time I was sure I had fashioned a score that would fool almost anyone. Still, I was unwilling to take another chance with a top flight Schubert scholar. Then, Johanna mentioned to me that she had an exceptional student, Stephanie Ellison, who was doing her dissertation on Schubert. When I learned that she had also studied conducting with Sir Charles, I couldn't believe my good fortune. Someone who was credible, but not yet sophisticated enough to pick up my deception. She was the perfect conduit."

"Starke followed her to Vienna?"

"Yes. He kept an eye on her every move. Mr. Starke is exceptionally talented at this kind of work."

"I don't doubt it. And, he left the notes on Stephanie's desk at the library?"

"Yes--the first two notes."

"And, then you switched to the girl. By the way, did she know what was really happening?"

"Of course not."

"How about the lady I met?"

"No. I never told her anything. But, I suspect she was beginning to wonder about some things I was doing. I really don't know how much she's been able to piece together."

Harry mused, "She was involved in the money transaction. She must have wondered about that."

"I told her it was completely legal and I needed money. She trusted me."

Harry nodded. "Tell me, Professor Cochrane, why did you bring the money into it at all? I checked into your background. You're a very wealthy man."

"True. The money was a ruse. If people thought I did it for the money, they wouldn't suspect what my real motive was."

"Which was revenge."

"I prefer the term rough justice."

"Johanna was part of your rough justice. She was a friend of yours."

"Yes."

"It didn't stop you from killing her."

Cochrane winced. "No. Her death was regrettable. I was in too deep at that point."

"And the security guard?"

Cochrane shrugged. "It couldn't be helped." Cochrane arose from the couch and began pacing about the room. He stopped and looked directly at Harry. "Tell me, Mr. Ellison, how did you come to suspect that I was behind these killings?"

Harry shrugged. "Johanna's files. The clues began there."

Cochrane protested, "But I destroyed the files when I searched her office."

Harry smiled faintly. "She had duplicates at home. Everything, her Schubert program, the analysis of your score--even a probability calculation of the odds that the score was--contrived."

Cochrane slapped his fist against his head. "Damn. I should have thought of that. You're very clever, Mr. Ellison."

Wasn't my idea," Harry said. "It was Debbie who thought of checking Johanna's home."

"I underestimated your companion."

"She's pretty, perky and sometimes that makes people underestimate how smart she really is. No, it was Debbie who set us in the right direction. She and Stephanie ran a computer analysis of your score, Professor Cochrane. It fit Dr. Hoffman's model like a glove. The chances of the match being random were something like one in a million, if I remember correctly. You may have been a bit too compulsive in using the model."

The tremor in Cochrane's finger reappeared. He was silent for a moment. He lifted his glass of wine to his lips, and took a deep drink before speaking. "From there, I imagine you eliminated the suspects one by one."

"The police did most of the work, Professor."

"I suspect you're being modest, Mr. Ellison. Is it fair to assume that the police know everything?"

"It is. As a matter of fact, I hear the sirens now."

Starke nodded. "They're coming. I have an Uzi in the basement. Should I try to stand them off?"

Cochrane shook his head. "No. We'll use Ellison as a bargaining chip."

They waited silently. In moments the house was surrounded. Floodlights began to scan the house, illuminating the front and back doors. The sounds of a chopper could be heard circling overhead.

A voice blared over a loud speaker: "This is Police Chief Cabot. Mr. Cochrane, can you hear me?"

Cochrane spoke quietly, "If you would be kind enough to open the window a bit, Mr. Starke."

Starke opened the window about a third of the way.

Cochrane called out, "I can hear you just fine, Mr. Cabot. Why in the world are you making all that noise? And those distasteful flood lights. Really, Chief!"

Harry smiled. Cochrane's cheek was amazing. However, Chief Cabot was not amused. "We're not interested in games, Cochrane. Release Mr. Ellison immediately."

Cochrane replied, "Why in the world would I want to do that? If Mr. Ellison were outside, you and your constabulary force would soon be inside. Chief, that wouldn't do at all."

"You can't escape, Cochrane."

"No. But we have Mr. Ellison. It's a stalemate, Mr. Cabot."

The chief did not reply. Cochrane spoke. "Let me make you an offer, Chief."

"Well?"

"Get me a small launch, filled with gasoline. There's a little beach 100 feet or so down the shore line. As you know, there's only rocks below the widow's walk. Leave the launch at the beach. We'll take Mr. Ellison to the beach with us and leave him there. Then we'll head for the open seas and take our chances."

"What makes you think you can survive out there?"

"I come from a long line of sailors, Chief Cabot."

"Interesting idea, Cochrane. But I won't buy it. There's nothing to stop you from killing Ellison at the beach."

"There's nothing to stop me from killing him here."

"If you do, you're a goner."

"One more murder wouldn't make me any more culpable than I am now. Better think about the launch, Chief."

"No way, Cochrane."

"Then Ellison's blood will be on your hands, Chief."

Suddenly, a voice came from the top of the stairs. It was a woman speaking. Harry turned quickly. He recognized her immediately. It was the woman he had supped with at the German restaurant in Washington, D.C.--the one who had given them the manuscript of the B Minor Symphony. She had a gun in her hand.

"There's been enough killings, Thaddeus. Let Mr. Ellison go."

Cochrane looked. "So you know, Anna?"

"I've known for a long time that something was wrong--very wrong. But I didn't know until tonight--until I heard you talking with Mr. Ellison that you..." Her voice broke. She looked plaintively at Cochrane. "How could you, Thaddeus?"

Cochrane did not respond. She looked at Harry. Her voice was firm. "Mr. Ellison, walk slowly to the door."

As Harry began walking, Starke drew a pistol from the inside of his coat and in the blur of an instant, fired at the woman. The bullet struck her and she collapsed on the floor. Starke turned toward Harry. "No further!" he yelled. Harry froze. Another voice came from the top of the stairs. "Drop it, Starke." It was Tony.

Starke whirled around and shot blindly. The bullet struck the staircase. Two shots followed. One came from Tony's revolver, another through the partially opened window. Both shots found their mark. Starke fell to the floor.

Debbie's voice came from the window. "Are you all right, Harry?"

"Yeah," Harry muttered, looking at the blood flowing from Starke. Harry turned toward Tony. "Cochrane has a gun, Tony. Keep him covered. I'll take it from him."

"Put your hands over your head," Tony said to Cochrane. Cochrane did so and Harry took the gun from inside his coat.

Harry turned towards Tony. "Boy, am I glad to see you. How did you get in the house?"

"The widow's walk. Did you hear the chopper?"

"Yeah, it was loud and clear. I had no idea they could drop you there. Was it tricky?"

Tony smiled. "Very tricky. They couldn't' get close enough. They had to use a long, flexible ladder. Still, I had to drop about six feet."

"Your leg okay?"

"Yeah. I think so."

Cochrane spoke, "Let me look at Anna. She may be alive."

Tony nodded. "Sure, go ahead."

Cochrane walked up the stairs and knelt over the fallen body. "She's alive," he called out. "Please call an ambulance."

Using a telephone that stood on an end table in the corner of the room, Harry dialed 911 while Tony examined Starke.

"He's dead," Tony said.

Suddenly, Cochrane bolted up the staircase.

"Damn," Tony said. "Open the door, Harry. Let Chief Cabot and his men in. I'm going after him."

"Be careful, Tony. They may have more guns up there."

Tony nodded, and then moved cautiously up the stairs. Harry unlocked the door, and then called out. "It's okay. Come on in."

Debbie, Chief Cabot, and four police officers entered the house. Right behind them was Jim Rafferty. Harry smiled. "Good to see you folks."

Debbie flew into his arms. She said nothing. She didn't have to; her tight grip around him said everything.

Tony's voice came from upstairs. "He's on the widow's walk. He's threatening to jump."

Harry spoke to Debbie. "I'm going up. Maybe I can talk him out of it."

"Okay," she said. "I'll go with you."

Harry and Debbie quickly walked up the stairs, followed by Chief Cabot. Tony was standing in dim light at the entrance to the walk. Cochrane was standing at the edge of the walk, beyond the protective wooden barrier, with only a narrow ledge separating him from the rocks below.

Harry called out, "Cochrane, it's me, Harry Ellison. Don't be foolish. Come over here. We'll try to help you."

"Help?" His voice was incredulous. "You help me? What a curious idea. No, Ellison. This has gone too far. There's only one way out. You know it and I know it."

Harry responded in a calm, clear voice. "No, Cochrane. Believe me. We can help you. Give us a chance."

Cochrane did not answer. He seemed to be considering what Harry was saying. Then, suddenly, a search light flooded his eyes. Startled, he threw his hands in front of his eyes to shield himself from the blinding light, and in so doing, shifted his body which was already precariously balanced on the edge of the structure. The involuntary movement proved disastrous. Losing his footing, he slipped over the edge. With his right hand, he made a desperate effort to grab onto the structure, but there was nothing for him to grip and he fell, dashing himself on the rocks below.

Chapter 30

Successful surgery was carried out on Anna Magdalena Furth in the late hours of the night, removing a bullet from her abdomen. Two days later she was removed from the hospital's intensive care unit and transferred to a private room to begin her recovery. On the following day, the attending physician gave permission to Tony to interview her.

Mrs. Furth was forthcoming in the interview, holding nothing back. She related how she was born in Vienna a decade after the end of the Second World War. She had been educated in a convent school and had received some university training in foreign languages. At the age of twenty-four, she married Gottfried Furth, a school teacher. They had one daughter, Constanze, and lived quiet, uneventful lives. When she was thirty-five, Gottfried experienced a heart attack and was out of work for many months. To support the family, Anna took a job working in Vienna's Stadbibliothek where she helped foreign scholars with translations of German materials. It was here that she met Thaddeus Cochrane who was researching his book on the life and music of Franz Schubert. Cochrane found her help indispensable and corresponded with her when he returned to the United States.

When Anna's daughter Constanze was twenty-three, she married Werner Schmidt, a civil engineer. The couple lived in Innsbruck. After several years of marriage Constanze gave birth to a daughter named Gretchen. Tragedy struck the family during the third year of Constanze's marriage. Gottfried, Constanze and her husband Werner were motoring in the Alps when their car was struck by another car driven by a man who had dozed at the wheel and lost control. Both cars plunged off of the highway into a ravine below. There were no survivors. The infant Gretchen who had been left with Anna now became Anna's responsibility.

Following the simultaneous death of her husband and daughter, Anna became deeply depressed and couldn't cope with the situation. She had no one to turn to. When Thaddeus Cochrane heard of the tragedy, he invited her to come to America to stay with him. She was grateful beyond words. Cochrane helped her obtain a visa. She moved to his newly built home near Salem, working as his secretary, doing the cooking, shopping, and looking after her granddaughter.

She knew that Thaddeus was working on a new "realization" of Schubert's B-Minor Symphony, but considered this was not unusual because other composers such as Brian Newbould had earlier attempted this feat with considerable success. She had no idea at the time that Cochrane would try to pass the score off as the original.

Her life with Thaddeus became less happy when Jonathan Starke moved into the household. Starke was a taciturn, unpleasant man but was fiercely loyal to Thaddeus. Sometimes Cochrane and Starke would go on trips together, but would say nothing about it to Anna. She knew that Starke possessed several guns which worried her; all that she could do was to make sure that her granddaughter stayed clear of the weapons. She suspected that Starke was not an American citizen, but an illegal alien from somewhere in Eastern Europe. She doubted that Starke was his real name.

Finally she described how Thaddeus had asked her and her granddaughter to help him in some business dealings. He said the transactions would be unusual but assured her that everything was perfectly legal. He explained that he was trying to raise money to settle some debts that he had incurred. Anna said she was skeptical from the start, but owed too much to Thaddeus to refuse. She related how her granddaughter had been coached to deposit the manuscript at the Library of Congress and she, herself, had been instructed to handle the transactions with Mr. Ellison and his niece.

Her uneasiness had increased steadily since that point. When she read about Sir Charles' press conference, she guessed much of what was happening. Still, she did not connect Thaddeus with the murders until the very end when she overheard the conversation in the living room. And then, taking one of Mr. Starke's guns, she tried to save Mr. Ellison. She smiled as she completed her narrative. "I'm glad he's okay. I like him. He's a nice man."

In the evening, Tony accompanied Harry and Debbie to the airport. They were catching the last flight to Washington while he stayed behind to clean up some final details with Chief Cabot. As they were about to board the airplane, Tony spoke to Debbie. "I was talking with your boss, Lieutenant Jackson on the phone. He wants to know whether you want to go to the Virgin Islands?"

Debbie smiled. "The Virgin Islands?"

"Yeah. They spotted Howard Jones there. Seems he's been cavorting with another con artist. A lady. She passed herself off as dean of a law school in the States. Can you believe it? She only had a mail order degree in nursery school education. When they finally found out about her, she skipped to the Virgin Islands and has taken up with Mr. Jones."

Debbie laughed. "What a pair."

"Interested in tracking them down?"

"Sure." She turned toward Harry. "You need a vacation in the sun, Lover?"

Harry smiled, "Why not."

Debbie turned to Tony and asked, "Can I take him along?"

"It's a free country, Debbie. But keep him out of trouble for a change."

Harry laughed. "No murders, no mysteries, just Mr. Jones and his dean...and a few good rum drinks."

Harry turned toward the waiting airplane. "See you, chum."

Epilogue

On the day scheduled, the symphony orchestra began its fall season. Every seat in Avery Fischer Hall was occupied. When Sir Charles Southwick walked onto the stage and took his customary place before the orchestra, there were only muted whispers from the audience, not the usual hearty round of applause. For a long moment as Sir Charles stood facing the orchestra, there was an almost palpable air of tension in the great hall. Then, slowly, the men and women of the orchestra arose from their chairs, first in groups of two or three, and then in larger groups, and then all--stood as one and began to applaud their conductor, giving him a resounding vote of confidence. As if on cue, the men and women in the audience began rising from their chairs and clapped in unison with the musicians. Responding to this show of affection and support, the now misty-eyed conductor turned toward the audience and bowed gratefully.

When the musicians and members of the audience returned to their seats, Sir Charles raised his baton and the concert began. The musicians seemed inspired and played both the Rossini Overture and the Mozart Symphony brilliantly. Then it was intermission time. When the orchestra returned, Sir Charles began the performance of the Schubert B Minor Symphony. The music came forth in all of its beauty, its majesty filling the hall. After the two movements of the unfinished symphony had been completed, Sir Charles turned to face a now hushed audience. He spoke slowly. "As you know, I had intended to play a completed realization of this symphony. Moreover, I must candidly admit to a personal error of judgment that the music we would be performing was in fact Schubert's own. I am terribly sorry about this. It should never have happened. I hope you will accept my profound apology for my failings in this regard. As most of you have undoubtedly read in Mister Rafferty's series of articles, this realization of Schubert's work has a trail of blood connected with it. I feel very deeply that it would be a disservice to the memories of three wonderful colleagues to perform this realization of the symphony. Schubert's masterpiece was unfinished. That apparently was his intention. And that is the way we shall leave it.

Southwick turned to face the orchestra. The men and women arose from their chairs and cheers filled the hall.

The End